MINE

LINZVONC

CONTENTS

1

GRETCHEN

"*M*iss Red? I don't suppose you could tear yourself away from your phone to participate in class, could you?"

I lifted my eyes to meet those of my teacher, Mrs. Saxton, who glared at me from the front of the classroom.

"Uh, I'm sorry...it was my mom..." My cheeks flushed as I lied, cramming the phone in my bag.

"Of course it was." She made a face, shaking her head as she spoke to the rest of the class. "So, I will need you to write an essay on whether romantic movies damage real-life relationships. You may find you can speak to your parents and family for insight."

A few cackles came from the class as my phone vibrated against my leg. I decided not to bother upsetting my teacher further by retrieving it, but the bell rang anyway.

I grabbed my phone, and the envelope icon showed I had a text message from Luke, my boyfriend.

> LUKE: Babes, gotta put tonight on ice. Big dinner at home- no phone zone- family shit. Love you.

I sighed, shoving my phone back into my bag.

"Girl, that's a sigh; what's wrong?" My best friend Rosie peered at me with concern.

I picked up my bag and followed Rosie out of the classroom door and into the carnage of the school corridor. Bodies filled every available space, and I groaned. I glanced at Rosie, who was waiting for an explanation.

"Luke has just canceled our date. He has 'family shit,' apparently."

Rosie lifted a perfectly arched brow. "Oh. Why don't you come with me and Sienna to The Lounge? she grinned, knowing I had no other plans.

"Yeah, why not?" I agreed, feeling a little brighter.

Just then, a loud crash came from the end of the corridor, distracting us from our conversation.

"Look where you are going, *dickhead*!"

I craned my neck round to see what all the commotion was about and saw Finn—a friend of Luke's—squaring up to a boy I had not seen before in school.

"Who's *that*, Rose?" I whispered, studying the boy.

"Ah, the new guy…" Rosie said. "I heard Clara and Krystal talking about him earlier. He's Clara's cousin. Cute hmm? Good for us single girls!"She cackled, sticking her tongue out at me.

I scrutinized him, trying not to stare. His dirty blond hair covered his face, yet the black t-shirt that clung to his broad body showed he could handle himself with Finn.

"Fuck you. You're the dickhead, *dickhead*," the new guy muttered.

Finn stepped forward, his fists clenched. Finn wouldn't think twice about socking this guy in the jaw, and something told me that would be one hell of a fight. I sighed with relief as Mr Whetton strode down the hallway towards the boys.

"Ah, Cal. I see you've met Finn, quite the star around here, aren't you?"

Even his name was heavenly. *Cal.*

Finn scowled at Cal. "Whatever, man. Welcome to the school, Cal."

He kept eye contact with Cal as he walked away, his face set in a firm line. Cal leaned against the locker, watching Finn with amusement. Sweet perfume filled the air as Clara approached us from the cafeteria. Clara was my boyfriend's cousin and the Queen Bee of the school. As she walked, she cut her eyes at those who dared to look at her, ensuring their gazes moved away. I detested Clara and her clique, made up of Krystal and Savannah, the popular girls in school.

"Cal," she called, flicking her platinum blond curls over her shoulder. "I've been dying to introduce you to my friends. Especially Krystal..."

Krystal followed Clara, wearing a tight denim skirt, high heels, and a revealing top. Someone needed to remind her we were at school, not a strip joint.

"With all due respect, Clara, I couldn't give less of a fuck. I'll catch you later." He turned and walked towards the exit, leaving Clara and Krystal standing open-mouthed after him.

Rosie and I exchanged a look of surprise as Clara narrowed her eyes at Cal.

"Well. He is rude, Clara," Krystal stood, hand on her hips as she followed him with her eyes. "Hot, though..." she added with a smirk.

Could it be that Cal was immune to the charms of Krystal Denning?

As he turned the corner, my stomach fluttered.

I sure hope so.

Suppressing a smile, I turned to follow Rosie into class.

Later that evening, I met up with my friends at The Lounge. Rosie was there, along with our other best friend, Sienna. We had been friends for years, and I was eternally grateful that I had not one but two best friends. Sienna was chatting to her boyfriend Ethan, and I sipped on my caramel latte, discussing with Rosie how the new guy, Cal, had dissed Clara and Krystal earlier.

"Finn said he's a prick," Ethan said, brushing his floppy chestnut hair out of his eyes.

"Well, that's it then," Sienna joked. "The mighty Finn has spoken…"She smacked his arm playfully and threw her crimson hair over one shoulder.

Ethan laughed, scanning her face with adoration. Ethan, Finn, and Luke had been tight for as long as we girls had, yet Finn was the alpha male. It bugged me how Ethan and Luke agreed with Finn about anything, as though they didn't have their own opinions.

"Nah, babe, Finn is sound. You don't start a new school and pick a fight with the golden boy, do you? Anyway, I am not gonna argue with you in that dress…" He leered, kissing her neck, much to our dismay. They still behaved like they'd just met despite being together for years.

Sickening.

"Ew, get a room, guys," Rosie said, rolling her eyes as Sienna pulled Ethan in for a kiss.

Ethan stood up, detangling himself from Sienna. "Right, baby. Gotta go, do you wanna ride home? Or you can stay at mine...." he said, staring at her chest while she stretched and yawned.

No prizes for guessing his motive...

"Yeah, I'll come to yours. I just need to grab up my stuff on the way," Sienna said, standing and lacing her fingers through Ethan's. "Later, girls." She smiled, blowing us both kisses.

Ethan gave a brief wave as they made their way to the door.

"Well," I declared. "I'm just going to nip to the little girl's room."

I slid out of the booth, heading to the restrooms. My hair became loose from its messy bun, so I flicked my head forward, gathering it using my fingers as a brush. This was the problem when you had such thick hair- it was unruly. I lifted my head back, colliding with someone. Releasing my hair, I rubbed my head, looking up to find Cal standing before me.

"Shit, I'm so sorry," my voice quivered beneath his penetrating gaze.

Boy, was he scary:

He shook his head, his lips curling into a sneer as he pushed past me, muttering under his breath, "It's not like there's not enough room in this shitty town."

Jeez. What crawled up his ass and died?

I stared after him as he walked out of The Lounge, the door slamming shut behind him. My veins hummed with adrenaline as Rosie hurried over to me.

"Babes!" She gasped, "Are you okay? What did he say?"

My head ached from hitting him, so I shrugged and said I just wanted to go home.

Rosie linked arms with me as she chuckled. "How was

the physical contact, though? He's a guy I wouldn't mind butting heads with." She giggled as I swatted her arm.

"Don't be a knob, Rose."

I made it home in one piece, falling onto my bed, fully clothed. Suddenly, my phone vibrated in my pocket.

LUKE: Sorry, babe. I just got back, and I'm wiped. See you tomorrow?

I was so annoyed I didn't reply. I closed his message and slipped into my comfy pajamas, falling into my bed gratefully.

My mind drifted back to Cal as my stomach tightened with excitement.

What was his deal?

I couldn't imagine it had been easy for him, transferring in his senior year. Especially to Winterburg, where nothing interesting ever happened.

I drifted off to sleep, his deep green eyes following me every step of the way.

2

GRETCHEN

*T*he next day, I considered what to wear.

It wasn't like it mattered; I always wore the same things. I settled on my skinny jeans, knee-high boots and a long black t-shirt, slicking on some lip gloss and mascara. Cold frosted my bedroom window, so I pulled on my coat and slipped my phone into my bag. As I walked the fifteen minutes to school, I felt relieved that I didn't live too far away; in warmer weather, it was a refreshing walk.

When I reached my locker, a pair of hands covering my eyes blocked my vision.

"Guess who?" A husky voice murmured in my ear as I whipped around, striking blue eyes inches away from mine.

"Luke," I said flatly, putting my hands on his chest and moving away to see him better. He wore a football jersey, his toned body visible through it. His helmet was in one hand as he ran the other through his jet-black hair while gazing at me.

I turned back to my locker and continued to put my things away while Luke leaned on the locker next to me, frowning at my reaction.

"Am I in trouble? I'm sorry about last night. My cousins

just moved here, and my parents insisted on having them over for dinner. Fucking pointless—one of them upped and left halfway through—apparently, he needed a smoke. But then he never came back." He rolled his eyes before focusing on me. "Anyway, do you forgive me?"

He gave me that puppy dog look that usually worked so well with me.

"Yes, but you can make it up to me later." I dropped a chaste kiss on his lips as his eyes lit up.

"That's a deal, right there. Gotta run, babe; I'll see you at lunch, yeah?"He winked at me as he walked in the gym's direction.

I grabbed my drink from my locker and opened it for a quick sip before class. I forgot to open it slowly, so orange soda exploded all over me. Luckily, the hallway was quiet with everyone in class, so I made my way to the restroom to clean up as best as I could.

Is there anything worse than being covered in sticky orange soda?

Grimacing, I left the restroom, still brushing my clothes with paper towels. If I hurried, I wouldn't be too late for class. I checked behind me to make sure I hadn't made too much of a mess near the locker; the janitor was a freak, and I wouldn't want to give him a reason to speak to me if I could avoid it. I turned back, walking straight into a hard chest.

"Shit!" I muttered as I looked up in horror to see Cal gazing at me.

"Are you trying to make a habit of this, *Raven*?" His lazy voice had a Brooklyn accent, ever so faintly, but it was there. He smirked when I lost my footing, scrunching the paper towels in my hands as I balanced myself on the wall beside me. A slow, sexy smile filled his mouth as he moved towards me, closing the distance between us. The heat from his body, combined with the faint whiff of cigarettes, made me light-headed, and I forcibly took a step backward, shaking myself mentally.

"*Raven*?" I scoffed. "My name is *Gretchen*." I stepped back, feeling more in control the further away from him I got.

He held his hands up in mock surrender as he chuckled, my skin tingling in response. "Yeah, okay, doll. Either way, that's the second time you've thrown yourself at me. It's getting a little embarrassing for you, not me," he smirked as he glanced down the corridor.

What?

I was furious. "*Excuse* me? I have not thrown myself at you, you jerk!"

I picked up my bag and stormed past him, hearing him laugh as I walked away, his delicious scent enveloping the surrounding air.

"Hey *Raven*, where's the gym?" He called after me.

I turned to face him, trying to ignore the butterflies fluttering through my stomach like a tornado. "Down there." I pointed with my finger before adding through gritted teeth, "And it's *Gretchen*."

He wasn't paying attention as he spun on his heel and turned the corner without a word.

Why did I even respond to Raven?!

I groaned, trying to avoid the way my heart was racing.

By lunch, I was drained. I slumped into my seat beside Rosie while Ethan and Sienna watched me unwrap my turkey sandwich with interest.

"What?" I frowned as they exchanged a strange look.

Sienna then cleared her throat, nodding to the corner of the cafeteria.

"Looks like someone isn't happy," Sienna said, my eyes following her gaze to where Krystal was having a heated conversation with Luke. She was showing her phone to him, and he had his hands up as he seemed to say he was sorry.

As she left, Luke grabbed her arm and went after her.

I swallowed the rest of my sandwich before dusting my hands off on my jeans. I followed them as Rosie called out after me.

"G? You want me to come with you?"

"No, babes, I'm cool. Back in a minute," I said, sending her a grateful smile. I pushed the cafeteria doors open to find Krystal and Luke beside the lockers.

"Is everything okay?" I asked, tilting my head in Luke's direction.

What was going on here? My gut told me something was off about this.

Krystal rolled her heavily made-up eyes in my direction, annoying me further. "Off to Mommy, baby boy," she said in a sing-song voice before she stormed through the double doors.

Luke turned to face me; his blue eyes clouded with annoyance. He smiled, reaching out for my hand. "Hey baby, sorry about that."

He looks super cute today, but that isn't the point.

"She isn't happy that she didn't get captain of the cheer-leading team. She seemed to think I could do something about it," Luke explained, tugging me closer to him.

Luke was the captain of the football team, and therefore, the cheerleaders seemed to believe he was theirs to order about and make demands of. I leaned forward, pulling him towards me to kiss him. He slid his arms around me as our kiss deepened, his tongue exploring my mouth as I ran my fingers down his back. I pulled away, kissing him again as he groaned.

"Babe, you're divine. Shall we skip the rest of school and go somewhere a little more discreet?" He winked at me suggestively as I swatted his arm. "Are you free on Saturday? Another family meal, I'm afraid. Only this time they invited you." He pulled me back towards him, kissing my neck as he did.

I closed my eyes, all thoughts of Krystal pushed away as Luke mumbled in my ear.

"You can stay in my room all night..."

3

GRETCHEN

I stared at my closet, as though if I waited long enough, a new outfit would appear.

I'd only been dating Luke for a little over a year, and I knew his family well; I had grown up with him, but part of me still wanted to impress them.

I settled on a black roll neck with tight jeans, sweeping my curls into a loose clip. I applied my usual mascara and lip gloss, aiming for a casual look. I packed a bag with a few things in case Luke got lucky, and I stayed over with a toothbrush, deodorant, and some clean clothes.

I pouted at myself in the mirror and decided I would do, skipping downstairs where my parents were drinking wine and playing Scrabble.

How idyllic.

"You look good, honey; where are you going?" My dad drawled, sipping his wine as he smiled at me. He was a silver fox with deep green eyes framed with long lashes I had inherited from him. My mom was the typical Californian blonde: waist-length hair, sparkling blue eyes, and tanned skin. We shared the same full mouth, naturally cherry red. She was often mistaken for my sister—although I wasn't sure that was too much of a compliment for me.

"I'm off to Luke's. Remember the dinner I told you about? I may stay at his house after- in the spare room, obviously..." My voice trailed off as I blushed under my dad's amused gaze.

"Honey, it's fine. You are eighteen now. If you tell us where you are going to be, we trust you. Just be good and keep us informed. Oh, and Gretchen? It will always be the spare room, *capiche*?"

My dad raised an eyebrow at me, and I cringed. I blew kisses at them both, slipping on my trusty black boots, when I heard Luke's car beeping its familiar horn. I called goodbye and left.

Luke whistled as I got in his car. "All this effort for me, babe?" he winked.

He wore a deep blue shirt that brought out the color in his eyes; his trousers were ironed to perfection, as though we were attending a wedding or something.

"Am I okay in this?" I asked, looking pointedly at his clothes, then waving a hand over mine.

"More than. How am I going to concentrate on anything but you tonight?" He murmured, and I blushed deeply.

I knew what he was referring to. We had been together long enough to take our relationship to the next level—but I was hesitant. If it was up to Luke, we would be at it twenty-four hours a day, seven days a week.

He pulled away from the curb whilst I fiddled with the radio to find some music.

"So, Clara can't make it. She has cheerleading practice." Luke grinned at me, knowing I had no tolerance for his cousin Clara.

"Clara? Is this your entire family?" I groaned inwardly at

the thought of spending the entire evening downstairs with Luke's family. They were nice enough, but they liked a drink more than most people, which could become awkward.

"Yeah, pretty much, babe. You'll be fine." He squeezed my leg as he swung the car into his driveway. Luke's family is well off; his dad was a successful writer and his house proved as much.

Luke parked the car, and I got out, inhaling deeply as we approached the house. His mother, Bella, opened the door to greet us, a beaming smile on her face.

"Gretchen! How lovely to see you! How are you?" She embraced me, smelling of expensive perfume and air-kissing each side of my face. I peeled off my boots as Luke wandered away to find us some drinks. "Go get settled in the lounge, darling." Bella gestured towards the large room behind the stairs, where I could hear laughter and music.

I walked in to find an elegant lady sitting on an armchair with a glass of champagne in her hand, smiling as her gaze fell upon me.

"Ah, Luke's little girlfriend has arrived; how sweet. Hello, dear."

A hand brushed my back, and I turned to see Luke grinning as he thrust a glass of champagne towards me.

Luke's little girlfriend? Gah!

I sipped my champagne, if nothing else, so I didn't have to reply.

"So that's Nanna, as you know. Pops is over there with the whiskey," Luke said as a ripple of laughter broke out from the red-faced man sitting beside the whiskey cabinet.

"You've met Aunt Sally and Uncle Brett," he continued as his gaze swept the room. "My brother Sam and his girlfriend Nancy."

I looked up in confusion; the last time I saw Sam, he was

dating a woman called Clare. He made eyes at me in desperation, warning me not to mention Clare.

"Hey, guys. Good to meet you, Nancy," I said.

Nancy checked her nails and barely glanced at me in response. She was immaculate to look at. Her blonde hair was perfectly in place on top of her head in a well-styled bun, with bright red lips and a sleek black playsuit. "Hey, Greta," she said in a bored tone.

I threw her a dark look as a small smirk played on her lips. Sam coughed to ease the tension between us. "Then there are the new guys in town." He raised his glass toward a woman in a beautiful silk dress, her caramel-colored hair gathered with a diamante clip, dark lashes framing the greenest eyes I thought I had seen somewhere before.

"I'm Alice, lovely. Nice to meet you. Drink up, you'll soon lose those nerves."

I liked her at once, warming to her instantly.

She smiled as she continued. "My sons are on their way, I'm sure they won't be long. We moved here literally last week. It is a lot smaller than New York, but at least we're closer to family."

"Sounds good." I smiled as Luke guided me over to a sofa.

The drinks flowed, and I felt myself relax until I heard a commotion at the front door, and Luke squeezed my knee.

"Looks like the brothers made it at long last," he said.

A man entered the room with the same green eyes as Alice, yet a mass of dark chocolate hair fell in waves around his shoulders.

"Hey everyone, I'm Drake..." His voice had a slow, confident drawl to it, and I noticed Nancy perk up and flutter her eyelashes at him.

"Hey Drake, I'm Nancy."

His eyes flashed over her as he gave her a smile.

Sam frowned with annoyance, but he still acknowledged Drake. "Alright, bro? Finally made it then...?"

Sam put his arm around Nancy, and Drake laughed, rubbing his neck awkwardly. "Yeah, sorry about that, guys. Car trouble."

More drinks flowed, and I excused myself to go to the restroom. I climbed the stairs, trying to remember which way it was; this floor alone had two large bathrooms and three bedrooms. I strode down the mirrored corridor and found the bathroom. After using the toilet, I checked my reflection and texted Rosie to tell her I missed her and that I was getting bored. The champagne was making my head hurt— it's not usual to get a hangover before experiencing any of the fun, right? My phone pinged back.

> ROSIE: But maybe it will be worth it later ;)

I pursed my lips when the bathroom door opened, and an intense green gaze swept over me. "Jesus!" I yelped.

It was *him*.

Cal.

He strode into the bathroom and closed the door behind him.

"Excuse me, I was just..." I stammered, unable to tear my eyes away from him.

He walked up to me, and he stared into my eyes, searching them with intrigue. Up close, I could see swirls of faint blue drizzling into a pond of emerald green, the color exploding beneath his full lashes.

"Why are you everywhere I go?" He murmured, my heart skipping about fifty beats.

What is it with that damn accent of his?

He was close to me now, and I couldn't help but notice that his breath smelt of a mixture of alcohol and cigarettes, but that just attracted me more. I turned my head; anything to break eye contact with him.

"Hey— I was the one in the toilet. Luckily, I had finished!" I retorted.

He didn't move a muscle as I leaned closer to him, my heart pounding in my ears. My body was moving of its own accord, held prisoner as his eyes moved down to my lips. His hands rest either side of me on the sink, his body pressing against mine.

I should have told him to move, but there was no way— every part of me was screaming for this man to touch me in any way possible. Then, without saying a word, he moved back and leaned against the door.

I flushed as his eyes trailed down my body, his tongue wetting his lips as he shook his head.

He was beautiful in every way.

His mouth was full, and he had a habit of biting his lip when he was silent.

My heart raced as I walked towards him and reached for the door handle. "I need to go, I'm—"

Cal gave me a crooked smile before moving away from the door. Pulling a hip flask out from his jacket pocket, he lifted it to his lips as I watched with fascination, my hand still on the door handle. He sucked on the lid, and I watched, mesmerized, as his throat swallowed the liquid with ease. He dropped his hand, the flask hovering close to his chest as he frowned at me.

"What are you staring at?" He asked, the corners of his mouth twitching with amusement.

I couldn't admit I was staring at his lips as he drank,

wondering what they would feel like on mine. "I don't know..." I admitted. "Sorry."

He raised his eyebrows, muttering as he did. "Come here."

It wasn't a command, but my body responded like it was, moving closer to him as he reached up and pulled my hair clip loose. My dark curls tumbled around my shoulders as he ran his hand through them. His finger then traced over my lips, and I felt myself moan. He studied me before stepping back, turning away from me so I couldn't see his expression.

"Man, I've gotta piss." He unbuckled his belt as he walked over to the toilet, and I grabbed my stuff and ran out of there.

I tried to calm myself down— nothing happened, except —well...

He'd played with my hair. Touched my lips.

Entirely normal behavior with a stranger in a bathroom.

Immense guilt swept through me at the thought of Luke waiting downstairs for me. I took a deep breath and made my way into the lounge, where everyone was still drinking like it was an Olympic sport.

I needed to speak to Rosie. If anyone would know what to make of this situation, it would be her.

Luke put his arm around me and whispered I was the most beautiful girl he had ever seen.

Nausea rose in my throat, and I asked him if we could skip the meal and just go to his room. His eyes widened, and a cheeky smile spread over his face.

Oh God.

"Guys, can you give us a shout when the food is ready? Gretchen and I are just going to my room for a bit." He stood up, pulling me up to him as the adults continued as though we hadn't moved at all. We made our way up the stairs, and I noticed someone coming down them, someone who gazed at me intensely.

"Cal, this is my girlfriend, Gretchen. Gretchen, this is my cousin, Cal..." Luke muttered as we met on the stairs awkwardly.

It was *him*. Cal. Luke's *cousin*.

Blood drained from my face as our eyes met. I had assumed that he was Clara's cousin on her mother's side. But no, he had to be *Luke's* cousin.

Cal looked at Luke and then at me. "Seriously?" Cal laughed with disbelief and shook his head, smirking at me when I swallowed, pushing my hair behind my ear.

Luke frowned with confusion and peered at me.

I wanted the floor to open and swallow me up, and I couldn't look at either of them.

"Happy fucking then," Cal muttered, pushing past us into the lounge.

Luke squeezed my hand and laughed. "I'm sorry, he is a bit of a prick."

My phone vibrated in my pocket, and I checked it, glad of the distraction.

> ROSIE: Any better? Hope it's got more interesting ;)

I followed Luke upstairs and into his room, deciding not to answer.

4

GRETCHEN

*A*ll I wanted to do was sit in front of the television and gorge on Nutella on toast, but I had to get ready for school. I had a habit of over-analyzing things, and technically, I hadn't kissed Cal, so why did I feel so guilty? Worst still, whenever I thought of Cal's beautiful face, butterflies went wild in my stomach. My breath left my body whenever he allowed those intense eyes to meet mine. Why did I think about him when I fell asleep and as soon as I woke up?

I felt *awful*.

My phone pinged, letting me know I had a text.

LUKE: Love you, baby.

I wanted to scream. How was I going to get through today? I texted back with a simple kiss and then stared at myself in the mirror. Maybe I would wear my hair down today, Cal preferred it that way.

Wait. What?

Pushing the thought aside, I ran some curl cream through the lengths of my hair and scrunched it up, making the curls wild and natural. I did my usual lip gloss and mascara but decided I wanted to make more of an effort. I pulled on my thick black tights and a honey-colored jumper dress before heading out to walk to school.

I was halfway there when I saw Cal. My chest tightened, and my steps slowed as I checked him out.

A cigarette dangled from his fingers, but he looked *incredible*. He had a grey beanie on with his blond hair escaping out at the sides. A white Ramones t-shirt sat over ripped skinny jeans and trainers. His jacket hung over his shoulder as he moved, clearly talking to someone, but I couldn't see who. I dawdled and moved to the right so I could see who it was. I saw a flash of a red skirt and her trademark knee-high boots.

He was talking to *Krystal*.

My heart sank. I watched as she flirted with him, leaning forward and pulling him towards her using the thin material of his t-shirt. She took the cigarette out of his mouth before pressing her lips to his, their heads moving against one another as they kissed.

I couldn't bear to watch.

His hands were all over her body, and I felt nausea wash over me. There was no other way to walk, so I crossed the street and strode as fast as I could past them. A car pulled up beside me, and I was relieved to see Sienna and Ethan.

"Need a lift babe?" Sienna called with a grin.

I climbed into the back, grateful to be hiding away from the sight of Cal with Krystal. It shouldn't have bothered me, but it did.

"Looks like Cal met Krystal," Ethan said, nodding behind us.

"So?" I snapped as his eyes widened in surprise.

"If you like that kind of thing," he said as we sped away.

"Many boys do because it is easy," I pointed out.

Ethan held his hands up, nodding in agreement.

Sienna remained strangely quiet, glancing at me in the rear-view mirror quizzically as we made the brief journey to school. When we pulled up, I jumped out swiftly so I could be away from Sienna's stares.

I didn't see Krystal for the rest of the day, but I thought about her constantly.

How was it kissing his mouth? God, even his hands were beautiful.

I tried to concentrate in my Psychology class, but it was pointless.

Maybe I need therapy myself.

The classroom door opened, and Cal walked in, looking idly for an empty seat. My heart thudded in my throat, and my body trembled from his sheer presence, but I stared out of the window, averting my eyes.

I groaned inwardly when I caught a whiff of his delicious scent, confirming that he was close. I stared hard at the front of the class when the teacher, Mr. Gane, spoke.

"I want you to do this with partners. This project will form a large part of your final mark, so put as much into this as you can, guys." He shuffled his papers, then glanced up at us. "I want to know the effects of talking therapy. I want you to do this in partners and then present to the class your findings. It is entirely up to you what you talk about, but as true psychology students, you must remain confidential. I have chosen your partners for you, as I want this to be an authentic experience." He called out names and eventually got to me. "You are with Cal Fallon, Gretchen."

My stomach dropped, and I turned to look for Cal. There he was, slumped over his desk, sleeping.

In class.

Rosie mouthed '*Oh my God*' to me as other girls just glared at me like I was the luckiest girl in the world.

So why did I feel so scared?

I gathered my things as the bell went, walking over to Cal's desk as I nudged his foot with mine. He woke with a start and looked at me through his sleepy, long lashes.

Sweet Jesus and all the orphans save me from this sexual devil.

"What do you want now?" He yawned as I took a deep breath.

This was important, this was my grades. Working as a therapist was my absolute dream, and I couldn't afford to mess this up at all.

"You and I are together," I babbled incoherently as he gazed at me.

"What are you talking about? You are so weird sometimes." He yawned again, this time leaning back in his chair. He rubbed his eyes and stretched, causing his t-shirt to ride up and expose the white blonde hairs on his tanned, taut stomach. He caught me staring at him and smirked, pulling his top up more. "Better view?"

I averted my eyes quickly, and I exhaled. "Listen, this is serious. You are my partner for this project. It means a lot to me. We have to do talking therapy..."

He was listening to me, actually *listening* to me.

Concentrate, Gretchen.

"It's important to you?" He murmured softly as my heart cartwheeled through my chest.

His voice, my God. It sounded like it was taking serious effort for him to speak.

"Okay, sweet. I can't really flunk class either, to be honest, but I reckon you won't need me to do much, will you? You seem like a bright girl."

I blinked in disbelief before I clenched my fists by my sides, narrowing my eyes at him. "I need you to do it *with* me, asshole. I can't talk to myself and present alone."

He burst out laughing, a beautiful sound that made me want to weep with longing. He smirked at me again, his blond hair falling into his eyes as he sighed dejectedly. "Tell you what, Raven. Come around to mine tonight. We will...talk." His eyes ran over me slowly before he dragged his eyes back to my face, which he continued to study. "Can you bring some pizza and beers?" He looked at me hopefully as I blinked myself back to reality.

What the actual hell was wrong with me?

"What?! I don't even know where you live," I scoffed, scrunching my nose up. "Pizza and beers? Hardly what therapists do, is it?"

He held his hand out. "Give me your phone."

Again, it was like a command, but this time, I tried to resist.

"What for?" I demanded hotly.

He groaned with exasperation as he spoke slowly, as though he was addressing a child. "Gretchen, can I have your phone so I can put my number in? I can text you my address unless you want to type it in yourself— either way, I don't care. I've got stuff to do till seven. Can you come after that?"

I handed him my phone, regretting it instantly when he saw my screensaver. My cheeks burned when I realized it was of me and Luke. He lifted his eyebrows as he exhaled slowly, typing away. I watched his fingers touch my screen, and for once, I was envious of a piece of technology.

"Done," he muttered with a tinge of annoyance, tossing my phone at me.

I caught it as he lifted himself out of his seat with ease, the muscles on his arms showing through his t-shirt. He caught me staring for the second time that day, I realized, my cheeks burning when he chuckled to himself, making me wonder what the hell he found so damn amusing.

"Babe, why are you still in here?" Luke walked back into the classroom, his voice trailing off when his eyes landed on the two of us. "Sup, Cal? I see you got my girl as your partner; make sure you get any secrets out of her, won't you?" He snorted, and I cringed when he laced his fingers through mine.

Cal looked at Luke in mock excitement. "Oh, I'm *sure* she is a deep ocean of secrets."

My face flushed with embarrassment as he left the room, his scent lingering in the air. He was annoyingly attractive yet obnoxious. I turned to Luke, who was staring after him, too, for reasons I didn't wish to know.

"Sorry you got him. Want me to have a word with Mr. Gane? Maybe we can convince him to give you someone semi-human," Luke muttered as his arms circled me.

I breathed in his scent, nothing like Cal's but somewhat still safe and comforting.

"It's okay; I think I can handle him," I murmured as he stroked my hair affectionately. I had a boyfriend, and this was strictly schoolwork.

So why is my stomach in knots?

5

GRETCHEN

*T*ime dragged. Not that I was watching it like a hawk. Every time I looked at the clock, it had hardly moved, somehow remaining at ten minutes to seven for about an hour.

I scrutinized myself in the mirror, happy with my choice of a loose hoodie and joggers. I checked Cal's address again on my phone, unable to believe he lived literally one block away from me. That explained how I saw him on my way to school most days.

I kept going back to my inbox, just to see the name *'Cal'* and the message with his address on it. It led to me dreaming up all kinds of messages. I gave myself a shake, deciding to just leave already. I was early, but I could walk slowly. I yelled to my Mom that I was off to do homework with a friend and that I wouldn't be late. I left the house and strolled to Cal's. His house was almost a carbon copy of mine, except it was a corner lot, meaning it was larger. I strode to the door and inhaled a deep breath before knocking.

I recognized his mother, Alice, as she answered the door

with a warm smile. "Hi, Gretchen, is Luke with you?" She peered behind me, looking confused.

"Ah, hey, Mrs Fallon. No, it's just me. Cal and I are psychology partners...." I shuffled on my feet, aware that my face was now beet red.

She nodded, stepping back for me to go inside. "I under-stand. Come in— Cal's room is on the top floor. Do you want a drink?"

I declined, and made my way up the stairs, looking for the next set of stairs to reach the top floor. My legs shook as I climbed up the ladder-like stairs to a dark wooden door, knocking softly. I heard his footsteps crossing the room, and the door swung open to reveal no other than Cal Fallon. He wore grey pants and a black vest that hung low over his chest, his incredible body on display for me to admire.

He studied me for a moment before he allowed the door to open wide enough for me to squeeze past him.

I held my breath, refusing to fall victim to that tantalizing scent again.

Okay, I'm in his room. Breathe.

"You're early—that's cute. Come in."

I needed to stop swooning every time he spoke. I was just another girl to him. I needed to behave like I had a boyfriend and a brain.

His bed was a mess, the curtains were closed, and there were clothes all over the floor. He sat on the bed and patted the space next to him.

"Why do you seem so scared whenever you're near me? We have to work together—you need to relax. I won't try anything with you, I promise." He grinned.

A flash of annoyance zipped through me as I remembered him with Krystal that morning.

What did I just say to myself?

Yet there I was, jealous that he had kissed the school slut. *Get a grip, Gretchen.*

"Yes, I know, I saw you with your girl this morning," I said before I could consider my words.

His eyes widened as he turned to look at me, bemused. "My *girl*, you say? When did you see me, anyway?"

I shrugged, my cheeks flushing. "Krystal. This morning, I passed you on the way to school."

He gazed at me and smiled. "Did you now? You should've said 'hey.'"

He didn't deny her being his girl; this annoyed me more than anything else.

"I didn't think you had any spare oxygen for conversation, Cal," I said, which only made him laugh. "Anyway," I huffed, reaching for my bag.

He stopped me, his hand on mine as I froze, electricity running between us as we touched. "Are you *jealous*? Could it be that Little Miss Girlfriend is jealous?"

He was so close to me that I couldn't breathe. I wanted to punch him for being right, but I made a face at him and moved his hand away from me, reaching back into my bag.

"What? Don't flatter yourself," I denied with an eye roll, refusing to look at him.

I pulled out two notebooks with a flourish, handing him one as he looked at me. "Here you go," I said, wondering why he was gazing at me like that.

"So, you spill all your darkest fantasies for me, I write them down and tell your horny-as-fuck boyfriend, so he can finally have his wicked way with you? Wonderful, happy to help." He laughed bitterly as he lit a cigarette.

I opened my mouth to respond, wondering how the hell he had worked out what was on Luke's mind constantly.

"What? Why are you so crude? Can you please open a

window, I don't smoke. Gross." My heart hammered against my chest as I thought about my darkest fantasies.

God, Cal was such a smug bastard.

He dutifully opened a window, then slumped down until he was cross-legged against the door, leaving me on the bed.

"Okay, so talking therapy is when you speak to someone about any negative feelings... so we explore that..." I said, avoiding his intense gaze.

He inhaled, distracting me entirely.

My words hitched in my throat as I tried to regain my composure. "There are different therapies. My personal favorite is interpersonal therapy. What about you?"

He leaned forward somewhat, his voice low. "Do I look like I do therapy? Let's do that personal one you like."

I moved down to his level on the floor, crossing my legs as I stared at him with unease.

Deep breath, Gretchen.

"First, we get to know one another."

6

GRETCHEN

*C*al shifted forward, his eyes on me. "How are we going to do that? I like your hair down, by the way," he said, motioning to my hair.

Just like that, I'm a mess. My cheeks reddened, and I was glad his room was dim. The last thing I needed was him noticing the effect he had on me.

"Excellent to hear, Cal. So, tell me about your life?"

He laughed, his emerald eyes twinkling as he shook his head. "What a shit question. Here's an idea: I'll ask you a question, be honest with me. Don't forget this is confidential. Neither of us can tell anyone anything. Or do you want to go first?"

I looked down at my hands. He was right; it *was* confidential. I looked him in the eyes as I decided to ask what I really wanted to know. "Why are you so rude to people?"

He shook his head as he stared at me in disbelief. "*That's* your question? Why am I rude to people?"

I stared back at him. "It's a simple question."

He whistled slowly before answering me. "Okay,

precious. I have little tolerance for people. I don't like anyone; it's better that way."

"But you like Krystal?" I shot back.

"No, Gretchen, you don't get to ask two questions. It's my turn," he reminded me as I folded my arms.

This was a bad idea.

"Fine, ask away," I said and lifted my chin defiantly.

"Are you happy with Luke?" He was brutally direct, but *why*?

Did he just want to make me uncomfortable? I opened my mouth to answer and he studied me. "What has that got to do with anything?!" I stammered.

"It's a perfectly valid question. It's your relationship. Are. You. Happy?" He repeated, his voice softer now, as his eyes searched my face intently.

I nodded confidently. "Yes. Well, I was..."

Was? Where did that come from?

I closed my eyes, hoping he hadn't noticed that last part.

"Are you going to elaborate? This *is* confidential," he cocked an eyebrow at me.

No such luck. Argh.

Despite barely knowing him, I *wanted* to talk to him, against my brain screaming signals in every different direction not to.

Something told me I could trust him.

"It's personal, though, Cal. I don't even know you," I said, fiddling with my nails.

"You wouldn't know a therapist. This is what this is for, isn't it? Why don't you ask me a question, then we can go back to that," he offered. I was relieved he had given me a get-out-of-jail-free card, and I considered my question.

"Have you ever been arrested?" I wasn't thinking straight. Why would a therapist ask that?

It's not truth or fucking dare Gretchen!

"Yup. My turn."

My heart leaped into my mouth. He'd been arrested? He didn't offer any elaboration, and I didn't dare ask.

Hair fell in front of his eyes, and he moved it away before he placed both hands on his knees.

The fact he had been arrested intrigued me, but I had to wait my turn; that was the deal.

"Elaborate," he said before he leaned back, a triumphant glint in his eyes.

Oh, fuck.

He wasn't letting this go.

I played with my fingernails, considering what to say. Part of me wanted to be honest with him, but that would reveal way too much. Besides, I wasn't even sure how I felt.

This was his *cousin*.

How could I trust him to be confidential?

"He is very sweet. We have been together for a little over a year. He treats me well..." My voice trailed off as he continued to stare at me with that intense gaze.

He gave nothing else away as he waited.

"I'm just not sure I want to be with him forever. Does that make sense? If you don't want to be with someone forever, what's the point in bothering?"

"Is that your question to me?" He raised an eyebrow.

"Yeah, it is."

I was eager for the attention to move away from me and my relationship, which, until now, I had thought was going well.

"I think we have relationships with different people to learn things. Learn how to behave, how to fuck, how to break up, and how to be."

When he said *fuck*, something danced within my stomach,

something unfamiliar yet delightful. What he said made complete sense. I bit my lip and looked at him as he continued.

"You said he makes you happy and that he is sweet. Is that what you want? Like, what really turns you on? Do you even know?" His expression didn't falter at all.

I swallowed, feeling ashamed that I couldn't even answer him.

What *did* I want? *Him*? Could I just say that?

"I don't know what I want, you're right," I whispered.

He raised his eyebrows again quizzically.

"As for what turns me on?" I cleared my throat, my stomach twisting with desire as I imagined it. "I want to kiss someone in the rain. I want someone to push me against a wall, kiss me hard, and pull my hair to the point of pain. I want to want someone so much they are all I think about."

I cannot bring myself to meet his eyes despite them burning into me.

Breathe, Gretchen.

When I finally lifted my eyes to him, he didn't speak, he just continued to stare at me. This time, I couldn't read his expression at all.

I asked him a question to change the course of the conversation.

"My turn. Do you like being single?" I asked, my voice barely above a whisper.

Where had this bravery come from?

He cleared his throat. "It's not about being single or being in a relationship. It would just *be*. I would have to feel things I had never felt before to be in a relationship of any kind. That would show me it was different, not just a fuck, or a crush. I've not felt like that yet," he cut his eyes at me. "Are you really making notes? It's confidential!"

I looked up guiltily from the notepad I'd grabbed to scribble in. "No, I was making key notes. Like needing a new emotion to experience something new."

His next question stopped me in my tracks. "Are you in love with him, Gretchen?"

His voice seemed different now, and I swallowed, replying quickly. "I love him, Cal. He's my boyfriend."

"That's not what I asked," he argued. "I asked if you were *in* love with him. Totally different." He looked at me as our eyes went to war. His emerald green ones won, and I dropped mine to the floor.

"I think I may not be," I admitted, as I blinked and realized I had tears in my eyes.

What the fuck was going on?

"I have to go. It's getting late," I mumbled, standing up as he stood with me, his hands tilting my face up to his as he looked at me with concern.

"Are you okay? Come here." He wrapped his arms around me, and I allowed myself to breathe him in; dizziness swept through me from a combination of my rapid heartbeat, crazy emotions, and that divine smell of his.

With Cal, I felt safe and secure and so far away from the world. I pulled myself away from him, and he grinned at me.

"I think I may be a shit therapist. They aren't meant to hug their clients, are they? Come on, Raven. I'll walk you home."

I didn't have the strength to argue, plus I wanted as much time with him as possible. We walked silently, side by side, as I stole the odd glance at him.

He seemed to be deep in thought, catching my eye now and then as I looked away.

When we reached my drive, I turned to him, grasping at any false confidence I had left. "Thanks. We will need to meet up again soon and try to pick some points out about whether it works—"

He put his finger to my lips, and I trembled beneath his touch. "Shh. Stop thinking. Get some rest; I will see you at school." He turned and walked away, lighting yet another cigarette.

I headed to my bedroom and logged onto my social media accounts on my laptop. There were new photos of Sienna & Ethan at the Rink, looking totally loved up. I clicked on my profile to see the photo of me and Luke after one of his games, looking loved up, too.

What the hell has happened to us?

I climb into bed, hearing the ping that alerts me to a text.

CAL: Confidential, I won't tell anyone. Night beautiful.

7

GRETCHEN

I woke with a start, the ringtone from my phone piercing my skull. I sat up, glancing around my room blearily. It must've only been around four a.m., judging by the darkness. I finally found my phone, and I swiped at the screen until it stopped making the damn noise.

"Hello?" I said groggily as I heard Sienna huffing down the phone.

"Gretchen. Tell me you are not in bed. I'm outside your house."

"At this hour?" I squeaked as she chuckled.

"It's almost eight, babe," she informed me, and I sat bolt upright.

I ended the call and checked the time to find Sienna wasn't joking. I stretched before I padded downstairs with a yawn. I answered the door as Sienna swept in, a flurry of perfume and glitter following her. I trudged back into the kitchen, delving into the fridge for the orange juice.

"Sienna, where's the fire?" My dad laughed as he walked into the kitchen, ruffling my hair.

"Morning, Mr. Red. I came early to remind Gretchen we

have the dance tonight. I'm not even sure she has an outfit."
She shot me a look, and I groaned.

"The dance? Argh."

"See?" She raised an eyebrow at my Dad as he chuckled.
Sienna returned her attention to me, her hands on her hips. "If
you're quick, we can hit the mall before school."

I slid some bread into the toaster, and she held her arms
up in dismay. "You haven't time for toast, Gretch!"

My mom sailed in at that point, smiling at Sienna. "There
is always time for breakfast." She poured herself coffee.
"Especially with Nutella."

Our eyes met as we shared a secret smile. We adored
Nutella.

"What are you wearing?" I asked Sienna, smothering my
barely toasted bread with Nutella.

"I have the most beautiful dress. Wait till you see it!"
Sienna grinned excitedly.

Twenty minutes later, we were in the mall, trying to find
me a dress.

"What about this? My God, Gretch, it's stunning."

I turned to see the dress Sienna was holding up. It was
strapless, a deep shade of emerald green.

"Wow, I do like that!"

Decision made.

I didn't care what I wore, I just needed *something*. I paid,
and we made our way back to Sienna's car.

"What would you have done if I hadn't mentioned
the dance this morning? Hmm? Where would you be
without me?" She grinned, and I stuck my tongue out
at her.

"I forgot about it. It's just not that exciting, is it?"

Sienna turned to gape at me. "Are you for real? The
annual dance is 'not that exciting'? Come on, what has

happened to you? Sorry, what would you class as exciting, my lady?"

"Oh, I dunno, Brad Pitt in Fight Club?" I offered as her eyes misted over.

"Hell yeah, in that red jacket? Gotta love a bad boy, hey Gretch?"

I chose not to acknowledge that and instead asked who Rosie was going with to the dance to change the subject.

"She mentioned something about a guy from her history class." Sienna frowned as she drove.

I nodded wordlessly as I replayed my conversation with Cal last night. "Si, do you think you and Ethan will be together forever?"

She parked at school and turned to look at me with an exasperated expression on her face. "You're acting strange, Gretch; what's going on? Are you and Luke okay?" She peered at me with concern yet again, my eyes filling with unexpected tears.

"I don't know, Si. I just don't know how I feel about him anymore."Admitting it to Sienna felt so different from admitting it to Cal last night.

Sienna hugged me tightly, her sweet perfume wrapping around me as she did. "Babes, this is okay; it will be okay Maybe you're just going through a rocky patch. Luke is amazing, and he is *so* into you. I would love to be with Ethan for the rest of my life, I couldn't imagine being with anyone else."

I dried my eyes, forcing a smile as I turned to her. "I know, hormones, hey?"

We got out of her car and walked up to the school, both stopping when I heard my name being called.

"Gretchen, wait."

It was Krystal. She tottered over to me in her high heels,

and I tried not to groan out loud. All I could see was her removing the cigarette from Cal's lips before she kissed him, and it twisted my stomach with agony and jealousy.

"What do you want, Krystal?" I folded my arms with annoyance as Sienna left us to it.

As usual, Krystal had on a super short minidress and a full face of makeup. She was a pretty girl underneath it all; she didn't need it.

"So, I don't like you. You don't like me, I hope not anyway." She made a face as she flicked her hair. "But we need to swap partners for Psych. They've partnered me with some loser, and I see they have partnered *you* with *my* boyfriend."

I glared at her with disbelief, unable to disguise my jealousy. "Cal is *your* boyfriend?"

She laughed in my face before smiling smugly. "What do you call someone who you spend most of your time naked with, exploring each other's bodies? Yes, *dumbass*, he is my boyfriend. So, we are swapping partners. Have a nice life." She stalked off, leaving me furious.

How dare Krystal think she can order me around? Cal was *my* partner! We had already started working together, too. More to the point, Cal had said she wasn't his girl. I clenched my fists as I trembled with rage. I was about to storm into school when I felt a hand on my shoulder.

"Hey, baby." It was Luke, his handsome face creased with worry. "Are you okay? What's up with Krystal?" His eyes followed Krystal with a strange expression on his face before he looked back at me. "You haven't answered my texts or calls?"

I blinked at him, only half-listening. "Sorry Luke, I'm just tired... and you know Krystal, always dependable to be a bitch."

He reached up to kiss me, but I stepped back, pointing towards the school as a way of explanation. "I can't, babe; I need to get to class; I'm already late..."

He frowned and looked at me suspiciously.

"Can we talk later, Luke?" I called over my shoulder, turning on my heel as I hurried into school, not waiting for his answer. I ran down the corridor despite the signs reminding me it was banned.

The day passed in a blur until I received a text from Luke asking me to meet him by the bleachers after school. I knew I couldn't avoid Luke much longer, with the dance being tonight. I made my way to the bleachers, finding him fresh from football practice. He was all sweaty and gorgeous, making me feel guilty for being such an awful girlfriend, but what could I do?

I can't help how I feel.

"Here you are," Luke said happily, tugging me into his arms. "What time shall I pick you up for the dance later?"

Why was it annoying me that he assumed we were going together? Of course, we would be; we were a couple, after all.

"Is seven good?" He murmured, tilting my head up to kiss my lips softly. "Are you okay?"

I noticed Krystal and Cal sitting on the bleachers behind him, leaning back against the bench whilst Krystal ran her hands down his chest, whispering in his ear. His presence alone left me breathless, and the familiar zing of electricity traveled through my body at the thought of him watching me. His aviators hid his eyes so I couldn't see where he was looking; I just hoped he wasn't watching us—how awkward.

I forced a smile as I moved my gaze back to Luke. "I just need to relax, I think. Tonight will be good for me. Can we enjoy the night with no pressure or questions?"

"Of course, baby. I'll meet you at seven. Can't wait to see

what you're wearing." He winked and patted my ass before I walked away.

I couldn't help but notice Cal was now alone as Krystal leaned forward, talking to her little posse. There's no doubt now that his eyes were on me, and he didn't seem pleased. I avoided his gaze and moved back towards school, refusing to allow him to make me feel guilty.

It's not like I'm his girlfriend.

8

GRETCHEN

*L*ater that evening, I made my way downstairs, trying not to trip in my heels. I lifted the green dress up as I walked, and Luke studied me with a low whistle.

My dad sent him a sharp glare, causing Luke to straighten up and smile politely. My mom then insisted on taking a million photos, and I posed, a fake smile plastered across my face.

"Guys please, I just want to go..." I groaned, sending Luke a desperate look as he held his hands up as a way of apology.

"Sorry, Mr. & Mrs. Red—ladies orders."

They both smiled and wished us a great evening, whilst I promised to be back at a reasonable time. The drive to the dance was silent, neither of us saying much to the other; which wasn't like us.

We pulled up outside and Luke turned to me, his eyes searching mine as he took my hands in his. "Babe, just have a good night tonight. I'll be there whenever you want me, okay"

I smiled gratefully, and we made our way into the dance.

They'd decorated the hall beautifully, and as we stepped in, my heels sank into the plush carpet that welcomed us. I spotted Rosie standing with Hal, a boy from our history class. We made our way over to them, and I embraced her tightly.

"Babe you look sensational!" I breathed. She really did: her hair was worn poker straight, her curvaceous body hugged by a full-length black dress with red slits, exposing her gorgeous legs. Her chocolate brown eyes were surrounded by smoky black glitter, whilst her lips painted a deep red. "Wow," I said, as she beamed at me.

"You think so? You look amazing as usual."

Hal excused himself to get us drinks when Ethan & Sienna turned up beside us. Poor guy—I could only guess he didn't feel too comfortable around people he didn't know too well.

Sienna looked gorgeous in a glitzy gold dress showing off her shiny red hair and tanned skin. Ethan couldn't take his eyes away from her, and she returned his heated gaze. It was typical for them to be this loved up, but I was relieved when Luke and Finn joined us, the latter appearing to be without a date.

"Girls, who wants to dance with me?" Finn held his arms open, his eyes on Rosie. "Rosie, you look incredible." His face changed as he stared at her, and he held his hand out to her. "May I have this dance?" He didn't wait for a response, his hand lacing with Rosie's, walking to the dance floor as she obediently followed him.

Sienna pressed a glass into my hand, whispering, "Down that; I popped some vodka in to make it work quicker." She winked at me, and I struggled to drink it. It tasted like rocket fuel.

As the night went on, I searched the dance floor for Cal. I knew he wouldn't come—dances didn't seem his thing.

I remembered Krystal's words about her relationship with him, and I knocked back the entire drink, signaling to Sienna for another.

Hal was standing on the side, watching Rosie and Finn with annoyance, who seemed to be close on the dance floor some ten songs later.

Sienna nudged me, nodding at Krystal across the room. "Look at her."

I followed her eyes to see Krystal standing on the side of the dance floor looking pissed off. "I wonder where her date is?" I mused, fishing for information from Sienna.

"Well," Sienna slurred, "Rumor has it she hasn't got one."

I looked back with surprise at Krystal, who was now speaking to Ray, another one of the football players. "It won't bother her for long," I remarked.

I searched for Luke, finding him dancing with Wes and Grey, two of his friends, as they tried to make the floss seem sexy.

I couldn't bring myself to watch.

My phone vibrated in my bag, and I pulled it out curiously, to see it was a text from Cal. My heart was in my mouth as I scanned the room.

Where was he?

I opened the text, my heart thumping in my chest when I read it.

CAL: Come outside.

9

GRETCHEN

*O*h, my *god.*

I spun around, catching Sienna's eyes as she lifted her brows at me. I mouthed to her, '*I'll be right back*', and she beamed at me before moving her attention back to Ethan. I stopped for a second, watching as Ethan dipped his head to hers, whispering things in her ear that made her throw her head back with laughter, the smug grin on his face showing how close they were. I swallowed down my envy, casting a glance at Luke, who was now doing some kind of peacock dance with his buddies.

My heart raced in my chest as I pushed through the throng of bodies, perfume, and aftershave clogging my airwaves. The music faded behind me, and I sucked in the cool air, pulling my bag under my arm. I had to address the reason I was out here when my boyfriend was inside.

What did Cal want?

I glanced around, seeking him out. My heels clicked on the tiled pathway as I scanned the area for him, wrapping my arms around my chest as I shivered in the chilly air. My eyes locked onto the silhouette of a figure leaning against a tree in the distance, in his usual jeans and t-shirt combo. My body relaxed as I walked over, offering him a polite smile.

His gaze traveled along the floor between us until it reached me, and my core tightened when he gave me a dark stare that told me he wasn't playing games.

The closer I got, the more I noticed my heart drumming in my chest, my body shivering not only from the cold but from his heated gaze.

"You look... *beautiful.* How is it going in there?" He murmured, his electric green eyes piercing into mine.

This wasn't the behavior I expected from someone's boyfriend.

His gaze journeyed down my body, stopping once he reached my hips. His eyes traveled back up to my eyes, and he stepped closer to me.

Being so attracted to him was painful. If Cal asks me, I'll leave with him right now.

I recalled Krystal's words from earlier that day, and I scowled, fixing him with a cool stare.

"Krystal isn't happy." I held my chin up. "She wants to swap psych partners. According to her, you should be hers, and I should be with whoever they have given her." My voice deceived me, showing the jealousy that raced through every fiber of my being. Being this close to him made me want to melt into his arms and ask him to take me home.

"Is that right?" He said, studying my face as I tried not to react. "I don't think that would be the best course of action, do you? I think we are good together. So, *fuck* Krystal."

Tingles shot all over my body when he said the word '*together*'. I knew he was referring to being stupid partners, but a trickle of excitement ran through me. I was beyond rationality when it came to Cal.

"That's your job, I gather." I folded my arms as I stared at him with what I hoped was utter disgust, and he frowned at me in confusion. I couldn't help being so fucking juvenile.

I was jealous.

"It isn't my job. I haven't fucked her." His eyes flashed at me, his hands dangerously close to mine.

Please let it be true.

I can't imagine him doing that with her. I don't want to imagine him doing it with anyone else.

"What you do and who you do it with is not my business, Cal; let's be honest here," I pointed out as he studied me with an intensity that made me shiver. I moved back again, creating more distance between us. The bark of the tree brushed against my back, and I exhaled to calm my senses, which were in overdrive.

He reached out, his fingers moving my hair from my face as his eyes followed the action. His gaze flickered back to me, and he gave me a lazy smile that set my ovaries on fire.

The rain poured around us, tiny droplets at first, becoming heavier by the second.

I glanced up at the sky with a groan. "I can't get wet!" I wailed, my eyes searching for shelter from the rain.

Cal put his hands on either side of me on the bark of the tree, pinning me in place. My eyes locked onto his as a nervous laugh escaped my lips.

I should have stopped him and asked him to move, but I did nothing. The words didn't come.

His warm hand slid around my waist, tugging me close to him. "What was it you said?" His breath was close to my ear, his masculine scent driving me crazy. His thumb repeated a pattern on the bare skin of my back, and I tried to summon the words to put a stop to this.

"Cal—" I stammered, my eyes drinking his in as he spoke.

"I want to kiss someone in the rain, someone to push me against a wall, kiss me hard, and pull my hair to the point of pain. I want to want someone so much they are all I think about," he quoted what I had said yesterday—word for word.

My heart stopped.

His face was close to mine, his lips hovering above my own as sparks of electricity flew between us. "Let me be of some assistance here."

His body was against mine, my bare skin prickling from the roughness of the bark on my back. I moaned with zero resistance as his lips pressed against mine, his tongue exploring my mouth slowly at first, as though he was testing the water to see what I wanted.

His hands laced with mine against the tree, and I gave into him. My knees almost gave way from the way he was kissing me, but for love or money, would I have moved.

I was lost in the moment.

The fantasies I'd had were *crushed* by reality. I kissed him back, my body screaming for his touch.

He pulled away, my mouth following his until he rested his forehead on mine, allowing our eyes to meet. He gave me that crooked smile, and he kissed me again, softer than before. He moved his mouth to my neck, dotting soft, fervent kisses along my throat as his hands moved, one slipping around my waist, the other cupping my chin as he moved further down to my collarbone.

I swore if he hadn't been holding my hands up, I'd have melted into a puddle of desire on the floor.

I've never felt like this, ever.

He broke away from me again, and this time, I was met with his deep green stare.

I tried to speak, but it was impossible.

Cal moved my curls back from my neck and traced his

finger along my collarbone, following the journey of his lips, my skin still sparking with fire from his kisses. All the while, he gazed at me with a heated expression. "I can't stop thinking about you, Raven."

My heart was going to explode out of my chest. He tugged me towards him, his fingers running down my back as I shivered.

"Are you cold?" He asked, shrugging his jacket off.

I allowed my eyes to skim over his brawn and his veiny, tanned forearms. He draped the jacket around my shoulders, his body heat still radiating from the material. I tugged it around me gratefully as he pulled me towards him by the collar of the jacket with a smirk.

"Is that better?"

"Yes, thank you," I breathed as he lifted my fingers to his lips and kissed them softly.

"I know what I'm about to say is wrong, but it doesn't feel like it," Cal murmured, gazing at me with such intensity I forgot my own name. "I want you to come home with me right now."

The air left my body in a whoosh at his words, and I held onto him as I closed my eyes.

His lips brushed against mine, his smoky yet addictive breath in my mouth as our tongues met. His hands skimmed the flesh below my dress, his fingers flickering against the soft skin of my inner thigh.

My breath hitched in my throat, and he stopped, dropping his hand from the place I wanted him to be so badly.

"This is what you are used to," I whispered as he slammed his hands on the tree, my eyes widening with surprise.

"No, it isn't— trust me. I can't get you out of my *fucking* mind. I've tried."

His confession made me smile stupidly, and all reason left my mind.

Except for one.

"I'm with Luke," I said, my fingernails dug into my palms as tears threatened to spill down my cheeks.

His eyes hardened. His finger grazed against my jaw as he tilted my head up. I gazed at him, knowing that I couldn't fight this, whatever it was. He dropped his lips to mine, and my hands laced around his neck, our mouths meeting fervently.

"Walk away then," Cal muttered against me, loosening his grip. I shook my head, my hands resting on his biceps. His eyes flickered with annoyance, and he shrugged. "Go, Gretchen. Back to your boyfriend, who you don't love."

"What's the alternative? I spend the night with his cousin?" I shot back, pursing my lips. "I'm not that kind of girl, Cal."

"The alternative is you come home with me," he said darkly, turning to gaze at me. "Because you can't deny this." His finger moved between us in a beckoning fashion, and my heart hammered in my chest at the movement.

He stepped forward, his eyes on mine the entire time. "Does he make you feel like I do?" Cal demanded, raising his eyebrows.

I folded my arms around myself, hugging my wet clothes to my body.

Cal *knew* that Luke didn't make me feel like he did.

No one did, and I'm convinced no one ever will again.

"No," I admitted, stepping closer to him. "But I'm not just leaving with you, Cal. I don't even know you." I raised my hand to cup his cheek, and he lifted his hand up to capture my palm with his lips, tugging me towards him.

"Then *get* to know me," he said as I closed my eyes. "Unless you say no, I'm going to keep fucking kissing you."

I lifted my mouth to his, knowing that I was powerless to resist Cal Fallon. When I kissed him, I knew it was over with Luke and me. I risked it all to be with this man who I barely knew.

"I'm going to hell," I whispered as he chuckled against my lips.

"You can ride there with me." His lips teased mine as we gave in to one another. "You coming home with me, Raven?"

His nickname for me was endearing, and I almost felt as long as he called me that, I wasn't Luke's Gretchen.

I was Cal's Raven.

"Luke will kill me," I whispered as I buried my head into his chest.

"You can't control how you feel," Cal scoffed, his hands running through my hair. "I'm not forcing you to do anything. I'm just asking you to choose who you want."

Any other guy would have done this slowly, but not Cal. It was now or never, and I have a suspicion it would be forever.

"Okay. Let's go," I breathed, and he smiled, a genuine smile that I had never seen on him before.

He led me away from the dance and into his car, my heart pounding erratically in my chest.

I wanted to get out of here, away from prying eyes, confusion, and, most importantly—my boyfriend.

Thoughts spun through my mind as we hurried to his car, our hands entwined. I wasn't proud of what I was doing, but the feelings and emotions that Cal invoked within me weren't to be challenged.

He drove carefully, without so much as glancing at me the entire drive.

We pulled up to his house, which was as I remembered, except now, darkness shrouded it. He walked around in front of the car, opening my door before slipping his hand into mine. My skin sizzled under his touch, and I followed him like he was a beacon in the night.

Breathe, Gretch.

It's just the hottest guy you've ever seen, taking you to his bedroom in your dress from the dance you were at with your boyfriend...

We climbed the last steps to his room and closed the door behind us. He stood in front of me, gazing at me, and I slid my heels off. I walked over to him, placing my hands on his chest nervously. He cupped my hand on his chest and kissed my fingers again.

"I don't know what I'm doing, Cal," I confessed, my voice low.

His eyes searched mine before he spoke. "Well, I do, but I want you to be absolutely sure it is what you want." His voice was hoarse with longing.

"Please stop kissing my fingers and kiss my lips," I begged.

Then his lips were on mine, his tongue urgently teasing me. I kissed him back fiercely, my hands now under his shirt.

"Fuck..." he whispered, pulling me onto his lap.

I pushed his shirt up, revealing toned abs. I wasted no time in dropping open-mouthed kisses onto his stomach as he hissed above me.

His hands stopped me from exploring his body further, tugging me up so I was straddling him.

I gazed into his eyes, my hair falling like a curtain around us.

"You remember that feeling I told you I would need, Gretchen?" He murmured lowly as I kissed his throat, devouring his scent in my mouth, my hands running down his back and his chest as I pushed him onto the bed.

"Yes," I breathed, dizzy with desire as he pulled me back.

"I've got it." He swallowed. "But against everything my body is telling me, I am *not* fucking you tonight."

I stared at him, his lips swollen from kissing me.

Did Cal just admit to having... feelings for me? Feelings he had never had before?

I wished I hadn't drunk that alcohol earlier because I couldn't remember every detail of our therapy session, which Cal was now referring to.

"You're not?" I couldn't hide the disappointment in my voice. He stroked my bare shoulders before sitting up, placing me next to him with ease. He tilted his head to look at me, his eyes scanning me as he exhaled loudly.

"No, I'm not. As hard as it is, when I do that, I want you to be mine. Do you understand? *Mine.*"

I stared at him. This god-like creature that was telling me he wanted me to be *his*. I knelt in front of him, sweeping his hair back so I could focus on him properly. It was time for me to be honest, too. "I haven't stopped thinking about you either."

He kissed me again, deeply, until my phone rang, shattering the blissful silence we had created.

"Shit." Cal's eyes narrowed as he nodded at my phone. "Is it him?"

I checked the display, relief coursing through me. "No, it's Sienna." I answered the call as Cal laid back on his bed, watching me through half-closed eyes.

"Babe, where the *fuck* are you? Luke's going crazy, saying you've left. Have you?"

My eyes drifted over to Cal, who smiled at me lazily. "I'm okay, Sienna. Tell him I will call him tomorrow. Will you cover for me? Please, Sienna, I'm telling my parents I'm at yours tonight."

Our eyes hadn't broken contact.

Sienna breathed her response slowly. "You're not going to tell me where you are, are you?"

"No," I whispered. "I can't. But I'm okay."

She agreed to cover for me, so I turned my phone off.

"Do you have anything I could sleep in?" I asked in a small voice, sinking down on the bed beside Cal.

"You could wear me?" He smirked, winking at me as we laced our fingers together.

"Easy there, Buffalo Bill," I joked as we laughed easily. I loved that he got my Silence of The Lambs reference.

He tossed me a t-shirt, tugging his own off to expose his chest as I sucked in a breath. That body was probably illegal somewhere in the world.

"Are you staying here?" He looked like the cat that had the cream.

"If that's okay..." I shrugged with a wide smile as he walked towards me and spun me around.

"Let me unzip your dress," he murmured, carefully sliding the zip down before stepping back. The dress fell as I reached for Cal's t-shirt.

"My God, you are fucking *perfect*," he whispered, his eyes wide as he studied me.

I pulled the t-shirt on before sliding into bed, my eyelids heavy and my tiredness sudden. Cal reached around me, his arm warm and strong, finding my hand as he kissed my shoulder.

"Goodnight, Raven," he whispered as I fell asleep with a smile on my face.

10

GRETCHEN

I woke to a pale blue wall that is unfamiliar and certainly not mine. I stirred when his warm arms surrounded me, pulling me close.

Oh. My. *God.*

I'm in Cal's bed.

The memories of last night returned to me hazily, and I closed my eyes. I turned to face him, finding him fast asleep. His lips were parted slightly, his long lashes resting on his cheeks. I gazed at him, my heart drumming in my chest. I leaned forward and kissed his lips tenderly as he groaned, his hands pulling me closer as he returned the kiss.

How was *this* my reality?

"Is this what lust feels like?" I wondered aloud as he wrinkled his nose up at me.

"Do you think that's what this is? You're the first girl I've ever slept next to and actually *slept*," he smirked as I hit him with a pillow. "Are you okay?" He looked at me, biting his lip.

I curled up next to him, my hands entwined with his. "This isn't *me*, Cal." I gestured between us. "Lying here with you whilst I'm in a relationship, with *your* cousin of all people," I admitted with a tired sigh.

Cal ran his fingers down my back, fixing me with his emerald gaze. "I know, I do. But what if you're meant to be with me? Then being with him is the wrong thing, isn't it? That makes this right?"

I smiled at his inane logic.

He leaned on his elbow so he was looking at me directly. I wasn't strong enough to resist his lazy morning smile or the fact he wasn't wearing any clothes over his muscular chest. He fell back onto the pillow, dragging me down with him as his arms circled my body, and I shivered with delight. "No one has to know yet," he said into my hair.

"So, what about Krystal?" I pouted.

She wouldn't let him go without a fight.

He leaned down and kissed me, making me almost forget my name. "Who?"

My heart hammered in my chest at his response when he spoke again; his voice was low and quiet.

"I don't think I've ever wanted anyone so much in my life," he groaned.

My cheeks ached from smiling, and I couldn't help but wonder how the hell I had attracted the attention of Cal Fallon. I pulled him down to me then, kissing him until he pulled away.

"I can't keep kissing you in my bed, Raven, without wanting to do wicked things to you." He swung his legs out of bed, stretching as I watched his back muscles ripple with each movement. "I'll get us some juice." He strode to the door, closing it softly behind him.

I peered at my phone to inspect the damage of leaving the dance so abruptly last night. Lots of messages greeted me from a very drunken Luke.

> LUKE: Where are you?

> Dammit, Gretchen! Tell me where you are!

> I can't believe you've left without even saying goodbye, what the fuck is wrong with you?

> Fuck you!

> I'm sorry, I love you so much.

> Sienna told me you're okay. You can talk to her and not me, huh? So WHO ARE YOU WITH?

I swallowed, texting Sienna straight away, reassuring her that I was fine and that I would be home soon. I didn't know what else to say.

> SIENNA: G, please call Luke. He has been out of his mind with worry.

Cal walked back in, handing me a tall glass of chilled orange juice. I filled him in on the texts from Luke, and he grimaced. "I know this is difficult for you...But you've got to go with what you want. Do you want me to talk to him for you?" His voice was colder now.

I shook my head, horrified.

"Shall I take you home?" Cal asked quietly.

I nodded, groaning as I realized the decisions I had to make. It wasn't going to be easy.

"Is anyone in?" I asked Cal in a small voice.

"No, you are my dirty little secret." He grinned, biting his lip again.

I dragged him towards me, kissing him again. This time,

he pushed me against the wall, lifting my legs around his waist, which was no easy feat.

"*God*, I *need* you. You're driving me crazy," he groaned, burying his face in my neck.

"*Cal*," I moaned into his neck, "I have to go..."

He stepped away from me, dropping me to my feet gently. "Tell me, Gretchen," he asked, "How badly do you want this?"

I drank him in and kissed his chest, then his neck, before our mouths smashed against each other again. We broke apart, his fingers tracing my jaw as his eyes searched mine. "So much," I whispered.

"You're *mine*," he muttered suddenly as my heart rate sped up. His hand ran through my hair, tugging it slightly as he nibbled on my lip softly.

I arched against him, feeling his hardness against me. Instead of feeling anxious like I did with Luke, I realized something else.

I wanted him.

My hand trailed down, but before I could reach for him, his hand clamped on mine, forcing it against the door.

"You're stopping me?" I panted as he stared at me, as though he was wrestling with his emotions.

His jaw clenched as he closed his eyes. "Not like this," he whispered.

I wanted him so much, and he was saying no. What was his deal?

I stood, smoothing my clothes down. "Shall we go then?" I said coolly as he raised his eyebrows. I moved to open the door when he pushed his hand on it, stopping me from leaving. My heart pounded in my chest as he brought his face close to mine.

"What's wrong?" He asked softly, searching my eyes with

his own green wonders. "Are you angry that I won't fuck you now, up against this door?" he trailed his fingers down my arm. "You have enough to think about without me adding even more."

Wow.

He was doing this for *me*.

He was right; I did have enough to think about, but then all I could imagine was him fucking me against the door. My insides were like jelly as he reached behind me and pulled the door open.

We made our way downstairs, my legs still shaking from our intimate doorway encounter.

A sharp knock on the door made me jump, my eyes widening in fear.

Cal frowned and looked at me. "Who the *fuck...*" He opened the door and in walked Drake, his brother.

"Morning. I forgot my keys. Been a heavy night," he explained as he looked at me in surprise. "Hey, aren't you Luke's girlfriend?" He sat on the kitchen worktop, drinking orange juice from the bottle.

What was it with the men in this family? Drake's tight t-shirt clung to every contour in his arms and his torso, and I tried not to stare.

"No, man, she's not," Cal growled, arms folded as he stood in front of me.

Drake raised his eyebrows at us and shrugged. "Whatever. I need to hit the hay. Have fun, kids." He jumped down from the counter, making his way upstairs as he smirked at me.

My cheeks burned as Cal turned me towards him and stroked my face tenderly. "If we are going to do this, Raven, you're gonna have to get used to people having a problem with it."

He brushed his finger over my cheek as he stared into my

eyes. I wanted him so much it hurt. I leaned up, gathering his hair in my hand as I pressed his head towards me, meeting his mouth with mine.

I still can't believe I get to do that— kiss Cal Fallon!

I felt like the luckiest girl in the world. Except now, I had to face reality.

Cal handed me his duffle coat, which I quickly zipped up.

"I'll get the car keys," he said as he made his way past me into the hall.

"We could walk; it's not far," I pointed out.

Cal laughed, looking pointedly at the heels I had worn last night in my hand. "It's your call, babe if you really wanna walk." He smirked at me as I rolled my eyes.

Smug bastard.

We made our way to the car, and I glanced around, terrified, in case we saw anyone we knew.

Cal leaned over to me, his eyes burning into mine. "Relax, it's early. Drake was just getting in from his night out; everyone will be asleep."

A few minutes later, he pulled up a little past my house and turned off the engine. He leaned back and watched me as I gathered my dress in one hand and my heels in the other. I looked at him longingly as I went to open the car door.

"How can I miss you when you are right in front of me?" I asked, my voice heavy with desire.

He smiled then before chuckling. "Is that your next question?"

I laughed and opened the door.

"Text me," he ordered, his eyes locked on mine as I nodded.

As if I wouldn't.

I climbed out of the car and made my way into the house, praying no one was up. The house was silent, and all I could hear was Cal's car driving away. I crept up the stairs and into my room, catching sight of myself in his clothes. I stripped them off before I pulled on my pajamas, using a makeup wipe to remove the sticky mascara. I had just climbed into bed when my phone pinged.

> CAL: Bed is cold without you.

A rush of excitement swept through me as I imagined him lying in bed thinking of me. I was about to respond when my phone pinged again.

> LUKE: Ring me. We need to talk.

My heart sank.
How can I be so happy yet so sad at the same time?
I texted Cal first without even thinking.

> GRETCHEN: Luke wants to talk. Don't know what to say.

> CAL: That you're mine?

My heart pounded in its prison, and desire swept through my body.

How had this happened? How am I supposed to explain this?

I dialed Rosie's number, not caring how early it was.

She eventually answered, whispering into the phone. "Babes, I'm asleep. I'll ring you later!" Then she hung up.

I stared at my phone in disbelief.

How rude!

I called Sienna, who answered on the first ring.

"Gretchen, what the *actual* fuck? Where are you?!"

I quickly explained that I was at home. "It's really complicated, Si, and I don't know how to explain..."

She abruptly cut me off. "The thing is, Gretchen, we were all at the dance, having a great time. Then you disappeared, and no one knew where you were. We were worried. Then Luke went looking for you, and he didn't come back!"

I winced at the mention of Luke as Sienna exhaled into the phone.

"So, what happened?"

I sighed as tears stung my eyes; this was going to be difficult. "I was with Cal."

I heard Sienna inhale sharply. "*Cal Fallon*? Are you shitting me, Gretchen? With him, how?"

I decided not to give her an answer, instead focusing on the consequences of my actions. "I need to call Luke, Si." I hung up and stared at my phone.

How was I going to explain this to Luke?

Luke answered straight away, his voice gruff. "Gretchen?"

Hearing his familiar voice made me want to cry.

"I'm so sorry, Luke."

He was silent at the other end. "Are you at home?" he asked.

I sniffled. "Yes, why?"

"I'm coming over."

11

GRETCHEN

*L*uke didn't wait for an answer and hung up.

Fuck.

I chewed on my fingernails, wondering what the hell I was going to say to Luke.

When the doorbell rang some fifteen minutes later, my body trembled. My heart was in my mouth as I made my way to the door, still thinking of what I was going to say to him. When I opened the door, all thoughts left my head, and his steely glare made me swallow hard.

I stared at the floor, unable to meet his glare. "Uh, come in."

Luke didn't take his eyes off me, following me silently to my room. I sat on my bed, my head in my hands, wishing I was anywhere but here.

He slumped into the chair in front of my desk, his posture heavy, already looking defeated, and I hadn't even told him anything about me and Cal yet.

Cal.

I tried to draw strength from how I felt when I was with Cal, remembering how happy I was earlier that morning. I owed it to Luke to tell him everything, and to end things between us before I took it further with Cal. Guilt twisted my stomach when I remembered how I would have handed my virginity to Cal on a plate this morning had he wanted to take it.

My cheeks flushed, and Luke frowned at me, moving his stare to the photos above my desk. Most of them were of us with our friends, in summer by the beach. The memories were beautiful, but they were just that: memories. Ocean-blue eyes moved to mine, and my stomach lurched with anxiety.

"Are you going to tell me what happened, Gretchen?" His voice broke, and a piece of my heart did too.

How to tell him this, that I've cheated on him with his cousin?

I knew I was skating on thin ice, but I *had* to tell him. "Last night... I'm sorry I left like I did."

Luke continued to stare at me, his eyes narrowing. His fingers drummed on the arms of my chair, his foot tapping repeatedly, a sure sign that he was angry.

"Where did you go? I came looking for you," he said slowly, crossing his arms.

I licked my lips and rubbed my hands on my legs.

This was it.

No amount of deep breaths calmed me, so I just bit the bullet and came out with it. "I was with Cal," I whispered, the air leaving his lungs as he inhaled sharply. My palms were sweating, my knees jiggling as I waited for him to say something.

Anything.

His eyes widened and his mouth opened, then closed before he finally spoke. "Say that again."

I didn't want to say it again, but his eyes commanded it.

"I went home with Cal."

His fists clenched so tightly I could see the white of his knuckles. I regretted telling him without Cal there, but then it would've only ended in a storm of testosterone.

"Why?" He spat, his voice laced with venom. He was standing now, and for the first time, I felt afraid of him.

I didn't think my explanation would suffice, so I opted for an apology. "Luke, I'm sorry..."

He paced my bedroom, running his hands through his hair. "So, let me get this straight," he barked, not meeting my eyes. "You spent last night with my cousin. Are you telling me it was a stupid mistake, Gretchen?"

My heart ached so much looking at his face, the face I had kissed so much over the past year. The face I thought I had fallen in love with.

I can't lie to him, not now.

I didn't want to be with him anymore; I wanted Cal, at any cost. It scared me that I felt as strongly as I did about Cal without truly knowing him, but all I had to go by was the way I felt when I was with him.

"I'm sorry..." I repeated, wringing my hands together. I had to say something else, but my mind was blank.

He glared at me with disgust. "Yeah, you said that. What are you sorry for?" He snapped, his voice dripping in sarcasm.

"For hurting you. I swear this happened so quickly..."

I knew I sounded like I was trying to make excuses for something you couldn't excuse. My mouth was dry, but my cheeks were flooded with tears.

Luke fell back into the chair, exhaling slowly. "I need to ask you something and I want the truth." His eyes swam with hurt, and I knew what he was going to ask me. "Did you sleep with him?"

I met his eyes then, shaking my head. "No, I didn't." I

didn't add that the only reason I didn't was because Cal has amazing self-control and I had none.

A look of relief passed over his face as he bowed his head. Sex was always the most important thing to Luke, and if he found out I had slept with Cal, I knew he would kill us both out of sheer jealousy.

"Luke—" I began as he raised his eyes to meet mine.

"I'm fucking gutted," he whispered, his eyes wide. "I can't talk to you right now." He left my room, the door slamming shut behind him as he did.

The tears blurred my vision then, a mixture of relief and sadness. I heard a soft knock at my door as my mom walked in, her silk robe trailing behind her.

"Baby, was that Luke? It's early...is everything okay? What's happened?" She sat beside me, wrapping her arms around me comfortingly.

"Oh, Mom, I don't even know where to start," I sobbed, letting out the emotion I had been holding in. She soothed me, stroking my hair as we sat in silence. I pulled away, looking into her lovely face, so full of concern. "I don't think I love Luke anymore."

She blinked a few times before speaking. "It's normal to fall out of love, baby. You are eighteen. Did he hurt you?"

Her eyes met mine, and I shook my head. "No, no, he didn't. It's not him...it's me," I cried.

She kissed the top of my head, rubbing my back before she held me. "Look, get yourself a shower and put your makeup on. Everything seems better when you look at the part, even if inside, you are crumbling. Why don't you call Rosie or Sienna? Surround yourself with your friends, baby." She smiled as she stood up.

She was right. I needed to take charge of the situation I had created.

I took a shower before putting my makeup on, my war paint, as I remember my Mom once telling me. My phone rang, and I tensed until I saw it was Rosie.

"Rose!"

"Hey, lady. Are you okay? Bit of an early call from you this morning..." She yawned down the phone as I apologized, pleading with her to meet me at The Lounge.

I dressed, checking my reflection in the mirror. I'd gone for an aqua-green jumper over ripped jeans; considering the weather, it should suffice. I took a deep breath and made my way out of the house, heading for the bus stop at the end of my street that would take me into town.

12

GRETCHEN

"*Y*ou spent the night with *Cal Fallon*?" Rosie gasped, and a few heads turned in our direction.

The Lounge was busy with mostly students from our school, seeing as it was a Sunday. We usually crashed here all day, getting high on caffeine.

"Please keep your voice down..." I hissed through gritted teeth, my eyes wide as my cheeks flushed. Not only would it be catastrophic if someone heard her, but they would also spread it around the school in less than an hour that I'd slept with him. I didn't want that for Luke, not when it wasn't true. I thought back to his eyes, the way he had looked at me with disappointment.

"Does Luke know?" Rosie asked, her eyes shining with curiosity and scandal.

"Yeah," I grimaced. "I told him this morning—it wasn't great."

Rosie winced, stirring her drink as she tilted her head at me, studying me with a mischievous expression. "I mean, I had my suspicions. I thought there was someone else, but *Cal*

Fallon? I did not see that one coming. *Fuck*! What was it like?"

I gazed dreamily in the distance as I remembered his lips on mine, his hands unzipping my dress...

"Hello?!" Rosie clicked her fingers in front of my face. I blinked at her, breaking out of my reverie.

"I'm sorry, it was amazing. I'm not gonna lie. I just feel bad..." I sipped on my drink, wondering how it was possible to feel so torn. I knew already that I wanted to be with Cal, and from his intensity, it was clear he wanted to be with me, too. My heart skipped a beat when I thought of him—until Rosie brought me back down to reality with a bump.

"No shit, you do. I bet you're looking forward to school tomorrow. Two of the hottest guys in school fighting over you." Her voice dripped with envy as she made a face at me.

It wasn't as exciting as she made it sound in reality, not when you cared for someone like I did for Luke. Then again, my feelings for Cal were escalating with each interaction. We had been texting non-stop, and I was wandering around with a smile on my face at the sheer thought of him. Then there was Luke, who was furious with me. I had to make things right.

"What am I gonna do, Rose?"

"I suppose you have to go with your heart." She shrugged, slurping on her drink. "I thought Cal seemed a bit of a prick if I am honest. Plus, he's been with Krystal, who is, let's be honest, the biggest slut in school."

I narrowed my eyes, seething at the thought of him with Krystal. I didn't want to think of his hands anywhere other than over me. It was natural for my friends to dislike him, more so now than before.

Sharing friends with your boyfriend is great until you break up.

"I think," Rosie continued, "If you aren't happy with Luke, you need to tell him and break it off. He deserves that, Gretch. You spent the night with Cal—hang on!" She wiped her mouth with her fingers, her eyes bulging. "Did you—"

I shook my head, grateful that Cal hadn't allowed me to have my wicked way with him that morning, or I would've felt even more of a jerk right about now.

"What? So, both said hot guys want to bone you, and you aren't giving it up to either of them? Can I be you for a day?" Rosie whined.

I rolled my eyes, opened my phone, and sent a text to Luke.

GRETCHEN: Can we talk?

"So, um, how was your night? I saw you dancing with Finn; that was quite the surprise..." I sounded like the coward I was, trying to deflect the subject away from me.

Rosie waved her hand dismissively. "You know what he's like. I just entertained him because I was drunk. I went home when we couldn't find you." Rosie moved the conversation back around to me, and I slumped back into my seat dejectedly.

"I know; I'm sorry again for just leaving. I just thought you and Finn seemed a little cozy on the dance floor..." I wiggled my eyebrows, hoping she would take the bait.

She laughed, wrinkling her nose up at me with amusement. "Cozy? Me and Finn? I can assure you we are anything but." She flicked her hair over her shoulder. "So, what are you doing today? Other than feeling sorry for yourself."

I groaned, dropping my head into my hands. I didn't feel sorry for myself— I felt guilty.

I was a cheater.

I'd hurt my boyfriend by shacking up with his cousin, of all people. He wouldn't ever forgive me, and I couldn't blame him.

"I should see Luke, but I don't think he wants to," I mumbled, checking my phone to find that he hadn't replied. I couldn't expect him to, considering everything that had happened.

"Well, I'm heading home, babes; I'm exhausted. Last night took it out of me." Rosie yawned again, sliding out of the booth. "Do you want to come back to mine for a bit?"

"No, I'm not the best company."

Rosie made a face as she reached for my hand. "Want a ride home?" She asked gently, smiling at me.

I shook my head as I gathered my things, forcing a smile. "No, thanks. I need to clear my head anyway; the walk will do me good."

She kissed the top of my head, pulling me in for a hug. "Love you, Gretch. Chin up, okay? You spent the night with the hottest guy in school, possibly the world!"

I smiled to myself as she walked away, swinging her keys around her fingers as she did. At least Rosie seemed happy. I left the Lounge and walked the long way home, taking the opportunity to think. I crossed the road and walked down a street lined with pretty houses, picket fences, kids playing outside, and sprinklers on the lawn. They looked so happy. I saw a little girl playing with her sister, chasing her around with what looked like a snail. The girl shrieked for her mother whilst the other laughed so hard she held her stomach. I smiled again, then I realized I was staring, so I made a move. At that point, my phone rang.

Luke.

I gulped before I answered the call. "Hey," I whispered. "Thanks for calling—"

"Where are you?" He interrupted, his voice sounding distant.

I had to get used to this coldness because I wasn't his girlfriend anymore. The thought made me sad because, more than anything, I knew we wouldn't be able to be friends anymore; it would change the dynamics of our friendship group, too.

What a pickle.

"Near The Lounge. I'm just walking home," I said, checking the road as I crossed it.

"That's a long way to walk. Stay there, I'll come and meet you," he commanded before ending the call.

I sighed, stuffing my hands in my pockets. I glanced around and sat on a low wall near a house. This was going to be even harder than this morning; I could feel it. He'd had time to mull it over, and I knew what this would do to him. He was possessive at the best of times—this was going to be a shit show.

Luke's car pulled onto the road some fifteen minutes later, tires squealing as he drew up beside me.

My stomach lurched with guilt when he dragged his eyes over me.

"Are you getting in?" He snapped, watching me as I crossed in front of his car.

With a deep breath, I climbed into the passenger seat beside him. The familiar scent of his aftershave greeted me, and I almost wept.

I didn't want to hurt him. I didn't mean to do this to us.

"Look, Gretchen," Luke said, his eyes meeting mine. "You made a mistake, right? I get it. He's a handsome guy. You got tipsy... We all make mistakes."

Wait... what?

He reached over, grabbing my hand. "We all fuck up." He gave a bitter laugh. "Was this the first time?" He gripped the steering wheel as he shifted towards me.

"Yes," I replied in a small voice.

Other than the time I nearly begged him to bend me over the sink in your bathroom...

I closed my eyes at the memory.

I'm such a bitch.

"Luke, I am sorry. I do like Cal—"

He leaned over, his hand sneaking behind my neck as he pressed his lips against mine, his tongue pushing into my mouth urgently. My back pressed against the car door as he kissed me, and I responded to him on autopilot, kissing him back, his familiar taste in my mouth. Dread swept over me when I realized that I was giving him false hope.

I didn't want Luke. I wanted Cal.

I put my hands on his shoulders and pushed him back, shaking my head as I did. "No, Luke."

He glared at me with disbelief, his face close to mine. "Why? Do you feel disloyal to *him*?" He spat the last word out in disgust. "I didn't think you felt disloyalty, Gretchen. You sure didn't last night."

I twisted away from him so that I was staring out of the window, my body trembling with guilt and anxiety.

Luke started the car and squealed away from the curb.

A trickle of fear seeped around my core as I pulled my seat belt on, asking him where we were heading.

He stared ahead in stony silence, not responding.

My mind raced. He was a nice guy; he wouldn't hurt me. He was hurting, that was all. My phone interrupted the awkward silence, and I reached for it until he snapped at me.

"Don't answer it. I just want your attention for a little while longer if you would be so kind."

I slumped back in my seat wordlessly.

He was incensed with rage, his jaw tightening as he drove, the car weaving in and out of lanes dangerously. "A *year*, Gretchen. Are you going to throw that away over a punk like him? Do you know anything about him? He's a fucking *dick*. I assume you know that he's got a temper?"

I remained silent, allowing him to continue.

"Oh, boy, has he got a temper. Why do you think they moved here?"

I glanced at him curiously as he continued with a sneer.

"Why don't you ask your lover *that*?"

The car veered to the left, and my heart thudded when I saw we were on a dirt track. It was only when he took a few more turns that I realized we were nearing my house.

"Home, sweet home, *honey*," he whispered bitterly.

I released my seat belt, my fingers trembling.

He's unhinged.

I had done this to him, but my instincts told me to get away from him.

"This is bullshit," he whispered as he grabbed the back of my head, pressing his lips down hard on mine again.

This time, I didn't kiss him back, and he tightened his grip on my hair.

"You want *him*, don't you?" He hissed, his eyes searching mine.

I'd never seen him like this, and when I reached out for the door handle, tears filled my eyes.

"Get out of my *fucking* car." Luke released me, staring ahead with a cold expression on his face, his knuckles whitening as he tightened his grip on the steering wheel.

My body trembled as I swung my legs out of the car, desperate to get away from him. The car door barely closed behind me before he sped away. I stood on the street, tears running down my cheeks.

What had I gotten myself into?

13

GRETCHEN

*W*alking into school the next day was like walking into a lion's den.

I tried to remain calm, but the constant whispering and wide-eyed expressions made me want to scream at the nosey gossipers.

Didn't they have anything better to do with their time?

Was our breakup the highlight of their week?

I exhaled and threw my books into my locker, my temper rising when they fell back out from all the crap I had piled in there.

"*Shit*," I mumbled as I leaned down to pick them up.

"You okay?" Rosie asked, her eyes filled with concern.

I crammed the books in, dragging out the two I needed. Whispers continued to fill the hallway, and I knew they were about me.

"Yeah, I will be. It's a shitty situation."

"You got that right, Gretchen." Boomed a voice, silencing the hallway instantly.

"Finn," Rosie warned as he pushed past her, his lips curled up in a sneer.

"You've ditched Luke for *that* prick? I can't believe you would do that to him. You *know* how much he adores you. Luke could've had *anyone*." He shook his head at me before walking down the hallway, his bag slung over his shoulder.

I turned to see Rosie staring after him in stunned silence.

"I deserved that," I whispered, biting my lip as my eyes filled with tears.

"Ugh. Just ignore him—what does he know?" Rosie mumbled, her voice trailing off as we saw Krystal standing at the bottom of the corridor, a wicked smile on her face. "What the fuck is she smiling at?"

I narrowed my eyes at her before following Rosie into class, preparing for even more grief. "Fuck knows." I sighed. I searched the room desperately for Cal, my eyes meeting the judgemental ones of my classmates. I slid into my seat and tried to ignore the stares from everyone, dragging my phone out of my bag.

GRETCHEN: Where are you?

CAL: Bit of something to deal with at home. I'll text you later...are you okay?

GRETCHEN: You aren't coming to school? Cal, don't leave me on my own here. It's horrible.

I stuck my phone in my bag and rubbed my eyes, as though by doing that it would erase this shit from my brain.

The door slammed open, and I jumped, a sinking feeling in my stomach when I saw Finn, Ethan and Luke walking in. Luke had dark circles around his eyes, which he trained on me.

Holy shit.

I stared out of the window, trying not to make eye contact with any of them. My leg jiggled when I heard the chair beside mine scrape across the floor, the familiar scent of Luke's cologne making my stomach do gymnastics. I dragged my book out of my bag, my phone dropping out between us on the floor.

Luke glanced down, his eyes falling on the digital envelope with 'Cal' on display. His eyes met mine, flashing darkly.

"Where is he? Left you to face the music alone? What a *lovely* guy." His voice was thick with sarcasm, the anger clear.

Sniggers spread around the class as he tilted his head to peer at me, his ocean-blue eyes churning with waves of anger. "Then again, I don't suppose he gives a shit about you or school."

The teacher cleared her throat, commanding our attention. She had no hope of me paying any form of attention today. I closed my eyes as tears filled them. Although I deserved that from Luke, it still didn't make it any easier to swallow.

I opened the text from Cal, my vision blurry.

CAL: Coming.

Relief coursed through me; I couldn't wait to see him. I was the bad bitch here, and it was a heavy cross to bear.

Luke glared at me from his seat, leaning forward towards me. "How could you do this to me?" He hissed at me, not bothering to keep his voice low.

"Luke, I've said I'm sorry..." I said, fully aware that everyone was ignoring the teacher to listen to our heated exchange.

Luke pointed at my phone, his eyes wide as he spoke

through gritted teeth. "Yeah? So why are you still fucking *texting* him?"

The teacher addressed us then, her hands on her hips as she glared at us from the front of the class. "Is everything alright there? If you would like to have a lover's tiff you can do that in your own time."

Laughter broke out around the room as my cheeks flushed with embarrassment.

"Fuck this," Luke growled, grabbing his bag as he stormed out of the class, followed by the teacher.

All eyes turned to me, and I retaliated without thinking. "This is none of your business; why are you all *so nosey*?!" I snapped, gathering my things and following Luke out of the class.

I found him sitting on a bench, his arms folded as the teacher walked back towards the class.

"Deal with your drama and get your asses back in here. We don't have time for these ridiculous games. I won't have it disrupting my class. In here working, or the principal's office. Your choice." She arched a brow at me, sending a warning glare to Luke as she strode away.

I stared at Luke, shifting my weight from one side of my body to the other as I tugged on my hair, a habit of mine. "I'm—"

"Sorry. Yes, you said. Do me a favor, Gretchen; don't fucking talk to me again. You've made your choice." He stood up, pushing past me back into the class.

I sat down on the bench, realizing I couldn't stay in school today. It was too much, too hard. I walked out of the exit, tears blurring my vision as I walked into a hard chest. I looked up to see Cal's beautiful green eyes narrowing as he tilted my head to his.

"I can't do this, Cal, it's fucking awful. Luke doesn't want to speak to me, and the entire school hates me." I sobbed as he wrapped his strong arms around me.

"Fuck this shit today. We don't need it," he muttered, and I followed him, sniveling to myself pitifully.

I had created this mess, yet I felt sorry for myself. I couldn't help the way I felt about Cal.

"Fancy skipping school, Raven?" He drawled as we reached his car, tossing my bag into the back casually. He stroked my hair out of my eyes as he gazed at me, his head tilted to the side.

I wasn't sure how we were this intense so quickly, but we were. "You're a dangerous influence, Fallon," I said, my breath catching as another sob threatened to rack my body.

"Yeah, I am. You coming?"

14

GRETCHEN

*A*s the car sped away from school, leaving everyone behind us, I relaxed into the seat, feeling safe and happy beside Cal. No one agreed with us being together, but when I was with him, none of that mattered. Most girls would kill to be in my position, sitting in a car with *Cal Fallon*—full name usage and everything.

His dirty blond hair was messy and pushed back away from his eyes, which looked slightly swollen and tired, but he was still the most attractive man I'd ever seen.

"Are you okay?" I asked when he looked over at me, my stomach flipping as his lips pulled into a reassuring smile.

"I'm alright, don't worry about me." He pulled off the main road into a deserted car park near a crappy local diner.

I frowned as he cut the engine, turning towards me as he did.

"What happened?" He murmured in a low tone, his gaze holding mine. He listened as I told him everything from start to finish, my eyes watering again when I remembered how angry Luke was.

"Raven, if you ever left me, I would be fucking *furious*. If you left me for someone *else*, well..." The sentence hung in the air, the understanding between us unspoken. The insane connection we had came with a powerful form of jealousy that we felt on both parts; the fact he referred to me as 'leaving him' despite us never having a conversation about us being official was a perfect example.

"I wouldn't," I said firmly, knowing it was true.

No one had ever made me feel this way before, and in such a short span of time.

He tilted his head to look at me. I could never describe his eyes as plain green; they were too vibrant, too deep. Animated with emotion, swirling against the darkness of his pupils as he moved closer to me, his scent driving me wild.

"No, you wouldn't. You won't ever want to leave me." He pulled me into his arms as I moaned beneath his touch. "Are you mine yet?" He breathed into my neck, his lips against mine, softly at first, before I parted my lips, unleashing his inner demon.

Unable to believe this creature wanted me as much as he did, I gasped against him as my tongue danced with his. "Yes," I breathed my excitement when he groaned into my mouth, pressing my head to his as he deepened the kiss. When I kissed Cal, I lost all sense of rationality. Reality faded into the background, and it was just us in our own world. But reality beckoned, as it always did.

"Cal." I pulled away from him reluctantly and stared into his eyes. "I need to go back to school. My parents will kill me if I don't."

He nodded as he started the car, his brow furrowed. "Whatever you want," he muttered, and fear leaped into my throat.

"Are you angry with me?" I asked, my chest tight with the thought of upsetting him.

A puzzled expression filled his face as he pulled out of the car park. "Why would I be mad at you?" He chuckled, turning back to gaze at me.

A flush of embarrassment washed over my body as I muttered under my breath, "You know... for not...."

"Fucking me in the seat of my car?" He finished my sentence, his eyebrows raised with amusement. "Not at all. It will be worth the wait, I know it," His hand squeezed my thigh. "Let's go face those fuckers."

When we got back to school, it was lunchtime, and a wave of nausea swept over me as we approached the entrance.

Cal squeezed my hand as we walked into school, lifting our joined hands up to me. "Is this okay?" He checked, a playful smile on his lips, and I almost burst with happiness.

"Yeah... although I don't think Luke will...."

Cal put a finger to my lips. "*Fuck Luke.*"

We walked into the cafeteria together, and a hush fell instantly.

My friends were sitting around our usual table, along with Luke. My heart was in my mouth when Cal and Luke made eye contact.

Ethan whispered something to Luke, and I couldn't help but notice the hurt in his eyes.

I pulled Cal towards an empty table away from them, but his resistance alarmed me.

"Cal," I whispered desperately. "Please..." I tugged at his arm, trying to stop the staring competition he seemed to be in with Luke.

Luke stood up and Ethan tried to pull him back down unsuccessfully.

Rosie stood, making her way over to us, glaring at Cal

with clear dislike. "Gretchen, why don't you guys leave? It's raw for Luke right now..."

My stomach clenched at my stupidity.

How could I even think this wouldn't end in a cockfight?

I stood to leave but Cal remained seated, tugging me back down beside him.

"Why? She's apologized. She can't help how she feels." His voice was low and strong, but Rosie scowled at him, prepared to do battle.

"Because it's *courtesy*, Cal. Less than twenty-four hours ago, Gretchen was his girlfriend, or did that slip your memory?"

He fixed his eyes on her, a stony expression on his face. "I thought you were *Gretchen's* best friend; I didn't realize you were the president of Luke's fan club."

Her eyes widened, her mouth open in shock as I groaned.

"*Cal!*" I exclaimed, shooting him an exasperated look "Rosie, I'm sorry, we should go..."

Rosie folded her arms and shook her head, walking back to the table wordlessly.

Why is she being so loyal to Luke suddenly?

I didn't voice this in front of Cal, as he would probably waste no time in telling her exactly what a shit friend she was without caring for our history.

Luke glared at us, Ethan and now Finn sat on either side of him as they watched us with grim expressions on their faces.

"Cal, please..." I pleaded with him, not knowing what he was capable of.

I didn't want Luke to antagonize him in any way, no matter how wronged he felt.

Cal finally turned and looked at me, his eyes narrowing. "He'll see it, eventually. He may as well get used to it." He lifted my hand to his lips and kissed it, my stomach filled with butterflies as his gaze swept over me. "But if you want to go, we'll go."

I nodded, relieved.

He swung his legs out from his seat, my hand still in his as he gestured for me to lead the way towards the exit.

"Cal." Luke's voice boomed through the cafeteria.

My body froze in response, my hand gripping Cal's as he turned slowly to face him.

"What?"

The entire school held its breath; I, for one, was most *definitely* holding mine.

Luke rose to his feet before folding his arms and nodding at me. "You're welcome to her. She's frigid as fuck."

His words cut through me like a knife.

Cal didn't blink as he tilted his head to the side, studying Luke pitifully.

Rosie's hand flew to her mouth as she stood up in my defense, her eyes flashing. "Luke, you can't say that!"

Luke put his hands in the air, ignoring her. "I'm a single guy now, girls. Let the fun begin." He smirked at me directly, sitting back down as a few whoops rose around the cafeteria. "Good luck, cuz. You will need it."

Cal turned to me, cupping my face so I was looking into his eyes. "Listen to me, he's hurting and behaving like a fucking *prick* because he has lost you. If you want me to deal with him, I will. But I think the fact he hasn't got you anymore is punishment enough. I really don't mind punching him in the mouth, though, the disrespectful little *bastard*."

Cal turned his head sideways towards Luke, who taunted him by opening his hands out in a beckoning gesture.

I shook my head as he put his arm around me, guiding me out of the cafeteria.

Rosie ran up behind us, her hand on my arm as I whirled around to face her. "Hey, Gretch, wait up."

Cal rolled his eyes and pulled out a cigarette as he leaned against a locker, a bored expression on his face.

"Can we have a minute?" Rosie hissed as he stiffened.

"Rose," I exclaimed, already exhausted with their hostility.

Cal looked into my eyes, kissing me tenderly. "I'll be outside."

I watched him leave longingly before I turned to Rosie, my eyes narrowed. "Rose, don't be mad with him, we can't help how we feel—"

She shook her head, interrupting me. "Listen to me. There are rumors—nasty rumors. You need to be careful."

"Rumours? Started by Luke probably," I huffed, my arms crossed.

"He is his *family*, Gretchen. He wouldn't spread rumors about Cal; you know how much he values family. Despite the stunt Cal has pulled, Luke isn't like that." She hugged me tightly. "I love you, Gretch, but please be careful." She turned and strolled back to the cafeteria as I stared after her.

My mind reeled as I pushed the doors open to find Cal.

What rumors? Who'd started them?

I realized I knew nothing about Cal, really, other than when I was with him, everything felt right.

But was that enough?

15

GRETCHEN

I had a relatively uneventful afternoon, avoiding Luke and his buddies. I made my way to the exit, my heart soaring when I saw Cal waiting for me.

He stared into the distance; his jaw clenched.

I stopped to study him, the crowds of bodies pushing past me as I did.

The wind blew his hair into his eyes, his hand lifting to push it away with irritation as his gaze fell on me. His lips curled into his trademark grin, and my stomach somersaulted beneath his heated gaze.

I skipped over to him, unable to keep away from him any longer.

His hands slid around my waist, his smoky lips against mine.

"I'm sorry for keeping you waiting," I murmured against him as he chuckled. A shiver ran down my body when he replied huskily.

"You are worth waiting for," he breathed into my neck.

My entire body was screaming for him, in every capacity. "So, what are we doing tonight?" I asked in between kisses.

A smile played on his lips when he moved back. "I can think of a few things." He winked as he kissed my forehead softly, his hands on my ass as I gulped nervously.

If his touch made me feel like this whilst I was clothed—

I silenced the thought before I lost it there and then.

"We still need to work on our presentation..." I reminded him weakly as his arm circled my waist, bringing me close enough to feel his hot breath on my face.

"Ah, yes, therapy. Come to mine now and we will work on our...presentation." He smirked, and I silenced him with my lips on his.

I'm intoxicated with happiness.

What Luke had said earlier was hurtful, but I also knew Cal was right; he was hurting. I followed Cal to his car, stopping when I found Luke sitting on the bonnet.

My stomach dropped as Cal released my hand, addressing Luke with his sharp tone. "Get the *fuck* off my car."

Luke slid down, standing squarely in front of Cal. "See, I thought we were sharing things, *cuz*," he spat, his eyes blazing. "Cars. Blood. *My girlfriend.*"

I reached for Cal, feeling his body stiffen as he replied.

"She's *not* your girlfriend," he corrected him, and I closed my eyes.

"Oh, but you're fucking her?" Luke growled, shoving Cal in the chest.

"Luke, stop—"

Luke ignored me, shoving Cal again.

Cal's eyes narrowed; his fists clenched at his sides. "I don't want to hurt you, Luke," he warned through gritted teeth.

Luke stepped closer, goading him again. "No? You should've thought about that before you touched *my* girl, you bastard." He swung his fist out suddenly, striking Cal's face.

I shrieked, trying to drag Luke away, but he pushed me onto the floor, his eyes black with rage.

"This is all *your* fucking fault. You could've said no, seeing as it's all you *ever* fucking said to me," he hissed.

I scrambled backward, the gravel beneath my hands cutting into my skin.

Luke's gaze dragged over me before a sadistic smirk formed on his face. "Did she tell you we kissed yesterday? *Twice* actually," he sneered, turning to Cal.

"Luke, *don't*!" I gasped, confusion passing over Cal's face as he registered what Luke was saying.

I clambered to my feet and stood closer to Cal, pointing my trembling finger at Luke. "That's bullshit, and you know it, Luke. You kissed me, and I kissed you back out of habit; I stopped straight away. It was *you* who forced yourself on me the second time *after* I had said no." I cried then. Hot, fat tears slid down my cheeks as Luke glared at me.

How had it come to this?

Cal grabbed Luke by the throat then and slammed him onto the bonnet of his car. "I asked you nicely. She doesn't want you. She wants *me*. She is *mine*. Get that into your *fucking* skull. If you ever touch her again, I will kill you, and *no one* will find you. Do you understand me?"

He was so calm it chilled me to my core.

Luke's hands tugged at Cal's that were wrapped around his throat as he struggled to breathe. His eyes met mine, and I jolted forward, calling out to Cal.

"Cal, let him go, let him go!" I begged, pulling at his arms.

Cal threw him onto the floor, before leaning down to his level. "Get the *fuck* away from us."

Luke sat up, gasping for breath. He stared at me in horror, spluttering in disbelief. "You chose *this*? This fucking *monster*?!" He rose slowly, his hand still on his throat as he trudged away.

"Oh, Luke," Cal called out, "She's not frigid. Not with *me*, anyway," he added, and Luke's face fell.

"But you said, Gretchen, you *said*..."

Cal moved in front of me, his eyes dark as he scowled at me. "Get in the car. Now," he barked, his voice laced with fury as he guided me to the passenger door.

Tears streamed down my face as I realized Cal's eye had swollen and blood trickled from his lip.

He slammed my door shut, moving to the driver's side at record speed. I gazed at his wounds, my hand at my mouth as he shook his head dismissively.

"I'm okay," he snapped, as I cupped his face. "So, you *kissed* him?" He curled his hand around the steering wheel as he turned to face me. "He kissed you, and you fucking *kissed him back*?" he uttered, as I reached for him, despite my terror.

"I did it because I am used to it! It's a shit reason, but it is the truth. I felt *nothing*, Cal, and I knew I was doing the right thing leaving him."

He started the ignition, and the car screeched away, causing me to fall into the side of the door. He glanced at me in concern as I held my hands up.

"I'm okay," I muttered.

"Don't kiss anyone else ever again. Those lips are *mine*," he said, and despite the dark tone in his voice, I was alive with passion. I should be worried, scared, or wary, but all I felt was content.

We drove to his house in silence.

When we walked in, we found his mother, Alice, at the kitchen table with a glass of white wine.

"Cal! What happened?" She glanced at me as I followed him in, exhausted from the day.

I sent a text to my Mom, telling her I was studying with Cal and that I would be home later.

It isn't far from the truth.

Cal reassured his Mom that he was alright and held his hand out to me. "Gretchen isn't with Luke anymore."

Alice stared at him with disappointment, her green eyes mirroring his before they flickered over to me. "Is that what this is? You had a fight with your *cousin* over *Gretchen*?"

I hung my head in shame as Cal ran his hands through his hair.

"She's with me now."

His mother looked over at me, and I tried not to meet her eyes.

The last thing I wanted was for her to dislike me because I was some kind of harlot.

"I see. Well, if you're happy, I'm happy. But try not to cause any more trouble with your cousin." Alice turned her emerald gaze to me. "I'm sure Luke is hurting, losing a beautiful girl such as yourself, Gretchen."

I blushed at the unexpected compliment as I smiled, "Thank you, Alice."

She nodded as she watched the two of us exchange a look, a wary expression on her face.

"But we have a project to work on. So, we'll do that now," Cal said and pulled me towards the stairs. Once in his room, he pulled me over to the bed. I kissed him carefully, avoiding his split lip as best as I could.

"I'm so sorry he hit you," I whispered, my mouth close to his.

He licked his lip, wincing slightly as he shrugged. "It's okay, you're worth it." He studied me, running his hands through my curls and then down my body. He continued to kiss me as he eased me down onto his bed, his hair falling into my eyes. "I *want* you. *All* of you..." he whispered, as his lips brushed against my jawline.

I allowed myself to relax in his arms, unable to fight my body's desire anymore. "Cal, I haven't... I haven't done this before," I stammered as my hands trembled with nerves.

He paused, staring at me, disbelief in his eyes. "You've never slept with anyone?"

I shook my head, biting my lip. His eyes moved to my mouth before he sat back and exhaled.

"I won't make you do anything you don't want to do. I can always have a cold shower, you know." He grinned at me, grimacing as his cut let out fresh blood.

I leaned forward, my lips brushing against his tenderly. "I don't want to wait. I want to be with you in every way possible..." I whispered, wrapping my legs around his waist. My heart thumped in my chest as he tugged me closer to him.

"I'm not gonna lie, I'm finding it difficult being with you, and not being able to fuck you the way I want to."

I sucked in a breath as he slid my top from my shoulders, dotting light kisses along them as I closed my eyes with delight.

"So, *do it then*," I breathed, terrified of what was about to happen, but I was certain it was what I wanted. He was the most beautiful man inside and out, and not being with him in this way felt wrong.

He gazed at me, his eyes meeting mine. "You're *perfect*, Gretchen, honest to fucking *God*. I've never felt this way, *ever*. But there are some things you need to know about me..."

I raised my fingers to his mouth, silencing him. "This first. Therapy after, yeah?"

He laughed then, climbing onto the bed with me, kissing me so hard I could taste his blood in my mouth.

16

GRETCHEN

*M*y nerves evaporated as his mouth moved expertly with mine. His tongue danced deliciously in my mouth as I moaned against him, his fingers drifted under my top, dragging against my skin as he gazed at me. His head moved down so his lips could meet the skin that was now cold without his touch.

I looked down, sucking in a breath.

His mop of blonde hair rested on my stomach as he trailed kisses down to the tip of my jeans. He peeked up at me as he loosened the buttons, and I sank my teeth into my lower lip with anticipation.

I was beyond nervous, but it was because his beauty made me that way. His manly presence left me in awe after years of dealing with mere boys. He may have been the same age, but he was worlds apart.

His lips grazed the bare skin left behind from the waistband of my jeans he had slid down ever so slightly. My breathing hitched as he sat up on his knees, tugging my jeans off as he discarded them on the floor. His heated gaze swept up my thighs, settling on my underwear, which I feared was soaked from his touch. He whipped off his t-shirt, dropping it to the floor as my breathing hitched in my throat, my lungs gasping for air as I studied his perfect form. He sank to his knees, his mouth littering soft kisses on my inner thighs as I inhaled sharply.

I'd done this before with Luke, and it wasn't something I'd ever enjoyed. But as Cal continued, his fingers lacing with mine as he moved further up towards my core, sliding my underwear down my thighs, he looked at me with a confidence I found exhilarating.

"Let me do this—I promise you'll enjoy it."

I sank back into the bed, my fingers gripping the sheets as he buried his head between my thighs. His tongue slid between my silky folds, and I shuddered with delight. I gasped as he sucked on my clit, his finger moving around the entrance to my core as I clenched instinctively.

"Relax, baby. I can stop anytime you want me to."

"*No*, don't stop," I mumbled, as his breath on my exposed core sent tingles and shivers through my body.

As he slid his finger inside of me, he muttered under his breath. "I won't last five minutes with you, you're so fucking *tight*."

I arched my back as he moved his mouth against me, my body bucking against him as he reduced me to a wreck. Every time I got close to my oblivion, he stopped, kissing me tenderly. "Cal, I'm ready," I gasped, pulling him up to me, his throbbing hardness pressing against my wet center as I shivered in delight.

"Oh, I don't know if you are, *Raven*," he murmured against me, his lips attacking my neck as he grabbed something from the bedside table.

As we kissed, I noted the taste of me on his tongue as he shifted me beneath him.

His breathing was heavy as he lifted the condom packet for me to approve. "Are you sure?"

"Cal, *please*," I whimpered as he tore it open with his teeth, pulling out the condom as I watched him roll it onto his enormous dick.

"I can stop anytime," he murmured again, as I nodded. I was part terrified, part desperate to feel him inside of me.

The head pressed against my entrance, and I bit my lip as I arched back. He continued to move slowly, gazing at me as I tried to ignore the agonizing pain.

Where was the pleasure everyone spoke of?

"Baby, it will hurt. It will feel better soon, I swear. Do you want me to stop?" He whispered as he held himself up on his forearms, gazing at me intensely as I shook my head.

"No. Just do it the way you think," I said, as I wriggled beneath him.

His mouth covered mine as he thrust into me.

My body tried to accommodate his size; my walls stretched around him, and he bit his lip as though it was causing him pain too.

After more kissing, a deep pressure filled me, and I moaned out loud.

"Okay, it's in, all the way. I'll go as slow as I can," Cal mumbled in my ear, his arms wrapping around my body.

As he moved inside of me, I gripped his back, and the pain subsided, replaced by an insanely pleasurable feeling. Combined with his delicious kisses and his voice in my ear, I saw what all the fuss was about.

"Oh *God*, yes." I moaned as he chuckled against me.

"Shh, you've gotta be quiet." He picked up pace, covering my mouth with his as I moaned against him. "I swear, I won't last if you keep moaning like that," he warned.

I didn't care, my fingernails dug into his back as he

groaned, his eyes closed, and his lips parted.

"You're *insane*, Gretchen."

I lifted my legs around him as he buried himself inside of me, my hands clawing at him as he lost himself.

His body was slick with sweat as his finger slid down to my core, massaging my sweet spot as I covered my mouth from crying out, as my body spasmed in a way I'd never experienced before.

"*Cal*," I moaned, and he seemed to halt for a minute, holding his breath as he gasped, grunting as he shuddered between my thighs.

I laid still, watching him hazily as he chuckled in my ear. "Are you okay? I'll take it out now, slowly."

I gazed at him as he moved from within me, leaving me feeling hollow.

How had I ever felt complete before?

He stood up, handing me some tissues as he smiled. "You're all wet."

I cringed, pushing the tissue between my thighs as I felt the intense wetness. I panicked when I saw blood on the tissue, but he soothed me.

"It's normal to bleed when it's your first time. Don't panic," he said, walking over to me as he helped slide my underwear back up, rubbing his hands on my thighs as he gazed at me. "Are you alright? How was it for you?"

I sat up, pushing my hair out of my eyes as I stared at him. "Are you for real right now? That was... mind-blowing. How many girls have you been with?' I demanded and his eyes widened.

"It's irrelevant," he said dismissively and I frowned.

"Why is it?" I asked as he held my gaze.

"Because now none exist. It's only you. I've got a feeling you're gonna be my forever."

17

GRETCHEN

I felt like everyone could see there was something different about me.

Did I look different? I felt different.

I'm so glad I didn't do it with anyone else.

Cal was perfect in *every* way. He took his time, continually asking me if I was okay throughout. I'd never felt yearning like it before; I almost got annoyed with how slow he was making us go. But then he took it to a different level entirely, and I felt as though those last moments were out of this world.

If I thought I wanted him before, it was nothing compared to the way I felt for him now. I leaned on my side and smiled at him, unable to deal with how delicious he was.

His perfectly sculpted body, all the way down to the V that sat above his boxers, sent a jolt down to my core, reminding me of what we had done.

"I don't suppose we could do more of that...." I whispered coyly as he lifted onto his elbow, dropping his lips to mine.

"Come here," he growled, pulling me close to him. "I fucking adore you."

I pulled the duvet up to my chin, snuggling closer to him. "I never want to go home," I murmured, burying my face into his neck and inhaling the delicious scent of his cologne.

He sat up, looking down at me. His expression was unreadable, his eyes harboring an internal battle that only he knew about. "Finish school first, then we will be together, *properly*."

I gazed up at him, speechless. "Are you serious?" I chuckled, unsure what he meant.

Either way, I'm here for it.

This man could ask me to jump off a cliff, and I would.

"You make me want to be a better person, Gretchen. You make me wish I could rewind my life and do things different-ly," he rubbed his head and seemed to be lost in thought.

"Rewind your life how?" I asked, my fingers trailing down his chest.

I knew this was dangerous territory, that Cal had secrets. But I wanted to know everything about him.

He sighed, capturing my fingers and lifting them to his lips. "I've done some unsavory things, babe, with some pretty nasty people. I would never want you to get involved with any of that, ever." His jaw clenched, and his eyes narrowed.

I shuddered, not because of him, but because of what he must've done. I sat up, pulling the duvet around me for modesty, my dark curls spilling over my shoulder.

"Do you want to tell me about it?" I murmured,

"Not today. Today's been strange as it is. But we just made it spectacular, didn't we?"

I blushed and held his gaze, allowing his hands to travel down my back before I answered. "Yeah, we did."

I reached over, grabbing my phone out of my bag to see I had received a text from my Mom asking me what time I was due home. I groaned, and Cal looked at me with exasperation.

"What now?"

"No, it's cool, just my mom wanting me home soon."

He laced his fingers through mine. "Until tomorrow, then?" he said softly.

I dressed quickly, still feeling weird about him seeing me naked.

He watched me as I slid my jeans back on whilst I leered at his tanned body, remembering my legs wrapped around it less than ten minutes earlier.

He caught me staring and chuckled softly. "Do you want me to walk you home like this, or shall I get dressed?" He winked at me, and I giggled in response.

'You might cause quite a stir walking around like that."

He walked over to me, kissing me slowly.

It felt different: more intense, more passionate.

"I don't want you to go," he muttered into my hair. "How long have we got left of school again?"

I met his gaze, and I bit my lip.

"Don't keep biting those lips, Raven. It's my job."

My heart thudded in my chest at his words. "You don't have to walk me home, you know," I pointed out half-heartedly.

He didn't respond other than to roll his eyes at me.

We made our way downstairs, and thankfully, I found no one was in. I had an image of his mother glaring at me like she knew what we had done. To be fair, if anyone was in, undoubtedly, they would have heard it.

Cal held my hand the entire walk home. "What are you doing to me, Raven?"

I tugged him into my arms, his mouth crushed against mine as we leaned up against a wall. His arms circled my body, and I stood on tiptoes to run my hand through his golden locks.

"Imagine being me; this is crazy," I mumbled against him.

"You're killing me, Princess." His thumb grazed my cheek as we kissed again before we ambled towards my house.

"Thanks for walking me home, Cal."

Our hands entwined, our fingers dragging along one another until we parted fully.

He waited at the end of the drive until I blew him a kiss from the front door, closing it behind me.

I leaned against the door and breathed in the delicious smell of beef casserole.

"Mm, something smells good," I declared, dropping my bag on the stairs before I walked into the kitchen.

My mom stood over the stove, stirring a large pot. She looked up at me with a wide smile, wiping her hands on a towel as she turned to me.

"Hey, stranger! I feel like I barely see you these days. Where have you been?"

I'm convinced she would take one look at me and just *know* what I've been doing, but she waited patiently for me to answer. She picked up a spoon and tested the food before adding more salt.

"I've been with Cal, studying, remember?"

Please believe me.

Mom put down the spoon, looking over at me with interest. "So, this Cal..." She raised her eyebrows, wanting me to elaborate.

I couldn't stop smiling before I gushed like a love-struck canary.

"He's nice, Mom, he's new in town. They don't live far from us."

She nodded before speaking quietly. "I see. Does this *Cal* have anything to do with you falling out of love with Luke?"

I flushed beneath her gaze and stared at the floor guiltily. "Um, maybe a little..." My voice trailed off as she wiped the kitchen counters down, frowning at me.

"Are we going to get to meet him?"

I rolled my eyes and headed towards the stairs, calling out behind me dismissively. "Yeah, I'm not sure when, though. I'm just going to shower."

I grinned to myself, pulling my phone out to find a text from Rosie.

> ROSIE: The Rink, tomorrow night, girls ONLY.

> GRETCHEN: Yes, thank you! Just what I need. Hope you are okay—lots to tell you... ;)

> ROSIE: OMG—you didn't!

I laughed to myself, skipping into the bathroom to have a shower.

Cal met me for school the next morning, and I couldn't help but beam at him when I saw him leaning against his car, waiting for me. His face looked a bit better; it was still swollen, but not as bad as it was yesterday.

I kissed him carefully, mindful of his cuts, which he responded to urgently, his hands sliding into the back pockets of my jeans to pull me closer to him.

"Morning, baby," he whispered, resting his forehead on mine.

"We could walk, you know; it's not far," I pointed out as he made a face at me.

"But this way, we get to make out more before school, no?" He smirked, his gaze journeying down my body.

I couldn't argue with that logic, so I climbed into the car willingly.

"What are you smiling about?" he asked gruffly when I noticed he didn't have his belt on.

"Nothing. You need your seatbelt on," I pointed out as he laughed, making no move to put it on.

We reached school, and when I got out, he put his hand on my arm. "Baby, I'm not going in today. I've got some things to take care of. I'll pick you up after and take you home. Will you be okay in there?" His eyes searched mine as I groaned.

"Cal, you can't keep skipping school."

He rolled his eyes before tilting my head to his. "Listen, beautiful. You don't need to worry about me; just focus on yourself."

I glared at him. "But what are you going to do when it's time to find a job, Cal? You need to pass—"

He looked at me with amusement, kissing my lips softly as I relented. "Are we having our first argument?" Cal murmured, nipping my teeth between his lips.

I gasped, running my tongue over my lip. "Maybe."

I kissed him intensely before I dragged myself off to class, aware he was watching me appreciatively.

I put my arm through Rosie's as I sighed, an enormous grin on my face.

"You seem very happy indeed." She nudged me. "How do you feel?"

I leaned back and pouted, unable to hide my euphoria. "Like a woman," I purred playfully as she giggled.

"So, where is he today?"

I bit my lip, avoiding her knowing stare. "He has some things to take care of..."

Rosie rolled her eyes with disbelief. "He's cutting school again. Attractive."

I nodded sadly. "I know, it's shitty. But you can't help who you fall in love with."

Her head whipped around to mine, her jaw dropping as she gasped. "Love?"

I stopped at my class, my cheeks burning as I giggled. I'd barely admitted as much to myself, but I had to be honest.

I was falling in love with Cal.

Rosie looked past me then, mouthing at me to *'turn around'* before walking away to her class.

I turned to see Luke striding towards me, followed by Finn. Finn strode past me to catch up with Rosie, and I braced myself for more verbal abuse from Luke.

"Hey." Luke stuffed his hands in his pockets as I stood perfectly still, waiting for him to speak. "I need to talk to you. It's not about us or anything like that," he added hastily, shuffling his feet on the floor.

I folded my arms and gazed at him coolly. I had no clue what he wanted to talk to me about, and I highly doubted it would be unrelated to us.

"Right. So, go on." I shrugged my shoulders, clearing my throat.

He fixed his blue eyes on mine, and I realized he wanted to speak privately.

Was he serious right now?

I didn't want to be on my own with this asshole after how he'd spoken to me.

"Not here. After class, meet me near the bleachers. Please?" He pleaded with me, and the look in his eyes told me I needed to be there.

Against my better judgment, I muttered that I would meet him later. I turned and walked back into the class, annoyed with myself for agreeing to meet him alone.

The bell rang out for the end of school, and I took a slow stroll to the bleachers to meet Luke. Being out here reminded me of the many football games I'd watched Luke play in, even when I was freezing, I'd been there for every game, the loyal girlfriend. I remembered when he scored the winning goal, how he ran up to me in the bleachers as everyone whooped and cheered around us. He'd kissed me in front of everyone, and I'd felt like the luckiest girl in the world.

My smile faded when I spotted Luke, his trademark blue jacket and helmet dangling from his fingers. I took a deep breath, forcing one foot in front of the other as I neared him, as pink talons crept around his waist. I stopped, my breath frozen in my lungs.

"You know I *love* fucking you. Always have." Luke laughed, his head moving to the right so he could kiss the neck of the girl in his arms.

Krystal's neck.

"At least you can be mine *officially* now." Krystal smirked as Luke's mouth silenced hers.

I felt nauseous, the realization that I wasn't the only bad one in our relationship. It seemed my boyfriend *hadn't* been waiting for me.

He'd been fucking Krystal.

"Sorry, am I interrupting anything?" I called out, walking towards them with an icy smile.

Luke whirled around, his eyes wide as he dropped his hands from Krystal, moving away from her as she narrowed her eyes at me.

"Gretchen, you're early," Luke frowned, rubbing the back of his neck awkwardly.

"Seems like you weren't expecting me," I huffed, shaking my head as Krystal rolled her eyes. "You have the audacity to kick off because I kissed Cal whilst we were together—"

"Yeah, and what?" Luke demanded, his eyes darkening with fury. "You shouldn't have fucking kissed him. You were with *me*."

"Um, *hello*?" Krystal snapped, folding her arms.

Luke glared at her before waving her away.

"This doesn't concern you," he muttered coldly, his eyes fixed on me.

Krystal's mouth dropped open, and she gasped. "Screw you, Luke! For the record, Gretchen, I've been sleeping with your boyfriend for at least a year. That's karma for you!"

Luke closed his eyes as Krystal stormed away, tugging her tiny skirt down as she did.

I felt numb. Every memory I'd ever created with Luke was now a lie.

The entire time we were together—he'd been with Krystal?

"That explains why she never liked me." I laughed bitterly, shaking my head. "All those secret meetings between you. They were nothing to do with the fucking cheerleading team, were they?"

"You're in no position to say fuck all to me—" Luke barked, walking forward and gripping my arm. "You did it with my *cousin*. You *fucked* my cousin, yet you didn't even let me do that with you."

I wriggled my arm away from him, stepping forward and poking him in his hard chest.

"You said this *wasn't* about us. So, you've been cheating on me this entire time. So what? We're over. Tell me what you want to say so I can go."

His chest heaved with every breath; his nostrils flared as he gritted his teeth together. "Has *Loverboy* told you anything about himself? Or do you not talk?"

I scrunched my eyes up, counting to ten in my head.

I'm so close to losing my shit with this asshole—

"Do you know why Cal moved here?"

I didn't want to hear this from Luke, of all people.

"Luke, don't you think Cal should tell me?" I exhaled with exasperation, my head already aching from the fuck-storm that was Krystal and Luke.

Our whole fucking relationship was a lie!

Luke laughed then, nodding his head enthusiastically. "Absolutely. He should have told you by now. The thing is, he's family. So, you will hear it from me and no one else— because no one else will know. If he thought anything of you, he would've told you that you could be in danger." He fixed his eyes on me, and they softened slightly as his shoulders sagged. "I *do* care about you. I didn't think for one second you would have left me to be with him, so it would have remained a secret. But you did, so now you need to know."

I frowned as he kicked the floor with his foot. I'd have left him a year ago had I known he was fucking Krystal behind my back.

Cal is my savior in more ways than one.

"He took part in a robbery. They got away with a fuck

load of money and jewelry. There was a girl there. She ended up in hospital."

I felt like I couldn't breathe, my heart hammering in my chest as he continued.

"The problem was, she was the daughter of a very important gangster in New York. Cal got arrested, sure. But then there was money on his head and all of his family."

I blinked furiously as I stared at Luke, my mouth suddenly dry. "They want to kill him?" I whispered, my words carried away by the breeze.

Luke looked at me with annoyance. "He is a *bad* fucking person, Gretchen. His family had to go into witness protection and move here. His name isn't even *Cal* fucking *Fallon*."

18

GRETCHEN

*M*y head spun.

This is serious. I'm an eighteen-year-old girl in love with a criminal.

I scolded myself, a criminal, according to Luke, who had many reasons to lie to me. I had a sinking feeling he wasn't lying, though.

My phone flashed on my desk, and I picked it up when I saw it was Cal. "Hey."

"Where are you?" Cal asked gruffly.

"I'm just getting ready to go to The Rink with the girls..." I explained as I grabbed my bag.

He fell silent on the other end.

"Can you pick me up after?" I asked sweetly.

"Yeah. Text me."

Just like that, he hung up, leaving me staring at the phone in my hand.

What was up with him?

I sighed, packing my skates in my bag. I skipped downstairs and out to Sienna's car: a gorgeous Fiat 500 in mint green. I needed to learn to drive; every time I saw Sienna's car, it reminded me of the fact. "Hey, girls!" I climbed into the back and grinned at my friends.

"Hey yourself," Rosie smiled cheerfully as she climbed back into the car after letting me get in. She turned around to face me, and we chatted casually on the way to The Rink.

I hadn't told anyone about Luke and Krystal, even though it was pure ammunition if ever I needed it; I wasn't that petty.

My phone vibrated in my bag, and I hunted through it until I found it, tugging it out to see it was a text.

> LUKE: I'm sorry about me and Krystal... I don't love her. Not like I love you.

Fuck you, Luke.

I shoved my phone back into my bag as I became aware of a pair of eyes staring at me.

"Who was that?" asked Rosie, her nose wrinkled as she continued to study me.

"Luke," I replied quietly, my head pounding. I needed a night away from drama, and it seemed to follow me, regardless.

"Everything okay? More hot guys fighting over you?" Rosie giggled nervously as Sienna nudged her.

"Luke texting is a good sign, right?" Sienna said hopefully as she swung into the parking lot.

I glanced out of the window, chewing on my lip. I knew it was difficult for Sienna, seeing as she was with Ethan. I felt bad for screwing up the dynamics of our friendship, but I was caring less and less the more secrets that came to the surface.

"I don't really want to talk about it, guys. Let's skate!" I suggested brightly as we walked into the stadium.

We joined the queue to pay, the sound of blades slicing through the ice in the distance. The cool air made me blow on my hands, and I rubbed them together to warm them up. I paid before I made my way down to the bleachers by the rink. I laced my skates up, humming to the music.

The ice glistened invitingly before me, and I yearned to slice through it with my recently sharpened skates. I hugged my coat closer to me as Rosie danced up beside me.

"Let's go," Rosie squealed, her excitement infectious as we made our way onto the ice.

The wind in my hair as I picked up speed soothed my soul. My feet moved effortlessly as Rosie appeared next to me, her hand slipping into mine as I gave her a small smile. We skated to the music in companionable silence, my thoughts filled with memories of being here with Luke. Rosie squeezed my hand, nodding towards the bar where they served the infamous orange hot chocolate.

"Feeling better?" Rosie smiled kindly as she blew on her hot chocolate.

We settled into the booth we usually occupied, the one that overlooked the entire rink.

My shoulders relaxed as I exhaled, nodding.

Rosie scanned my face with a frown, her eyes filled with concern.

"Yeah, I needed this. It clears the mind." I frowned as I glanced around us. "Where's Sienna?"

Rosie sipped her hot cocoa and followed my gaze. She whipped her head around in different directions until she groaned. "Oh, God."

Sienna was skating beside Ethan, followed by Finn and *Luke*.

Luke grinned at Finn, his gaze on the floor as he skated. He moved over the ice with annoying ease, his dark hair in his eyes as he looked up towards me, our eyes locked on one another for the briefest of moments. But it was enough for an entire conversation. He looked away, his face crumpled beneath my steely gaze.

"*Shit*, Gretch, I'm sorry. I honestly didn't know he would be here." Rosie's face fell with dismay, her fingers on her forehead as she closed her eyes. "I said *girls only*."

"I don't want to spend my evening with my ex; I really don't," I mumbled as I rose to my feet. There was no way I was doing this, playing at being civil. Not with the guy that had cheated on me for the past year.

No fucking way.

"I'm leaving."

"What? No, no way!" Rosie laced her arm through mine, ducking under the DJ booth to where some tables lay hidden from view.

"I think we'll be safe in here." Rosie glanced anxiously behind us at the rink, her cheeks flushed. "Do you really hate him that much?"

"I'm so sorry, Rosie. It's not just me that fucked up; Luke isn't innocent in this." I sniffed, knowing I had to tell someone the truth.

Rosie hummed in response, whipping her head up to me as she did a double take. "What?"

"Luke was sleeping with Krystal through our entire relationship," I explained as I laughed hollowly. "He's a fucking *hypocrite*."

Rosie looked like I'd slapped her; her mouth formed into an O as she struggled to find words. "Please tell me you're lying, Gretchen," Rosie whispered, her head in her hands. "Luke loves you—"

Oh boy, he has a funny way of showing it.

"I don't care now, Rosie. I'm with Cal." I shrugged as two shadows fell over the table.

Sienna and Ethan.

"Here you are!" Sienna smiled, oblivious to Rosie's glare.

We sat and chatted for a while until Finn and Luke wandered over.

Luke pushed his hands into his jeans pockets, his eyes on me.

I avoided his stare as Rosie nudged her leg against mine under the table in what I could only imagine was empathy. I knew she was pissed; she had promised a girls' night out, and this felt like I was back in school again.

I asked Ethan if I could squeeze past him, explaining to the girls I needed to go.

Sienna frowned, but Rosie shot her a dark look.

"Want me to walk with you?" Rosie asked as she rose to her feet.

"Funny how you leave when we turn up," Finn said drily, his eyes narrowing at me.

I had understood his animosity when I'd thought Luke was the wounded party, but now I wondered if he had known all along. I doubted Luke would've kept it to himself.

"Fuck off, Finn, it's got nothing to do with you," I muttered.

He ignored me, sitting down beside Ethan. He then told us all how much better it was for Luke to be single and how cheating never paid off.

"Shut up, Finn," Luke snapped as Finn looked up at him with surprise.

"She fucking cheated on you, man—"

"Just let her go," Luke said as he turned away.

"It wasn't just me, though, was it?" I breathed, my voice laced with bitterness. "Did you tell your friends, Luke?"

Luke shook his head, his eyes filled with regret. Finn exchanged a look with Ethan before nodding at me.

"Is that your next move, Gretchen? Slinging shit at Luke—"

"I cheated on her," Luke declared, his eyes fixed on mine.

I breathed with relief as Luke stared at me.

"*What?!* With *who*?!" Sienna shrieked as she jumped to her feet. "You've let the entire school slate her while all along *you* were cheating on *her*?"

I dropped my eyes to the floor, my body exhausted from the drama.

Luke's jaw clenched as he tilted his head to Sienna, as he shrugged. "Krystal."

Ethan groaned, dropping his head into his hands as Sienna gaped at Luke.

Finn was silent, his disgust clear.

"You're better off without each other then," he muttered as Ethan nodded.

I knew Finn's parents had divorced over his Dad having an affair, so this was low, even for him.

Luke avoided his gaze. Instead, he focused on me.

"Well, it's been lovely, but I'm leaving," I snapped before he tried to talk to me.

I tugged my phone out of my pocket as I headed up to the seats to unlace my skates. My fingers trembled, my heart still in a whirlwind from Luke's confession to our friends. I knew he did that to save me from getting any more shit from Finn, but I refused to feel grateful.

> GRETCHEN: I'm ready if you are?

> CAL: Always ready to see you. Gimme fifteen.

I looked up to see Luke headed towards me, a determined look on his face. His legs strode up the steps two at a time, and I dropped my skates to the floor. I couldn't get my trainers on quick enough as his voice boomed my name.

"Gretchen."

> CAL: Almost there. Happy to warm you up if you're cold…

"Gretchen.," Luke repeated with a hint of impatience.

"*What*, Luke?!" I retorted as I glanced at my phone.

The thought of Cal warming me up was enough to thaw out this entire stadium.

I slipped my blade guards on as Luke's hand gripped mine, dragging it to his chest against his heart.

"I love you, Gretchen," he swallowed.

I moved my hand back like I'd been burnt. His ocean-blue eyes gazed at me, pleading with me to say it back.

"We could go back to normal if we love each other enough—"

"Luke! You cheated on me *for a year*!" I hissed as I pushed past him, dragging my skates with me.

Despite being with Cal, it still hurt me. I'd adored him, and until Cal, I'd never so much as looked at someone else.

"It wasn't like I was with her every fucking day, Gretch," Luke protested as he jogged beside me.

I shot him a look of disgust as I pushed through the exit.

"Come on, Gretchen, for fuck's sake," Luke snapped, his hand on mine as he tugged me back towards him.

"You don't get it, do you?" I cried. "I fucked up by hurting you, but I didn't sleep with him! You, though? You slept with Krystal for—"

"Because you wouldn't!" Luke yelled. His eyes bulged as he grabbed my arms. "I swear—"

"No, Luke, we're over." I shook my head at him as I backed away.

"For him? Come on, I am the better man, not that fucking *criminal*—" Then his gaze moved behind me, his eyes darkening. "What a fucking surprise," Luke muttered.

I felt his presence before I saw him, but then the tell-tale scent of smoke and cologne wrapped around me like a second skin, and I knew.

Cal was here.

I turned to see the black leather jacket that he wore over the white t-shirt, his messy blonde hair loose to his neck. But it was his eyes that drew me in, the way they flickered over to me, the smile that told me I was safe. I exhaled, and I moved into his arms, muttering that we needed to leave.

"You and I are going to have a real problem," Cal warned Luke, his thumb dragging across my cheek as he gazed at me. He frowned, turning his attention back to Luke. "If you don't leave *my* girl alone."

Luke scoffed; his lips twisted into a sneer. "She won't stay with you. What can you give her? You won't even finish school, you're a deadbeat—"

"But he *isn't* a cheat," I hissed as Cal rolled his eyes. "Leave me alone, Luke. Please."

A battle of wills locked their eyes together, chaos threatening to escape at any moment.

"*Cal*," I pleaded, my fingers on his jaw as I turned his head towards me.

His eyes met mine, and I smiled, stroking his face as I studied him. His eyes hid his real age; the pain and hurt mirrored in them told me stories his lips didn't. He nodded so briefly that I almost missed it.

Luke muttered something, and I ignored him, sliding my hand into Cal's.

I didn't care about Luke anymore, but I didn't want them to fight. It was exhausting.

"Coming to mine?" Cal drawled, his arm around my shoulders.

"I'd love to, but I need to be home at some point tonight. My mom is getting suspicious that she's not seeing me much lately," I explained as we reached Cal's car. I went to open the door, but Cal spun me around, so he pressed me between his body and the car.

"He called me a criminal, and you didn't flinch," Cal said as his breath fanned my cheek. His fingers slipped into my back pockets, his eyes on my lips as he held his breath.

"Luke spoke to me today," I admitted, "He told me some things…" My voice trailed off as he lifted a brow.

"Some *things*, Raven?"

Jesus. He isn't taking any prisoners tonight.

Yet, as I met his intense gaze, I felt no fear; I just wanted to know everything about him. "You're not called Cal, are you?"

He closed his eyes, exhaling into my face as I cupped his cheek.

"Please tell me," I said softly.

"Luke is a fucking *dead man*," he rasped through gritted teeth.

"I want to know who you are—"

"It's complicated," he barked, slamming his hands either side of me on the car.

My heart raced in my chest; my eyes darted around us anxiously as I swallowed. "Who are you, really?" I demanded, refusing to back down. I wanted to know who this man was. The stories he hid so well, I wanted to hear them.

"I can't tell you that," he breathed, "Please understand, I can't tell you a great deal other than I *really* fucked up. I tried to tell you the other night..." He trailed off as he watched Luke come out of the stadium, his head bowed and his hands in his pockets. He looked crushed, but the hatred in Cal's eyes scared me.

"I want to *kill* that bastard for ever having you. Do you know what it does to me *every* time I see him? I *hate* him. Now he has told you something that was mine to tell."

"Whoever the fuck you are, tell me what you did. I need to know who I am falling in love with!" I exclaimed as I moved his face to mine.

His eyes widened as he swallowed, his brow furrowed. "You're falling in love with me? It's been three days..." His voice trailed off when I narrowed my eyes.

"Tell me about it. I spend a year with someone who I don't sleep with or fall in love with. I spend three days with a stranger, and I do both."

He stroked my face, and I closed my eyes, his fingertips invoking demons deep within me I didn't know existed.

Being with Cal was like swimming in wild waters, your lungs desperate for air as you fought your way to the surface. Cal was that first breath you took, that deep, relieved inhalation. Cal was my oxygen.

"I don't want to hurt you," he whispered hoarsely.

"Then don't."

Cal exhaled, looking at me sadly. "When I was a kid, I just wanted to be rich. I spent my days researching rich people. What did they do to get to where they were?"

I listened closely, afraid to interrupt.

"Some were bankers, most were famous, and some invented things. I didn't want to be rich from inheritance; I wanted to earn my money myself. When I went to school, I made out I didn't have much money. I smoked pot, I stole, and I lied. My parents didn't know what to do. They tried moving me schools, but I still ended up with the crowd I felt that I identified with. The ones that were cool, but for the wrong reasons. Anyway, there was a girl at our school. She was rich and arrived at school with her driver, designer clothes, and bags. Her pops was stupidly loaded." He closed his eyes. "Someone suggested we rob her house. They'd researched it. All I can tell you is that I did what I was told to do. I was only *fifteen*."

I slid my fingers into his hand and clasped it tightly.

"We broke in. All I had to do was throw the loot onto the ground. Easy. Except the girl was home."

I could barely breathe as he continued.

"She was fifteen, too. I can promise you I had no part in what happened to her. But I didn't stop it either. I was a coward. I was there with boys of my age and up. The oldest was a man in his forties." He leaned his head back, and I saw the raw pain in his eyes, the way they crinkled up in the corners as though he watched the memory play out on a screen only he could see. "They left her for dead. I just ran, and I didn't look back."

I couldn't imagine the trauma my man had been through. I squeezed his hand tightly as I lifted it to my lips. "So, what happened?" I mumbled against it, closing my eyes as he cleared his throat.

"Well, she survived. Only just. Turns out her dad was rich illegally as well as legally; he had his fingers in all the pies. We were all caught. There were six of us in total. Four are now dead."

He smiled wistfully, and I gasped.

"I got a hefty fine, which my family paid, and we moved here under witness protection. I don't know how long I will be here, though; her father won't let me get away with it. I may have to keep moving, Gretchen."

I froze as I absorbed the information. My heart hammered

against my chest painfully. "But *you* didn't hurt his daughter," I argued as he bowed his head.

"No, I didn't. But I didn't stop them, did I? That's as good as doing it—in his eyes." His voice was so soft I barely heard the last part. "I understand if you want to end this. I don't want you to get hurt. If they find me, which I think they will, I don't want them coming for you. You mean too much, and I couldn't protect you, no matter how much I would try." His voice choked with emotion, his forehead resting against mine.

I reached for him, my hands wrapped around his neck. "I won't lie to you; I'm terrified. But I meant what I said—I'm falling for you. I can't be without you."

I mean it.

His life was at risk, which made mine at risk, too. But could I really break off with him and carry on like he never existed?

What if something happens to him?

I shuddered at the thought.

He kissed my head before his lips grazed against mine. "Now you see why school doesn't matter overly to me." He chuckled. "I'm just focusing on surviving." His eyes filled with regret and anguish.

I want to soothe him, but I don't know how. "Can we go somewhere, *anywhere* where no one will know us?" I asked him, no longer caring about anyone or anything else.

He searched my eyes, pressing his lips against mine as he nodded. He moved away from me, and we both got into the car.

After a while, we pulled onto the freeway, pulling into the second motel we passed.

"What was wrong with the first one?" I yawned as I stretched my tired limbs.

"Nothing. But I never use the first one I get to," Cal

mumbled as he turned the engine off. He pulled a wad of cash from his pocket, ignoring my raised eyebrows when he handed it to me. "Go get us a room."

I strode to the reception door and pushed it open. A bell rang somewhere, announcing my arrival. A bored-looking man played with his phone, paying me no attention.

"Yeah?" He drawled out without lifting his head up.

"Uh, I need a room?" I stammered as I licked my lips nervously.

"Fifty bucks. Seventy if you want WIFI."

I handed the cash over, and he gave me the key.

No questions asked.

Was it really that easy to rent a room?

Cal read the room number on the key and held my hand as he led the way to our new home for the night. The room was basic: a bed in the middle and a small TV set on a stand at the end of the bed. The bathroom was at the other end.

"Well, I don't think it's too bad," I declared as I slung my bag on the bed.

Cal stood against the door and watched me without seeing me. His eyes glazed over, and I knew he was lost in another memory.

I beckoned him over, and he strolled towards me, the slow, steady walk he had mastered so well. I moved his hair out of his eyes as he turned to look at me. My heart burst with love for this man; he had been through so much, and some-how, the universe saw fit to give him to me.

"I meant what I said, Raven. You don't need a part in any of this," he said gruffly, his eyes filled with misery.

A lump rose in my throat as I stroked his face. "I know that... but I can't imagine myself not being with you," I swal-lowed as he held my face in his hands.

His eyes locked on mine, and I saw his jaw tighten. "You could go back to your life, living the American dream."

"Ever since the minute I met you, I knew I would have to have you in my life in any capacity...I literally don't know how I existed before you," I confessed as he shifted and broke eye contact first.

I'm terrified.

The thought of him cutting off my oxygen was enough to make me weep.

"I really didn't want to fall in love with you, you know," he murmured. I held my breath as he rested his forehead against mine, and blood filled my ears with anticipation. "But then I did..." his green gaze bored into mine.

We fell onto the bed, our limbs tangled together as our mouths searched the other urgently. It felt as though there was no world other than the one we existed in right at that moment.

He whipped his t-shirt off, revealing his tanned torso. I clawed my shirt off, my hair covering my face as I did. He reached behind me and unclipped my bra with ease, my breasts revealed as he bit his lip.

I laid back on the bed as he leaned down, soft lips grazed against my stomach before they trailed down to my waistband.

He smirked as he slid his fingers into my jeans and underwear, which he tossed to the floor moments later. My breathing deepened as he loosened the buckle on his belt impatiently. I stared at his body in awe as he climbed back on the bed.

His warm body sent me into oblivion with each touch whilst my fingers explored him like an ocean I was desperate to navigate. It was only my second time with him, yet there were no nerves. I wanted him so much it was a visceral yearning.

It was softer, calmer, and slower.

Each move pleasured one, if not both of us, our bodies in sync throughout. His touch drove me insane, and I never wanted it to end.

The pleasure was *intense.*

He held me after, his fingers on my arm as they drew invisible patterns.

"That was amazing, wasn't it?" I grinned as I reached for my clothes.

"I'm struggling to label it; it was fucking delicious. *You* are fucking delicious." His eyes wandered over me as I dressed. "Do you feel okay?"

I loved that he didn't want to hurt me. I nodded happily, yawning as I crept into bed next to him. My body curled against his, and I savored the warmth he gave me. My eyelids drooped, and his lips brushed against them softly.

"Get some sleep, beautiful," he murmured as I fell asleep to the sound of his breathing.

19

GRETCHEN

I knew my parents would ground me.

In fact, I thought they would murder me, so grounded was an improvement. I was eighteen, and I'd spent the night away from home without touching base with my parents once. In hindsight, I could've sent a text; I was so wrapped up in Cal I didn't think of them, and I was in serious shit.

Mom was puce, her eyes wide as she gestured to me with rage. "She is *changing*, Ted. Trust me, I was her age once. This is not a good sign." Mom glared at me. "Staying out all night without thinking to tell us where she was? She barely sees her friends—there's some new boy called Cal she is hanging around with—"

"Leave Cal out of it," I interrupted as my dad raised his eyebrows in surprise.

"Don't you understand how scared we were? We didn't know if something had happened to you. We woke up this morning to see your bed empty; all your things gone. Then you walk in wearing the clothes you wore yesterday?" He murmurs, his voice full of hurt. "What's happening, Gretchen?"

"You wouldn't understand," I whispered as my Mom folded her arms, narrowing her eyes.

"Actually, I think I might. Luke came over last night to see you."

I looked up in shock. "What?"

"He's *worried* about you. So are we, Gretchen. Luke said this boy is his cousin. He said his last school expelled him for fighting and that he skips school regularly."

She cursed under her breath, her hand rubbing her temples, as my Dad's mouth opened, then closed as he stared at me with disappointment.

A surge of hatred towards Luke zipped through my body, knowing that he did this on purpose to fuck me over.

"Good *God*, Gretchen, I absolutely forbid you to see him anymore. What were you thinking?!" My dad demanded, his eyes flashing with anger.

I cried then, huge sobs that racked my body at his thunderous tone.

"Go to your room, Gretchen; you're grounded. Completely. Until you are out of college," he yelled, walking away from us.

My mother was furious, avoiding my desperate gaze.

I grabbed my bag and ran up the stairs to my room, my chest heaving with the thought of not seeing Cal anymore. I had to calm down, but I just couldn't; I was dizzy and nauseous, my heart rate going through the roof as I tried to breathe normally.

Why is Luke doing this to us?

So he was hurting, but he had his tongue down Krystal's throat earlier, so it couldn't be that bad.

My door opened, and my father stood in the doorway,

disappointment etched on his face. His jaw clenched as he studied me.

"Give me your phone and your laptop. I will not have you communicating with *him*. We'll take you to school and drop you off from now on. The only way you could see him would be at school, and by the sounds of that, he doesn't go." He shook his head in disbelief. "This is for your own good."

I threw myself onto my bed and sobbed into my pillow as my father disconnected my laptop and left my room quietly.

Why are my parents so controlling and involved?

I couldn't wait until I could leave and do whatever I pleased.

Until then, how was I going to cope?

CAL

It had begun.

A letter addressed to *Leonardo Cape* arrived today.

I stared out of my window into the street, the familiar fury rising within me. I punched the wall, hot white pain shooting up my arm.

"*Fuck*!"

The door opened behind me.

"Bro. What's wrong?"

I turned to see Drake watching me warily from the doorway, his eyes filled with anxiety as he watched me rub my hand.

"As usual, fucking *everything*."

I threw the letter at him as he unfolded his arms and read it quietly. He lifted his eyes to mine finally, heartache all over his face.

"We left you to it. You needed to live a normal life... but

stealing your cousin's girl wasn't really the best idea, knowing what he knows about you."

He attempted to smile, but it faded too quickly to be genuine. He closed the door behind him before he walked over to me. "I love you, even though you've fucked up quite a lot over the years. You know what I think?"

I closed my eyes, not wanting to hear what he had to say.

"Mom and Dad like it here. They've been through so much." His voice was quiet. "I think we should leave. You and me."

I whirled around, my eyes wide with anger.

He can't be serious.

"*What*?"

Drake's eyes fixed on mine. "Yeah. You heard me. Leave. I'll come with you. Fuck school. Fuck the girl; if you care about her, then this is the best thing you can do for her. If anyone finds out you care for her, she is as good as dead anyway."

Nausea swept through me.

How have all my shitty decisions led me to someone so fucking incredible, yet I can't be with her?

"I *can't* leave her, Drake. I've ruined her fucking life. She'll be alone if I am not here."

Drake sighed and searched the letter in his hand. "You don't seem to have much of a choice."

20

GRETCHEN

*M*y parents had cooled down after a few days. They'd agreed I could have my phone back, but I remained grounded.

I scrolled through my social media idly, catching up on the events I had missed in such a brief space of time. I hadn't heard from Cal, but I didn't know if that was because my parents had been extreme and blocked him on my phone or whether he had simply tried not to contact me.

Pushing the thought out of my mind, I got dressed for school.

I couldn't wait to see Cal; I just hoped that he would be at school today, if only to see me.

I swept my curls into a clip and slid on a faded blue t-shirt and jeans. I glanced in the mirror, relieved to see my eyes weren't so swollen from crying anymore. I remembered Cal's preference for my hair down, so I took the clip out, letting the curls fall around my shoulders.

My phone pinged, and I grabbed it excitedly; my heart sank a little when I saw it was from Rosie.

ROSIE: Can we talk today? Miss you.

I typed back a quick reply and grabbed my bag.

My mom was waiting for me at the kitchen table, car keys in hand.

"Ready?" She snapped, her eyes narrowing at me.

She was still bitter, purely because I had worried her so much. I couldn't understand it because whenever I thought of that night with Cal, I realized it was so worth it.

Mom pushed the chair away as she rose, her blue eyes piercing into mine. "Keep away from Cal, for your own good. I can't force you, but I am trying to help you. Now get in the car, please."

I nodded glumly.

I can't keep away from him if I try.

Nothing compared to him, ever.

We left the house, and my eyes searched the road, just in case Cal was waiting for me. Disappointment filled my stomach when I saw that he wasn't there, and I slouched into the passenger seat of my mom's car. We rode in silence until she dropped me off outside school.

"I'll pick you up after school."

"Mom, I—"

"No, Gretchen. You don't get to say anything about this. Until you learn how to behave like an adult, we will treat you like a child."

She leaned over me, opened the car door, and signaled for me to get out.

I climbed out and watched her drive away.

Jeez, she was truly pissed.

I don't get it—I'm safe.

It clearly didn't matter; this was her way of dealing with it. I followed the throng of people making their way painfully slowly to school, and I searched for the face I needed to see more than anything.

No sign of Cal.

I spotted Sienna leaning on her car, wrapped in a winter coat. She waved wildly when she saw me, and I trudged over to her as she held her arms out.

"Hey, are you okay? I texted you and called you, with no reply! Were you with Loverboy?'" Her eyes rolled playfully as she spoke, her arm linked with mine as we strolled into school.

"It's complicated. I'm sorry I didn't get back to you. My dad took my phone from me…" I explained with a loud sigh as I unhooked my black leather bag from my shoulder.

The sound of a basketball being bounced resonated through the hallway, cut my sentence short, and I pursed my lips.

"No shit—why?" Sienna exclaimed, her eyes wide as she peered at me with surprise.

I understood—I wasn't the rebellious type.

I pulled my books out and slammed my locker shut as I turned to face her. "I spent the night with Cal, and I didn't tell my parents where I was."

Sienna made a face as she placed her hands on her hips and peered at me curiously. "Okay, who are you, and what have you done with Gretchen? You're a real rebel now!"

She said this proudly at first, but her expression changed when she saw the sadness in my eyes.

"Luke went to my house, and of course, I wasn't there," I muttered, ducking as I narrowly missed the basketball that was still being tossed around.

Sienna's eyes flashed as she threw her hair over her shoulder with a frown, showing she was clearly as confused as I was about the whole situation. "Why the fuck did Luke go to your house?" Sienna asked.

"I know, right? I saw him the other day with Krystal—"

"Well, I mean, there's moving on, and then there's *that*. He's a cheating bastard. I refuse to speak to him again," Sienna declared. "But why turn up at yours?" Sienna fumbled in her bag for a moment before slipping gum into her mouth, offering me one as she did.

I muttered my thanks before I popped a piece in my mouth.

We wandered through the crowds, and the different voices and sounds dulling our conversation allowed me time to think.

"To see me, but I wasn't there. So, he told my parents Cal was a punk, pretty much. Then I didn't come back home…" I shrugged, allowing her to piece together the rest in her head.

"Oh no… So, they took your phone away?"

I nodded as we made our way into our Psychology Class. "I can't see him anymore, and I'm grounded for life."

My eyes threatened to fill with tears again as she squeezed my arm.

"This is horrendous, Gretchen. Listen, we will talk more after class, okay?" Sienna nodded at me kindly before she made her way to her seat.

My eyes swept over the empty seats behind me, and my chest tightened.

I noticed Luke walking in, his hair clearly still wet from the shower. His eyes met mine briefly, but he avoided my furious glare and instead attempted to talk to Finn. Finn glanced at me and gave me a half smile, which I coolly ignored and stared out of the window. I hoped Luke didn't expect me to speak to him. I wanted to poke his eyes out with my nails for looking so relaxed and happy, not like someone who was actively ruining two lives.

Cal didn't show up that day. Or the next, or the one after that.

Against my parents' strict orders, I texted him, but he didn't reply. My heart felt like it was being crushed.

I was in the library one afternoon, my feet curled under me, reading my favorite book. Whenever I felt stressed, reading always soothed my soul.

The rain lashed on the windows, the sky dark and foreboding. I shivered and pulled my hoodie around me tighter for the extra warmth. I flipped my hair over to the side and leaned back, trying to get back to the book.

I was so absorbed I didn't realize how much time had passed when the bell rang.

I sat up to gather my things, dropping my book in the process. I leaned down to pick it up when someone else's fingers beat me to it. I glanced up in surprise to see Luke, who handed me the book whilst I marveled at his audacity. I snatched it from him, pushing it deep into my bag. He looked at his feet, his hands stuffed into his pockets.

"I know you hate me, Gretch." He put his hands up, his eyes wide and genuine. "But I need to explain...I did that for you, not for me."

I swiveled my legs down and stood to face him. "Is that right?" I said indignantly, as my body trembled. "Well, thank you, but I'd much rather you hadn't bothered."

I was tired of apologizing to Luke, taking his name-calling, and now this. I moved to go past him when he grabbed my wrist.

"Wait," he begged, as I pulled my arm from him like I had been burnt and turned to face him.

"No, I won't, Luke. Don't ever think you have done anything for me. I never want to speak to you again."

Hurt swam in his eyes as I spun on my heel and stormed away.

My eyes were blurry and filled with tears as I made my way out of the school, heading for my Mom's car, which was waiting in the pouring rain. I slammed the door behind me as I climbed in, tears spilling down my face.

My mom peered at me with concern. "What's happened?" She attempted to push my hair out of my eyes, but I moved away stubbornly. She drew her hand back gradually as I shook my head, then stared out of the window glumly.

Mom didn't get it, did she?

My life was falling apart in front of my eyes, and all she could do was ask what had happened.

How could I say, '*Mom, I'm in love with a felon who I stayed out all night fucking, and for some reason, you won't let me see him, and now my ex is making my life as hard as possible? Oh, and I haven't heard from Cal in fucking days.*'

My tears fell silently as I stared out the window, refusing to communicate with my mom.

Time passed, and I struggled to function.

I was going to school, avoiding everyone, coming home and crying, sleeping then repeating the pattern. I hadn't heard from Cal, and I was worried something had happened to him. He wouldn't just leave me, not without explaining it to me first. My mind was in overdrive, my thoughts meshing into chaos I couldn't even begin to make sense of.

My parents were happy, though; I heard them laughing at ridiculously mundane TV shows and living their lives. *Together.*

I felt empty inside, but I was powerless. The only options

I had were to break more rules to go and see Cal at his house or sit and wallow in self-pity.

I laid in the darkness, listening to the silence. My phone pinged, and instead of leaping up like I had been, I ignored it, slipping the volume key to silent.

I don't want to speak to anyone.

Without Cal in my life, I couldn't exist successfully.

I remembered his arms around me and felt my heart breaking with longing: his soft lips on mine, his striking eyes gazing at me. His fingers laced with mine as we lay in bed in a world that was totally our own. The pain I felt pretty much every day was becoming so familiar I felt like I had to do something.

A knock at my door interrupted my thoughts, and I turned on my side, refusing to acknowledge it.

I'm too angry and hurt.

The door opened softly, and the bed dipped as someone put their weight on it.

"Gretchen." My father's voice invoked a fresh lot of tears to spill down my cheeks. "Gretchen, you need to look at me, honey."

His voice was soft and calm, but I shook my head.

Didn't he know the damage was done?

My father sighed as he sipped from his glass of wine. There was a silence between us until he spoke again. "The day you were born was the happiest day of my life. I didn't think I could've loved anyone like I loved your mother until I met you."

I closed my eyes as he continued.

"You always have amazed me. I watched you learn to walk, to talk, to laugh. I love the person you have become. You are intelligent, beautiful, and *usually* very sensible." He chuckled at this part. "When you didn't come home the other night when we couldn't reach you...I haven't ever felt fear like it. Then Luke came over and told us about this boy you were seeing, and I actually hoped you were with him."

I opened my eyes in surprise.

"The thought of you being with someone who cared about you was a damn sight better than those I was imagining." His voice broke a little then, and I sat up. He glanced over at me, his eyes wet. "Your mother and I didn't sleep at all that night. I wanted to call the police, but your mother knew it had something to do with this boy." He shook his head. "Mothers are always right, you know," he added gently as I stared at my hands. "So, anyway, Gretchen. We were so worried. I'm sorry you feel so sad; it kills me to see you this way. I don't want you anywhere near someone who could hurt you."

My head snapped up at this. "Cal cares about me, Dad, he really does. He would *never* hurt me. I love him."

He acknowledged this sadly before he gave me a tender smile. "I thought as much. If that's the case, nothing or no one will keep you apart. So, you have a curfew, young lady, but you aren't grounded anymore. One red flag, and you are back to being grounded. If your grades slide, it stops. Am I clear?"

I threw my arms around him. "Thank you, Dad."

Immediately, I wanted to bolt to Cal's house in my pajamas, barefoot. I needed him so much that I felt like I was gradually dying inside.

Dad patted my arm and kissed my head. "Please, Gretchen, don't ever do that to us again."

I squeezed him tightly and nodded. "I won't."

21

GRETCHEN

*T*hat winter was the longest I'd ever known.

They say absence makes the heart grow fonder and that time heals all wounds. I wasn't entirely sure which applied to me, if any. I'd been trying to move forward, but it felt like I was doing it with a rock attached to my back.

My dreams were so vivid, so painfully real, bringing intense joy and comfort, then shattering upon waking. I sometimes thought I saw Cal in crowds of people—I have since read that this is a form of a coping mechanism, the brain comforting us in a time of extreme grief or sadness.

Because that is what this feels like...like he has died.

I walked past his house every day, which was always empty. No sign of life, but there's no for sale sign either. I've knocked on and peered through windows. I've sat on the porch and sobbed like a madwoman, but still, nothing.

How could he just leave me?

I can only imagine he had no choice, and that *terrifies* me.

I've found it easier the past few months; I have started ice skating again. I read more, and I spent more time in my room. I recently got accepted to the college I wanted. I should have been elated—my parents certainly were. Nothing held any excitement for me anymore. I knew it sounded maudlin, but I never felt like I did when I was with Cal.

The end of the school year loomed, which inevitably brought prom, but I wouldn't be going. The last time there was a dance was the happiest day of my life—how could I put myself through that again? I had, however, promised to go dress shopping with Rosie and Sienna.

So, this was where I found myself in the mall, waiting by the doors impatiently. I watched an elderly couple laughing together as they walked past me, a private joke only they would understand. The familiar pang in my chest arrived, and I breathed through it deeply. The one good thing about my new college was its location—it wasn't anywhere near Winterburg, and I didn't know anyone who was going there.

I noticed Rosie walking towards me, drawing approving glances from a group of guys from the year below us as they called out to her. Jeans that looked like someone had sprayed them on encased her slender frame, with a cropped long-sleeved shirt; her skin glowed, and her eyes shone. She giggled with excitement as she walked up to me and pulled me into an enormous hug.

"Hey, girl! How are you? I can't wait to pick my dress! Thank you so much for being here with me; I know it must be hard for you." She stuck her bottom lip out in an attempt at humor, presumably to lighten the mood.

I plastered a fake smile on for her benefit while taking her arm. "Do you have a color in mind?"

We linked arms as we walked into the mall, the stores all showcasing their most beautiful dresses in the windows.

"Yes, and no. I was thinking, gold? Or maybe red? Like a dark red, obviously." She wandered over to look at a dress, and I spotted Sienna in the distance.

"Sorry I am late," she said breathlessly. "How are you, Gretchen? I'm so glad you're here today. I need a green dress. Emerald green."

I held my hands up, laughing. "Okay, let's see if we can get you both ready for the ball!"

Sienna peered at me sadly. "I can't believe you aren't coming, Gretchen. So many boys would have loved to take you!"

I shook my head. "Si, really, this isn't as big of a thing for me as it is for you, so please don't worry about me."

I tried not to think about what I would do if Cal was here. He would've taken me to prom for sure.

We walked into *Camille*, one of the largest dress shops.

"So, what's with the green theme Sienna?" I cleared my throat, desperate to change the subject.

I noticed Rosie texting on her phone and tried to sneak a peek. She clutched the phone to her chest and giggled.

"Nope, you're not seeing who I am texting."

I shrugged and walked around the store, my fingers touching the different fabrics, the embellishments shimmering under the store lights. I turned to see the girls gasping over a deep crimson dress in a mermaid off-the-shoulder split-front style.

Rosie selected her size eagerly, and I walked with her to the changing rooms to try it on.

"Oh, my God, it is so *tight,* Gretch." I heard her wailing as she wriggled around. "Almost got it!"

She pulled back the curtain a few minutes later, and I gasped at her.

"*Shit*, Rosie…"

"How is it possible that this is the dress?! The first one I have tried on?!" She twirled around, and I clapped my hands happily.

"You look amazing, I bet your secret date will feel like the luckiest man in the world!"

She laughed as she fixed a diamond choker around her slender throat. She was beaming; she knew how good she looked. "I'm sure he will. Stop fishing; it's a tradition in my family that we never share our date's name until the actual prom. Even to my bestie." She gave me a puppy dog smile that made me laugh, and I let it go.

I felt a pang of regret that I wouldn't be doing this tonight, but I knew there was no way I could—not without Cal.

Rosie scurried off to get changed, and as I came out, Sienna passed me in a flurry of green.

I sat in the plush red armchair reserved for people giving their verdicts on the dresses, pulling my phone out to see an empty screen. I slid my phone away and smiled as Sienna came out in the first of what would be many dresses.

A few hours later we were sat in Guilty Pleasures, finishing our delicious ice cream, a comfortable silence between us. We'd gossiped about who was going with whom to prom, the latest scandal being that Luke was taking Krystal. It didn't matter to me at all; being with Luke felt like a lifetime ago.

As the girls hugged me goodbye before they headed off for their hair and makeup appointments, I gulped down tears.

"Ah, group hug!" Sienna cried.

"I feel like such a shitty friend." Rosie sobbed as she pulled away. "How can you *not* be coming to prom...?"

I wiped her eyes and squeezed her hands. "This is my decision, okay? Don't you dare let this ruin your night. You'll make memories that you will remember forever! But will you do me a favor? Can you please text me the name of your date?!" I swallowed a lump in my throat.

Sienna rolled her eyes and started reeling off names of potential dates, which Rosie ignored, turning to me.

"Yes! It's just a silly family tradition…" She blushed.

We said our goodbyes, and I walked back to the car park, slipping my earphones into the socket of the phone to play my latest mix. I walked down the stairs, not looking where I was going. I exited out onto the street, the sky already dull, the clouds dark, the air charged with the promise of a storm.

I pulled my coat around me until I reached the bus stop, music blaring in my ears. I didn't notice the car pull up beside me until it was blocking the bus stop, and a familiar head leaned out the window.

Luke.

"Gretchen, let me give you a ride. Please."

I took my earphones out and walked over to the car.

Luke's blue eyes filled with concern as he motioned to the seat beside him.

I just can't with this boy.

What made him think I would ever get in a car with him again? Better yet, why did he want me to?

"Luke, I would rather walk. Please leave me alone." I went to put my earphones back in when he touched my arm.

"You know what, Gretchen? We both kinda fucked up this past year. You hurt me. But then I was a dick, and I upset you. I'm sorry." He seemed genuine, and I finally met his gaze with mine.

"I love him, Luke. I'm sorry that I hurt you, but you and I have nothing else to say to each other."

I noticed the pain in his eyes when he nodded.

"I know, but you know what, G, he isn't here, and I *am*. I just want to be friends," he mumbled, his eyes on mine.

Part of me wanted to scream at him and beg for any information on Cal, but I couldn't bring myself to.

"Thank you, Luke; I appreciate your offer of a ride. I hope you understand why I am saying no. Have fun tonight." I said this as firmly as I could, aware his eyes were still on me. I stepped back as the rain fell.

He gazed at me for a beat before smiling sadly, pulling away from the curb with speed.

The bus eventually made its way towards me like a beacon in the night, and I gratefully climbed on board. I sat by the window and stared out into the darkness, the music filling my ears.

I couldn't banish the thoughts in my mind that were always there, reminding me that once I had felt *something* instead of this constant state of emptiness.

When I got off the bus, the rain was pouring. I considered my friends in their beautiful dresses, having to contend with this weather, as my boots disappeared into the small puddles that formed on the ground. I walked past Cal's house, my heart rate increasing as always, to see it shrouded in darkness. I stood for a minute. The tears that fell from my face blended with the rain, making it impossible to tell the difference.

Will this pain ever end? Will the thoughts ever go away?

I pushed away from the fence, heading towards my home, and left the memories behind.

The rain slammed onto the sidewalk, falling so heavily I could barely see in front of me.

Typical Winterburg rain.

I didn't mind it tonight; it soothed my soul.

An orange glow burned in front of me for a split second, stopping me in my tracks. I searched for it again, but it had disappeared.

More mind tricks, Gretchen.

Maybe I was finally losing it, hallucinating along with everything else. I shook my head and moved faster, my head down now against the elements. I ran up the drive to my house, peeling off my coat and calling out to my parents.

It was warm and welcoming in the house, and I was grateful to be away from the world. I wandered into the kitchen to find a note from my parents letting me know they had gone out for dinner. I knew they felt guilty for my unhappiness, but it wasn't their fault. I tugged the elastic from my hair and flipped my head over, shaking the curls out. I flipped my head back and left it loose. I headed upstairs, thoughts of a bath and a book coming to mind.

I slung my dirty clothes into the laundry as I unclipped my bra with relief.

What is it about taking your bra off at the end of the day? Total relief.

My phone pinged, and I reached over to see it was Rosie.

ROSIE: Finn.

I gasped.

Finn? He was her date to prom? How did I not guess?

A million questions run through my mind as I text her back.

GRETCHEN: OMG! Have fun, I love you!

I walked into the bathroom smiling to myself as I imagined Finn's eyes falling out of their sockets when he laid eyes on his date in that dress. I turned the taps on, reveling in hearing the rain battering the windows outside. I drizzled some bath cream into the hot water and watched idly as the water turned soapy and full of bubbles. Just then, the doorbell rang, and I frowned.

Who could that be?

This concerned me; Luke seemed to have a hard time leaving me alone. But surely, he would be at prom or getting ready for prom?

If it was him, I would lose my shit.

I'll hand deliver him to Krystal in a body bag.

I grabbed a towel and quickly turned the taps off, making my way downstairs. I tried to look through the glass at who it was, aware that whoever was on the other side wore a hat through the blurry glass. Cautiously, I leaned close to the door.

"Who is it?" I demanded.

No answer. I felt uneasy.

Why would someone ring the bell then not answer when asked who it was?

It *had* to be Luke.

Fuck, fuck, fuck.

I gripped my towel around my body tighter, wondering what the hell I was going to do.

The doorbell rang again.

"Who is it?! I'm not answering the door until you tell me who it is!" I yelled, my heart pounding with terror.

"It's me."

22

GRETCHEN

J could barely breathe, my fingers fumbling with the lock as I opened the door.

That voice...It couldn't be.

My mind reeled in shock at the sight of him as he leaned against the doorway, his dirty blonde hair longer than I remembered, a beard on his face.

It can't be.

"Do you always answer the door dressed like that?" His eyes twinkled as he drank me in, his hands stroking the beard on his chin softly. The black skinny jeans hugged his legs, the thin white t-shirt soaked through from the rain, exposing his skin and incredible body. I took in his rough beard and intense green eyes that stared into mine.

"Cal?" I tried to sound strong, but my voice shook violently as a wave of dizziness overpowered me.

"I must be hallucinating," I mumbled, tears filling my eyes as I blinked rapidly.

He strode towards me, his long legs closing the distance between us easily. His mouth met mine roughly, his hands in my hair as he kissed me fiercely. At first, he was holding me upright, but then I returned the kiss, my heart racing and jumping around ecstatically in my chest. He kicked the door shut behind him, and he pulled away so he could see me properly.

I cried, hot tears of anger falling down my cheeks. "What the *fuck*, Cal?" I stammered, my voice barely audible as he closed his eyes, exhaling loudly. "You *bastard*!"

"I know." His voice was gruff with emotion.

He smelled so good; my body screamed for him in every capacity, but the tears continued as I shoved him in the chest.

"You fucking *left* me! Just left. Do you have any idea what you have done to me? You can't just walk in here expecting to pick up where we left off like nothing has happened! I thought you loved me!" I sobbed again, my heart shattering to a million pieces. My body hunched over as I tried to remain calm.

He grabbed my shoulders and put his face up to mine, his eyes blazing. "I've got some explaining to do if you'll let me. But don't for one second think I stopped loving you. I've thought about you *every* single minute of *every* day." His thumb ran under my eyes, wiping away the tears. "I'm *so* fucking sorry, baby. But I didn't have a choice."

I stared at him, unable to believe he was my reality.

"But I'm here now," he mumbled, pulling me towards him as he buried his face into my curls.

I breathed in his familiar scent, wrapping my arms around his muscular body. My mouth littered urgent kisses on his throat until he turned his mouth to mine, and once again, we kissed so intensely that I thought I was going to bear physical marks from it.

I grabbed his hand, which was around my head, pulling me deeper into him.

"My parents will be back soon," I stammered as I backed away slowly.

He breathed heavily, kissing my throat whilst his fingers slid under my towel.

"I've missed you so much." He groaned, my body responding to the touch it had yearned for months despite my brain screaming at it to remain still.

I pulled away, holding my hand against his chest, the other gripping my towel.

He leaned back against the door and watched me, a confused expression on his stunning face.

"Give me a minute. Stay there," I ordered, turning towards the stairs.

I ran upstairs and pulled the plug from the bath. I dropped my towel and slid on my underwear, spraying some deodorant before slipping my hoodie on. I pulled on jeans and boots and picked my jacket up.

He is back.

As much as I wanted to have his body wrapped around mine for the rest of my life, I deserved some answers.

I made my way downstairs to see him with his hands in his pockets, his broad chest still wet from the rain. He looked solemn, and my heart skipped a beat.

What was he going to say? What could possibly explain leaving me without even a text?

"My parents will be back soon," I repeated urgently. "I need to hear why, when, where, but most of all, *why!*" I folded my arms in front of me.

"Come with me," he commanded gruffly. His hand held mine, and the other opened the door.

Regardless of everything he had put me through, I felt powerless to fight this. I wanted my explanation, and more than anything, I wanted *him.*

I followed Cal outside, relieved to see the rain wasn't as heavy as it had been earlier. His car was parked opposite my house, and I climbed into the familiar passenger side. I clipped my seat belt in as the car screeched away, the wipers clearing the sodden windshield.

Cal flicked the heaters on to clear the windows, which would take a while, given how cold it was.

Why am I thinking about the fucking windows?

I didn't ask where we were going because I didn't really care. I texted my parents to say I'd gone for some food and I would be back later—I wouldn't make that mistake twice—and stared at the road ahead of us.

The rain wasn't letting up at all, making the road hard to see at the speed Cal drove. We were soon on the freeway, and I took this moment to sneak a look at him. He fixed his eyes on the road, concentration on his beautiful face. I wanted to pinch myself.

I can't believe he is here.

My phone pinged, causing him to glance over at me.

I could've told him it was from my parents, but I wanted him to wonder who it was. I allowed myself a smile and slid the phone back into my jacket.

He frowned and chewed on his lip, deep in thought.

We pulled off the freeway, heading through roads that all seemed the same as the one before that. I didn't know this area too well, so I asked him where we were going.

"Won't be long, Raven, you'll see."

The mention of my pet name on his lips made me shiver with longing, but I couldn't shake the anger. "You don't get to call me that anymore," I snapped haughtily.

He lifted his eyebrows as he pulled onto a dirt road surrounded by trees and shrubs. We made our way up a long and narrow driveway, and as my eyes focused, a house came into view that you couldn't see from the road.

"You live here?" I murmured, despite my anger.

He nodded and got out of the car, and I did the same. The house was beautiful, with shutters adorning the windows, ivy climbing up the old brickwork, and steps leading to a rustic porch.

Cal retrieved his key from his pocket and opened the door, confirming that, yes, he lived here and that he wasn't breaking in.

I followed him inside, walking into a hallway with shiny wooden floors, a sweeping white staircase, and mirrors on the dark walls.

Cal slung off his jacket, tossing it on the banister, then peeled his wet t-shirt off. I gulped as I watched the muscles on his back rippling and averted my eyes to the floor.

Don't get distracted.

He walked into the kitchen and opened the fridge, pulling out two beers. He popped the lids off and gestured for me to follow him. He handed me a beer and threw himself down on a grey sofa covered with blankets, raising his bottle to me as he took a sip.

I placed my beer down without touching the contents and continued to stand, my arms folded as I waited.

He sighed, knowing full well what needed to be done. "This hasn't been the easiest thing for me either, Gretchen."

I remained silent, purely because I couldn't be trusted to not tell him to fuck himself.

How dare he?!

He rubbed his head, his strong, tanned body still glistening with rain. "I couldn't contact you. I had to make a decision quickly," he confessed, his eyes on me the whole time. He inhaled slowly before he sipped more of his beer.

"Couldn't or wouldn't?" I whispered.

He looked at me directly and continued like I hadn't spoken. "I got a letter, Gretchen. They addressed it to '*L Cape.*' It was handwritten."

I frowned, confused.

Who is L Cape?

Why would that make him leave?

I bit my lip to stop myself from interrupting.

"No one knew my address or my real name, aside from family. The letter told me that my identity was no longer a secret and that it was only a matter of time until I joined the others." His voice was flat as he stared at the floor.

My heart was in my mouth. "The New York father?"

He nodded silently. "Me and Drake split. You were in danger—I couldn't remain here, fucking around like we were just two teenagers in love." He smiled sadly. "I didn't know what he knew *if* he knew about you, but I couldn't risk it. I couldn't risk *you*."

I took a huge slug of beer at that point before I sank into a beanbag on the floor in front of him. "You were in danger, and you left? I thought the worst. I thought you were dead…" I shook my head in confusion. "I don't get it. You ran again, but you've come back. I don't understand."

He didn't raise his eyes to look at me but winced as though he knew what he was going to say would shock me. "I went back to New York, Gretchen."

23

GRETCHEN

*I*f I wasn't sitting down, I would've collapsed.

"What?" I cried then, not sure what had happened or how he was still alive in front of me. "You're in witness protection!" I hissed, stunned by his sheer stupidity.

He raised his beautiful green eyes to mine, and I sobbed harder.

"I need you to tell me what happened to you," I whispered as my hands trembled.

Cal shook his head slightly, his expression unreadable. He peeled the label from the beer bottle, and absentmindedly, I remember reading that it was a sign of sexual frustration.

Why does that make me feel happier?

I jumped when he spoke gruffly.

"It was fucking *hard*, Raven. But you're safe now; that's all that matters. I want to tell you everything, I just... can't, okay? Not yet. Give me time, please." He held his face in his hands, and I crawled forward to where he was.

I peeled his hands away from his face and looked at him.

"It's been *months*," he murmured, pain in his eyes. "I get that you may have moved on, and if you have, I swear I will never bother you again." He cupped my face in his hands before he continued. "You deserve to be happy with a decent human being who isn't in trouble with less desirable fuckheads."

I cut him off with my lips on his.

He pulled me onto his lap effortlessly, his fingers sliding up my back as I kissed him harder. I ran my nails down his chest, biting his neck as he lifted me up to throw me down onto the sofa. I gasped and looked up at him in awe as he pulled my jeans and panties down, tossing them aside. He kneeled over me, unbuckling his belt without taking his eyes away from me once. I surprised him as I took control, pushing him down onto the sofa and straddling him. I lifted my hoodie off to sit on him naked. He pulled his jeans down, and I felt him against me, and I moaned softly. I leaned forward and kissed him slowly on his face, his lips, his throat.

I couldn't get enough of him.

His hands skimmed my body greedily, his fingers tracing down my thigh until he slipped a finger easily inside of me. My body squirmed, my hips thrusting as I sank my teeth into my lip.

Heat coursed through me, his eyes holding mine as he finger-fucked me. I reached down and grabbed his dick, which was now solid. He lifted me easily by the hips as he entered me.

I arched back in pleasure as I lifted myself up and back down on him, the full length of him inside of me.

"You're fucking *perfect*," he muttered into my ear as our bodies rocked in perfect rhythm.

I woke a little after two a.m. when Cal shook my shoulders softly.

"Raven, wake up." His voice was urgent, worried.

I sat up in confusion to find I was drenched in sweat and naked. I took in my surroundings, my gaze resting on Cal, who was watching me with concern.

"Cal, what's wrong?"

I couldn't believe we were entwined together on his sofa.

"You were having a nightmare," he murmured, kissing my head.

I'd dreamt he was dead. I'd dreamt of it before, but this seemed so final. I had watched his casket being lowered to the ground and people walking away sadly. I dug my hands into the soil, screaming his name.

"I'll get you some water," he mumbled as he got up from the sofa, and I pulled the throw around me, shuddering despite the warmth of the house.

I watched Cal pad over from the sink, a glass of water in his hand. I could watch him all day. I couldn't help but stare at his body, which he smirked at.

"Seen enough?"

"No," I retorted as he sat on the sofa, his hand running up and down my leg reassuringly. I swallowed the water gratefully and checked my phone.

He watched me as I put it back on the floor and sighed contentedly.

"Is everything alright?" His tone was casual, but I knew I'd worried him.

"Yeah, my parents bought that I was staying at Rosie's. I think they would let tonight slide either way with it being prom." I shrugged, sipping the water before placing it on the floor beside my phone.

"Prom?" Cal echoed faintly; his arms wrapped around me as he scattered kisses all over me.

"I was hardly going to go, was I?"

"I bet you had lots of opportunities to go. I can't even imagine how much attention you got the minute I was out of the picture. It kills me, actually." His hand found mine as he brought it to his lips.

"You're *mine*. You always have been Raven, and you always will be. I just hope you always want to be."

I smiled as I nodded my head. "Always, baby."

His eyes clouded over with something, which soon passed.

"Are you back now? For real?" I asked anxiously. I needed to know; there was no way I was going through that hell ever again.

His finger stroked my cheek. "I left because I *had* to. I'm here now, and there is no reason for me to have to leave again, know that."

I frowned, and despite myself, I asked what I most wanted to hear the answer to. "What happened in New York?"

His eyes narrowed. "I know you need the truth, but I just don't think I can tell you. Not yet. But I will *never* leave you again. Okay?"

I realized he suddenly seemed a lot older than his eighteen years.

"Can we sleep in a proper bed now?" I grinned as he yawned and smiled at me.

I couldn't push it—not at two a.m.

I stood up, bringing the throw with me. I followed him upstairs as my mind raced with the possibilities of what had happened to Cal in New York.

His bedroom was simple. Floor length curtains adorned

the windows, a thick grey rug on the varnished floor. His bed was up against a plain wall; white sheets lay crumpled on the mattress, an ashtray on the floor. I rolled my eyes; some things don't change.

Then again, the image of a naked Cal smoking in bed... Yum.

I crawled into the bed as tiredness overtook me.

Cal slid into bed beside me and kissed my head before he exhaled. "I can't tell you how much I've missed you."

I smiled in response as my eyes closed, our fingers laced together.

24

GRETCHEN

*T*he next morning was Saturday.

I turned over to see the empty bed beside me, as an ice-like grip took hold of my heart.

Where is Cal?

I looked around the room and spotted a pile of clothes strewn over an armchair in the corner. I made my way over to it, slipping Cal's *Ramones* t-shirt on that only just covered my butt. As I walked out of the door, I was hit by the delicious smell of bacon cooking. I hadn't even realized how hungry I was as I hurried down the stairs.

Cal was beside the stove, wearing just grey bottoms as he frowned at the pan with concentration. I took pleasure in watching him whilst he was unaware I was there. He looked fucking delicious. Suddenly, I wasn't hungry for the bacon.

He turned his head to me, and an enormous smile broke over his face. "Morning, you." He opened his arms out, and I slipped into them.

"I could get used to this," I murmured, kissing his mouth.

"There's orange juice in the fridge; help yourself." He

nodded at the fridge as I took the juice out, searching in the cupboards for the glasses.

The first cupboard had nothing in it at all, and the second one had three plates and some mugs. I frowned and went to open the third and final cupboard.

"Yeah, it's right at the back, baby, whatever you are looking for." Cal watched me hungrily as the t-shirt raised up to give him a wonderful view of my naked self.

I rolled my eyes and instructed him to find the glasses himself as I made my way to a stool by the kitchen bar.

How did he get this house? Who does it belong to?

I gazed around it, imagining that it was ours. I remembered my phone on the side and leaned over to grab it. My parents had texted me asking how I was today and if I had fun.

Oh, if they only knew, I smirked to myself.

Cal slid a bacon sandwich over to me, and I thanked him as I took a bite.

"So, do you have any plans today?" He leaned on the counter before taking a bite of his own sandwich.

"No, do you?" As I responded, crumbs of bread escaped from my mouth, and he laughed, shaking his head.

"I wondered if you wanted to go to LA?" He said it so casually that my mouth dropped open.

LA?! That's over two thousand miles away.

"How are we going to do that?" I asked, staring at him.

Cal smiled and winked at me. "Do you think we could get a night away or not?"

I laughed nervously. "Are you serious? First, that's a flight away from here. The nearest airport is Minneapolis. What would I tell my parents I need my passport for?"

He nodded with understanding. "Yeah, we can do it another time. Maybe for your birthday?" His eyes met mine.

"My birthday?!" I squealed with excitement before I hesitated. "I would love that, But Cal, I need my parents to be okay with us."

I stared at the remnants of my breakfast. He walked around the table, swiveling my stool around so he stood in between my legs.

"Hey," he whispered, lifting my head back. "I'd love that. I want to be with you. Whatever I have to do, I'll do."

He was thinking of my birthday, which was six months away.

He will do anything to be with me.

Tears threatened to spill down my face as our mouths met. It wasn't a long walk back to the sofa...

I couldn't bear to be away from Cal, but I knew I had to return home, or my parents would become suspicious. He drove me home, our fingers laced together as much as we could.

"When will I see you next?" I asked as he drew up beside my house. "It's not like you are nearby anymore." I cast a sad look in his old home's direction.

He turned towards me, kissing my hand. "I'll take you for dinner later," he said.

"What will I tell my parents? I can't keep lying." I dropped my head down, groaning with frustration.

Why is everything so difficult?

He watched me for a moment, biting on his lip, "Right, come with me. Let's do this." He got out of the car and walked around to open my door.

I stay seated, confused. "I'm sorry, do what?"

He smiled at me mischievously before he chuckled. "Come on. If this goes wrong, I promise you—I won't leave."

I stared at him open-mouthed as he leaned on the car door, a smile on his lips.

"Baby, if I have learned anything at all, it's that life is too short. I love you. Let me meet your parents."

25

GRETCHEN

I slid my legs out of the car, my heart in my mouth as I considered every possibility that could go wrong. "Cal—"

He put his finger to my lips and shut the car door behind me. He leaned against me, his lips pressed against mine. "Let's go."

I was breathless from his kiss, his touch, *damn,* even his presence.

He laced his fingers through mine again and led the way up the driveway towards my home.

"They thought I was at Rosie's," I hissed, my eyes widening as he smiled at me, ringing the buzzer.

"Cal, I don't ring the buzzer at home." I bit back nervous laughter as the door swung open to reveal my mom.

Her eyes creased with confusion when she saw Cal before she moved her gaze to me. She stared back at him and widened her eyes. "Gretchen?" she said with uncertainty.

He stepped forward, moving his hair out of his eyes. "Hi, Mrs. Red. I think it's time we met. I'm Cal."

Their eyes met, and I watched as my mom went through a

million different emotions. She grimaced, then glanced back at me; my cheeks flushed with happiness, and my eyes that shone with emotion and adoration.

"I thought you stayed at Rosie's last night, Gretchen?" She was looking back at Cal, who didn't miss a beat.

"She did; I gave her a ride home this morning, as I didn't want her walking home alone." He shot her a winning smile as her face relaxed.

"I see. So, are you going to come in, *Cal*?"

I nearly fell over when she said this, but he nodded and held his hand out for me to go first.

I walked in, staring at my mom as she closed the door.

"So, Cal. It's good to meet you, but I have to say, I thought you and Gretchen had cooled it off somewhat?" She sounded almost hopeful until he laughed.

"No. I gave Gretchen some space to concentrate on her studies. I know how much she wants to be a therapist."

He sat down in the chair beside him. I stared at him: this smooth talker who seemed to have the answers to everything. He glanced back over at my mother, who watched him skeptically.

She cleared her throat and fixed him with her fierce gaze. "So graduation is soon. What are your plans, Cal?"

He frowned as he appeared to be deep in thought. "Well, to be honest, I'm not sure which path is best to take. I could follow my father down the acting route, or I could stick with sports therapy, which I am better at, to be honest."

He laughed, and I couldn't hide my surprise as I took this information in.

He's interested in sports therapy? His dad's an actor?!

His eyes met mine, and he tilted his head to the side, acknowledging my confusion.

"I assume you won't be keeping my daughter out

overnight anymore without letting us know first, right?" My mom's voice had softened somewhat, but she still made it clear she meant business.

Cal held his hands up, his eyes wide. "Ma'am, I can only apologize about that. It won't happen again."

We were all quiet for a moment until he rose from his chair while smiling at my mom.

"It was a pleasure to meet you, but I have to head home. I have some things to take care of." He paused for a moment. "Oh, Gretchen, I didn't know if you were free this evening, but would you like to go out to dinner with me?"

My mom folded her arms, looking at me with wide eyes.

I couldn't have loved him any more than I did right then.

"I would love to, and Mom, I will be back home straight after. Promise."

Mom pursed her lips and nodded. "Does Cal know you're going to New York University?" She sounded so proud, beaming at me as my eyes met Cal's.

The color drained from his face as he recognized the name and the location. He recovered rapidly as he nodded. "It's fantastic news, I'm so proud of her. That's what tonight is about—celebrating." His voice hadn't changed at all.

Wow, an expert liar.

Mom nodded in approval. "We are very proud of her; I know she will excel at all she does."

I walked Cal to the door as he waved goodbye to my mom. I pulled the door closed behind me and leaned against it with my eyes closed.

"I'm sorry I didn't tell you…" I mumbled, refusing to meet his gaze. "You weren't around, I didn't know…"

He nodded, grimacing. "New York, eh?"

I gulped, unable to take the pain in his tone.

He stood up straight as he leaned over, and his lips grazed against mine. "I'll pick you up later, about seven?"

He walked down the steps from the porch, walking backward so he could still see me.

I couldn't stop gawking at his beautiful face, his hair in his eyes. "So, the beard—are you gonna lose it?"

He snorted and ran his hand over it nonchalantly. "Hmm, you seemed to like it this morning?" He smirked and strode to his car.

My eyes followed him longingly as he swept his hair back, pulling on his aviators to avoid the glare of the bright sun.

He studied me one last time before he drove off back in the direction we had come.

I groaned, not sure what to think. There was so much to consider.

What happened to him in New York?

What would happen when I go to New York?

How did he feel about it?

My mind buzzed with the questions as I made my way back to the house.

Mom was sitting at the kitchen table, coffee in hand. Her sapphire eyes locked onto mine when I strolled in, a small grin on her lips. "He was...interesting. I can't think what you see in him."

We both laughed suddenly, thawing the ice between us.

I took a seat in front of my Mom, who examined me with interest. "Everything okay, honey?" She asked.

"It's complicated, Mom... I am so in love with him."

She didn't respond. Instead, she sipped her coffee in silence.

"He's all I think about. I know me going to New York is going to be a big thing for him...but I also know he supports me entirely." I sighed, absentmindedly playing with one of my dark spirals as it tumbled over my shoulder.

"I don't doubt you are in love with him. I think it's clear you are both in love. I know long distance is hard. Where will he be able to study sports therapy?" She cocked her head to the side.

I looked back at her, answering her honestly. "I have no idea."

She shrugged, reaching for my hand. "If it's meant to work, it will. Now, why don't you have a relaxing day before your date tonight? I have to nip to the store if you need a ride to the mall."

I wanted to pinch myself. My mom understood for once.

I beamed and grabbed my phone, dialing Rosie's number. She answered with a yawn, asking what time it was.

"Rosie, I need to see you. I need your help."

26

GRETCHEN

J peered at the reflection in the mirror, barely recognising the woman staring back at me.

I'd met Rosie at the mall earlier that day, begging her to help me look sensational for my date.

Rosie had squealed and danced at the news Cal was back, then she went into diva mode, dragging me to the hair salon.

I wasn't holding out much hope they could fit me in; it was a Saturday, after all.

A petite blonde girl called Molly had a cancellation and was all too excited to get her hands on my unruly mop. She had scrubbed, snipped, and blow-dried to within an inch of her life. I was astounded that someone so small could have such strength!

She teased my hair into silky curls that tumbled down my shoulders, complete with caramel highlights. Molly ran some hair product through my hair, and some three hours later, after walking in, I was done.

Rosie stared at me, agape, as I paid Molly and added a heavy tip.

Wow.

I felt almost awkward, not wanting to mess up the curls.

Rosie walked over, whistling. "Ouch. Cal is going to die! You look *insanely* hot, momma!"

I giggled, linking arms with her as we made our way out of the salon, watched by a smiling Molly.

The next stop was all the stores—we trawled through so many—Rosie was getting agitated because she didn't know where I was going that evening.

GRETCHEN: Where are we going tonight? Need to know how to dress...!

CAL: Dress however the fuck you like—you won't be wearing it long. We are going somewhere nice, I promise.

I had butterflies in my tummy as I read it.

Rosie rolled her eyes. "They really do just think with their cocks, don't they?"

I shrugged, remembering that morning with a shiver. In the end, we settled on a simple yet figure-hugging black dress, the back exposed.

Later that evening, I stared at myself in the mirror again, chewing on my lip as I waited for Cal to pick me up. I wore a diamante choker, and I had gone all the way with the makeup, going as far as to follow a tutorial on YouTube on 'smoky eyes' and nude lips. I'd just finished the lip liner on my lips as the buzzer rang.

I squealed, grabbing my black fur-collared jacket. I carefully walked down the stairs in my heels and tried not to slip.

My dad had answered the door and was standing at the bottom of the stairs talking with Cal, a relaxed expression on his face—clearly, Mom had filled him in.

I smiled as they broke off their conversation to watch me descend the stairs.

Mom walked in from the kitchen, her eyes falling on me as she smiled in delight, her hands flying to her mouth as tears filled her eyes. I felt for them—they didn't get to see me go to prom; this was as good as that to them.

But it was Cal who took my breath away, his jaw dropping as he watched me stride toward him.

"You look beautiful; I am a lucky man." He was trying to behave in front of my parents, but as his eyes drank me in, I saw his thoughts were not that of a respectable man, more likely depraved.

My father watched him, as did I.

He wore a black suit that showed off his brawn to perfection, and a crisp white shirt and skinny black tie completed his outfit. His long hair had been cut back to its previous length and slicked back, drawing attention to his chiseled jawline, which was now devoid of any hairs.

He lifted my hand to his and kissed it softly while his eyes remained on mine.

My parents stood watching us, then my mom came over to kiss me on both cheeks. She whispered, "Be safe, and if you aren't coming home, text me."

I looked at her in surprise, and she winked, sliding an arm around my dad's waist.

"Have a good night, honey, and Cal, look after her." My father raised his eyebrows at him as he said this, and Cal nodded his head.

"Absolutely, Mr. Red, you have my word."

My father crossed his arms and watched us leave, his chest puffed out with pride. We left into the chilly evening air as the door closed behind us.

"Cal, you look *amazing*. Can we just go to your place?" I

murmured huskily as he held my hand, gesturing in front of him.

"Or the back of this?"

I followed his gaze to a sleek black limo stretched out in front of my house. I gasped, halting as I took it in. "A *limo*?!"

Cal laughed, clearly pleased with my reaction.

A driver stood at the door, which he held open for me, holding his hand out as I climbed in.

I'd never been in a limo before, and I couldn't believe my eyes. I slid into a seat that curled its way from the door and around the length of the limo, a bar in front of that complete with champagne on ice. I turned to see a huge bouquet of roses lying next to the champagne, with a note attached. My heart thudded in my chest as Cal slid into the seat next to me, kissing my shoulders.

"You look and smell good enough to eat." He looked up at me then, following my gaze to the roses. He handed me the bouquet, and I reached for the note. I realized the limo was moving, and I squealed with excitement. I slid the note out, and it simply read:

Mine.

27

GRETCHEN

*T*he limousine sped through the streets of Winterburg as I sipped champagne in between kissing the most amazing man I had ever met.

"Where are we going?" I uttered, glad I had gone with nude lips that evening, considering how much we were kissing.

His lips curved into the smile I adored as he gazed back at me.

How did I get this lucky?

He was gorgeous but also addictive on another thousand levels.

He leaned back against the leather seat and ran a hand through his hair, the other entwined with mine. "Somewhere different. You missed prom so…" He shrugged, looking down.

I rolled my eyes and savored my champagne as the cold bubbles made their way down my throat. I can't remember feeling this happy.

Cal watched me, an unreadable expression on his face.

"What?!" I giggled as I bit my lip.

He dropped his finger over my knuckles before he lifted my hand to his handsome mouth. His green eyes found mine, and an electric bolt shot through my body.

I swore he had magical powers. There was no other explanation.

Voodoo maybe?

As I pondered this, the limousine slowed before coming to a halt. I stared at Cal as he smirked.

The door opened, and the chauffeur held his hand out for me to get out. As I stepped out, the wind met me, taking my breath away. I gasped when I realized we were at the marina.

"Cal?!" I whirled around to him, my eyes wide as I searched his. "What are we doing at the marina?"

He chuckled as he swung me around to face the direction behind me. "We're spending the evening on that..." He nodded to a beautiful yacht in the near distance.

It was lit up against the dark, and I squealed with excitement.

He beamed at my reaction, grabbing my hand after tipping the limo driver.

My heart thudded in my chest as I gawked at the yacht.

Roses adorned the rails that surrounded the ramp, and small lanterns lined the path to it. I went to walk on it but Cal stopped me, removing first my heels, then his shoes. I peered at him, puzzled, as he winked at me.

"You need to take your shoes off before you walk aboard a yacht, my lady. It may damage the decks."

I was relieved I wouldn't have to navigate the yacht in heels.

I stepped up the slope and board.

A girl in a crisp white shirt approached me, her hair swept up into an elegant French twist, and she handed me yet another icy glass of bubbles. I thanked her and spun around to take in my surroundings.

Cal's arms slipped around my waist as his lips brushed my neck. "Do you like it?" His voice trembled with uncertainty, very out of character for him.

I rubbed his palm and whispered how much I loved it, and he led me by the hand to a table circled by more small lanterns, candles, and even more roses.

The chairs were soft, with at least room for three people on each side.

I slid into one, and Cal slipped in opposite me, his eyes twinkling with happiness.

The attendant came over, and we ordered our food: chicken for me and steak for Cal... and even more champagne.

"You look amazing, Gretchen," he breathed as his eyes drank me in.

I blushed, and he noticed, smiling further as he leaned back into his chair.

The attendant poured more champagne and fluttered her eyelashes at Cal when he acknowledged her.

"No problem, Sir." She swung her hips as she sauntered away, casting a sly glance behind her to see if he was checking her out, though all she saw was my furious glare.

"Does she want to offer to take you below?" I muttered, annoyed that she had the audacity to flirt with my boyfriend on our date.

This was the trouble with being with someone as hot as Cal.

He lifted his eyebrows and flashed me a wicked grin. "Now *that* is an idea. We should go below at some point, Raven," he licked his lips suggestively, and my face burned.

It must have been the bubbly because I was contemplating doing it.

After dinner, Cal and I retired to the other end of the yacht and stared at the sky together, complete with a thick blanket to shield us from the cold.

I couldn't believe how many stars were visible; it was such a clear night.

"It's so beautiful," I murmured.

Cal pulled me towards him, our lips meeting with urgency as his mouth explored mine. I pulled his hair as he tugged me onto his lap. We kissed with raw passion, his lips biting mine as I moaned with desire. He pulled me further down onto him, the blanket covering us. Waves lapped the boat as it rocked, creating the most wonderful moment. He pulled away from me, and I groaned.

"I think it's time for a dance."

I frowned at him with a perplexed smile. "What? Here? But…"

He lifted me to my feet. He turned, holding out his hand, which I took as I laughed to myself.

At that point, the lights on the yacht went out, and I gasped, moving closer to Cal, who muttered against my neck. "It's okay."

I stared up at him, beaming. I stood in the dark beneath the stars, on a yacht, in a dress and bare feet, whilst Cal held me in his arms. He swayed with me to invisible music, and tears pricked my eyes.

I sniffed, and he tipped my head back to look at him.

"I worship you, you know that? Nothing will ever tear us apart again." His voice was strong yet sweet, his lips brushing against mine. "I adore you, too. *So* much."

Our mouths met as we danced under the stars.

28

GRETCHEN

I woke up the next morning naked in Cal's arms. I looked up at him and watched as his lips moved with each breath, his chest rising and falling slowly.

He looked as content as I felt.

I peeled myself away from the warmth of the bed and made my way to the bathroom. I stared at myself in the mirror, realizing that my make-up from last night was still on. Much of it was on the pillow, too.

I ran the water in the shower and waited until the temperature was hot enough to step into. I stepped into the steam as it covered my body, running my hands over my face and my hair as I hummed to myself. I washed my hair, massaging the conditioner in before I rinsed it out. I shivered when I remembered what Cal did for me last night. My smile was so wide that I thought my face would burst with happiness.

I didn't hear the footsteps that came into the bathroom and jumped out of my skin when I heard a deep voice.

"Well, you must be the reason he isn't answering any of my calls."

I gasped, and I grabbed my towel from the top of the

shower, my hands twisting at the taps to stop the water. Through the steam, I saw a muscular man towering in the doorway, his eyes running over my body as he watched me with a lazy grin on his face. I gulped, wrapping the surrounding towel in horror.

Who the hell is this?!

Why is he staring at me like I am his breakfast?

"What the fuck are you doing in my house?!" Cal growled, relief washing over me like a tidal wave when I heard his voice.

The man continued to assault me with his eyes as his hand moved to his belt.

Oh, God.

His depraved thoughts didn't need to be said. The leer he gave me spoke volumes.

"See, I was just telling this young lady here now I understand why you haven't returned my calls." his voice was thick with a New York accent, and panic took over. My entire body shook in response to the situation.

Cal pushed in front of him, creating a barrier between us.

I cowered behind him as he barked at the stranger.

"What the *fuck* is this, Andre?!"

I hid behind Cal, my heart pounding in my chest so hard it vibrated around my entire being. I knew nothing would happen to me whilst Cal was there, but I was still out of my depth, and it terrified me.

Andre spoke again. "Let's go downstairs. Let the girl...get dressed." He licked his lips, and I shuddered.

Cal remained in place as the man stepped backward out of the bathroom, his dark eyes flashing towards me. Cal's eyes were wide with fear, which made me nauseous. "Get dressed, and don't worry. You're safe with me."

He kissed my head, his eyes fixed on mine before he turned in the same direction the creepy Andre guy had gone.

I grabbed a stray t-shirt and some jeans that were way too big for me, tugging them onto my damp body. I wanted to cry with frustration; I didn't even have any clothes here that fit me. I found a hoodie and pulled it on, grateful for the larger size. My hair was dripping wet as heavy curls formed. I grabbed a towel and scrunched some moisture out, and I realized my hands were shaking. I tiptoed to the stairs and listened to the voices as best as I could. I heard the vibration of their voices, but I couldn't make out what they were saying. All I could think of was what I was going to do if something happened to Cal. I screamed inwardly, desperately trying to calm myself down.

How did we go from dancing on a yacht last night to hiding upstairs from a lecherous prick who had let himself into Cal's house?

I gripped the handrail as the voices got louder and less muffled.

"If you had answered my calls, I wouldn't have had to make this trip, especially Leo."

Leo?! Who the fuck was Leo?

My heart punched in my chest.

"I told you. This is all over now. What the fuck are you doing here?!" Cal demanded, his voice so cold it sent chills down my spine.

"You can't ignore what happened. Does your pretty little girlfriend know?" Andre sneered.

"Don't even mention her. Forget you ever saw her," Cal warned.

"It's hard, though; she is such a hot little thing. Remember the last little thing you had? I liked her a lot, too."

There was a loud bang before I heard Cal speak.

"You come to *my* house, let yourself in, and fucking stare at my girlfriend in the shower?! You are one sick fuck!"

Andre laughed. "But we are alike, are we not, Leo?" His voice was softer now.

"No, we aren't, we're nothing alike," Cal spat.

I wanted to hold him back, but I knew I needed to stay upstairs.

"You deserve to die," Cal snarled. His voice was menacing. I had never heard him like that before, *ever*.

"I'll pay your little girlfriend a visit. Hopefully, she hasn't got dressed; I much preferred her naked."

I gasped then, my feet sliding on the floor as I ran to the bathroom and locked the door. My heart pounded in my chest, my ears filled with the sound of rushing blood. Nausea filled my throat from pure fear. Tears streamed down my face as I heard footsteps racing up the stairs, followed by scuffles and hollering.

"You are a weak little boy. She needs a man. When I have finished with you, I will make sure she knows what a man feels like."

His vile words made me retch, but I racked my brain, thinking of what I could do. My phone wasn't in the bathroom, and if I went out there, I'd be at risk.

I couldn't leave Cal, though.

Andre was bigger than Cal and clearly fought dirty. I glanced around the bathroom, searching for anything I could use as a weapon.

Fuck!

All I could see were bottles of shampoo and shower gel.

Bangs from outside the door startled me, then a thud slammed against it.

As sweat dripped down my back, my fight or flight kicked in.

Fuck this.

I opened the door gradually, peeking through the crack in the door; I couldn't see anything. I opened the door more, and the crack expanded to allow me to see legs sprawled beside the bedroom door. I wept as I walked towards them, and I prayed they weren't Cal's.

They weren't moving.

I walked forward, my hand over my mouth as I saw Andre.

I recoiled at the blood that covered his face, and as I crept forward, I jumped at the sight of Cal leaning against the wall, his right eye swollen shut, his face purple with bruises. Andre had split Cal's lip open, the blood trickled down his chin as he stared ahead.

"Baby," I whispered. He didn't look at me; he didn't even blink. "I'll call an ambulance, okay?" I looked around for my phone desperately, spotting it on the stand beside Cal's bed as I ran over.

"*Don't,*" Cal hissed.

I stared at him, stunned. "But—"

"No. He needs to die, okay? I'll explain. But he needs to." His voice was eerily calm. He nodded towards his phone, which was on the floor near the bed. "Can you pass me that? I'm not sure I can move just yet." He tried to smile and winced.

My mind raced as I handed him his phone.

What is going on?!

Andre was a rotten apple, but did he deserve to die?

I slumped onto the floor against the bed, closing my eyes.

Suddenly, Andre gurgled and coughed, and Cal's eyes widened as he jumped up, roaring with pain as he did, his hand clapping over Andre's mouth and nose.

I froze, covering my eyes as Andre tried to fight Cal

pointlessly. His eyes were wide as he tried to speak, but Cal stared at him as he leaned in close to his ear.

"This is for Lucia, you sick fucker," he spat in his face as the light faded from Andre's eyes. Cal didn't remove his hands, pushing down repeatedly until he was sure he was dead.

I choked out a sob then, and Cal whipped his head towards me as though he'd just remembered I was there. He leaned back and reached for his phone as he beckoned me to his side.

I shook my head.

No.

Cal made a call, his hands on his head. "Can I speak to Verno? It's Leo."

I stared at him, a million questions in my head.

Leo Cape?

Was this his name?

His real name?

I closed my eyes and tried to breathe.

I was sitting in a room with a corpse who, moments before, was going to kill my boyfriend before doing unthinkable things to me.

Cal didn't have a choice. Well, *Leo* didn't.

My head spun as I realized I had zero grip on reality.

I listened as Cal explained to Verno that Andre was dead and that he needed someone to remove him.

Remove him?

A fresh wave of nausea swept over me as the room spun; was I now an accessory to murder?

Cal hung up as he crawled over to me, my hands in his blood-stained ones. "I will tell you everything. Just please listen to me."

My hands shook uncontrollably, but I nodded, desperate

for him to shed some light on what the hell had just happened.

"Okay." Cal took a deep breath. "First, we need to get out of here. Let me clean myself up."

He stood, grimacing as he did. I helped him to the shower as he washed away the blood. Deep black bruises appeared on his ribs and chest, and my heart ached. He winced as he washed, but he was soon out and drying himself. He dressed with my help, and as we stepped over the body of Andre, Cal drew me close to him. We made our way downstairs and outside to his car.

29

GRETCHEN

"*Y*ou're leaving him there?!" I stared at Cal aghast.

He nodded and reversed down the drive and onto the road before speeding away. "Text your parents. We have to talk without interruptions," he commanded, and I shot off a text to my Mom.

I had texted her last night to gush about my evening before falling asleep. I realized my hands were still shaking as we pulled into a diner close by.

We walked in, and it relieved me to see it was empty, so we chose a booth towards the back as a server came over and took our orders.

I stared at Cal, waiting for him to speak.

He met my gaze and nodded.

"What the fuck just happened?" I whispered.

"So, New York. The house we broke into. It belonged to my then-girlfriend." He had the grace to look down then before he continued. "Lucia. No one knew we were seeing each other. She wasn't supposed to be there." He closed his eyes, clearly remembering that night. "We were almost done. She came in and saw us all."

I didn't know what to say, so I just remained quiet.

The server came over, placing our milkshakes in front of us, which we both left untouched.

"You could do with the sugar for shock." Cal nodded at mine. I folded my arms and stared at him.

"Carry on."

He looked at me through those beautiful dark eyelashes. "I told her to run," he whispered, his eyes hardening. "She didn't. They dragged her upstairs. I tried to stop them. But they were men, Gretchen. I was too young. I lied to you before—I didn't run...But they weren't about to let me stop them. They punched me hard enough to knock me out. When I came to, there were police everywhere."

I realized tears were running down my face.

He was struggling now, his face creased with emotion. "She never told them we were seeing each other. The police assumed I had a part in it."

I swallowed, barely able to breathe as I imagined a young Cal going through this.

"I had a good lawyer. Lucia survived, but only just. She can never have children, and she doesn't leave her house. She has no life, not really." His voice was filled with remorse and agony. "I admitted to taking part in the robbery, but not what happened to her. Not *that*. not ever," he said with disgust. "So yeah, Verno was Lucia's old man. He wanted me dead. In his eyes, even if I didn't touch her, I didn't help her either."

I reached out and held his hand, and he looked at me in surprise. "Go on," I pleaded. My voice was broken, but I wanted him to tell me everything.

"I got a fine and a caution. I was the youngest. Four of the men went to prison for what they did. They got five fucking years. It was a mockery of the justice system. So, Verno created his own justice system. They died in jail," he said without emotion.

"So, Andre?" I asked, "What did he do?"

Cal's face changed to that of hatred. "He was vile, Raven, really fucking bad. To the core. He went on the run. I never heard from him or saw him until today. He was the worst of them all—what he did to her—" He shook his head as if it would erase the memory. "It was just me and him left, and Verno wanted us both dead."

I stared at him, trying to process everything he had just told me. I reached forward and drank my milkshake in a few gulps.

I wish it was wine.

Cal observed me before he spoke. "He must've found out she was my...girlfriend."

He looked like he was in physical pain.

I couldn't even comprehend what he was telling me.

We sat in silence as I absorbed what he had said.

"So that's why you killed him today," I whispered, my voice lower than a whisper.

He didn't confirm this, but he didn't have to. His face said it all.

"He would have hurt you, Gretchen. I couldn't let that happen again—no way. I just couldn't. What he is capable of —" He closed his eyes as his hand tightened around mine.

Cal had killed a man.

For *me.*

For Lucia, too, I realized.

He had killed an awful man who would have killed us both if given the chance.

"So, the body—" I started before Cal placed a finger to his lips to silence me.

"Will be removed. I have to go back to meet with Verno. I have to end this, baby."

What? Is he insane? Verno will kill him!

"No, Cal. *No*. I'm going with you," I stammered, wondering why I was saying this.

Love is blind and fucking stupid, too.

His eyes met mine, ice cold as I sat back in fear. "No, Gretchen, you're not. This is *not* up for debate. I need you to be safe. I also need you to know how much I love you, okay? No matter what," his eyes burned into mine as he grabbed my hand and squeezed it. "I can't believe what you had to see today. I am *so* sorry. So *fucking* sorry. I think you need time to process—"

This time, I snapped. "No. *No*, I don't. Because you don't get to choose who you fall in love with. I fucking *love you*. You *saved me*."

His eyes shone with love as he gazed at me. "I killed a man, and you still want to be with me?" He smiled. "I'm going to get you home. I have to be back at mine shortly."

30

GRETCHEN

*T*he plane touched down on the runway, and I stared out of the window in excitement.

New York City.

Anything is possible!

I leaned back in my chair and waited for the seatbelt sign to come off so I could grab my bag. This past year had been such a whirlwind, I felt like I had aged ten years. I was finally off to college to pursue my dream of being a therapist.

I glanced around the cabin and noticed most people were business passengers or families on a trip. I felt a pang of loneliness, but I swallowed it down.

Time to be brave, Gretchen.

I took my phone off flight mode and sent my parents a text to let them know I had landed.

This is so exciting!

I had arranged accommodation with the University; it was off-campus but close to Manhattan, so I was ecstatic. Easy access to shopping and heavenly food. I was nervous, though; there would be so much going on here, and I was just from a small town.

I reached up and grabbed my bag when the sign went off, allowing my body to stretch. I followed the group of impatient passengers from the plane through the jetway and into the airport. It was lively and busy, and my heart lurched with excitement.

MOM: Good luck, baby! Be safe!

I grinned as I made my way to the baggage claim, spotting my bright pink suitcase. I heaved it off the conveyor belt and looked for the signs to the taxi line, slipping through the crowd. I already preferred the buzz of the city—everyone was on their phones and moving quickly, going about their business. I took a free paper from someone handing them out and made my way out of the revolving doors and into the crisp New York air.

I checked my email on my phone for the address. I was concentrating so much I didn't notice someone hurtling towards me.

"Oh, *shit*, I am sorry. I didn't mean to literally fall into you."

I looked up and saw a handsome guy with a football jersey on, grinning at me, his hand extended towards me.

"I'm Josh."

I hesitated before I replied. "I don't talk to strangers," I mumbled, swiping through my phone as he studied me.

"No, that's a good point to make, actually. What brings you to New York?"

I found the address and glanced around for a cab. There was a long line of them and a queue of people waiting.

I made my way over to the line with Josh in tow.

He was certainly persistent.

"Look, Josh, I mean this in the nicest way. I'm not interested in you or anyone else." I smiled and moved away from him. "I have a boyfriend."

His face fell as he held his hands up. "I'm sorry, just a sucker for a pretty face."

I laughed as he moved on to another girl, who seemed a little more receptive than I.

Eventually, I was in a cab, riding through the bright lights of the city, heading for my apartment. I was excited to meet my roommate. The rent was surprisingly good, so I had hoped it wouldn't be in too bad an area.

I marveled at the skyline as it fell into view, and I got that famous New York gawp I had heard about. The cab made its way through the traffic, the driver reluctantly answering my many questions. He seemed bored to tears, to be honest. I sat back in my seat and marveled that I was finally here.

Slowly but surely, my cab pulled onto a residential street that was very pretty, considering it was still quite central. I pulled out my money and paid him, being sure to give him a tip as he pulled my luggage from the trunk for me.

I longed for Cal suddenly, feeling vulnerable.

He hadn't been in touch before I left, telling me he was shitty at goodbyes but that we would try the long-distance thing. I sighed, pulling my suitcase up to the steps to the door that read '11A'.

I searched my phone once more, making sure I was pressing the correct buzzer. I waited patiently as I heard foot-steps come towards the door, and I gulped, trying not to be nervous. This was, after all, my new roommate.

The door opened to reveal a striking brunette with large brown eyes studying me.

"I'm Gretchen. You must be…" I racked my brain to recall her name.

"Nancy," she drawled and moved back so I could walk in,

not offering to help at all. She wore black thigh-high boots, which left a gap of flesh between them, and a long red shirt that hung over one shoulder. Her dark hair was poker straight, and her lips were painted red. She closed the door behind me as I dragged my case in awkwardly.

She folded her arms and sighed. "So, we share the top floor." She eyed my bags. "There's no elevator, so it's gonna be a struggle with your things." She reached into her pocket and pulled out a silver key. "This is yours. I'll see you around." She turned on her heel and walked out of the door I had just come in.

I closed my eyes and wished more than anything Cal was here.

How the hell am I going to get this case to the top floor?!

Why is my roommate such a bitch?

She literally had waited to let me in, then she had left without offering to help.

Ugh, was this what all New Yorkers were like? I gazed at the stairs, trying to think of a solution.

My phone beeped, and I felt my heart lurch when I saw it was Cal.

CAL: Settling in okay? I miss you already.

Tears pricked my eyes as I imagined him back in Winterburg, in his cozy house, all alone. *He better be alone*, I thought, texting him back quickly.

GRETCHEN: Roommate isn't too friendly. I've got to get my case up three flights of stairs. Any suggestions?

I tried to be jovial, but I just sat on my suitcase in frustration.

> CAL: Leave it downstairs and pay someone
> to take it up for you later. Are you okay,
> Raven?

I laughed despite myself. That was *so* Cal—Pay someone to sort it for you.

I typed back my response as I heard footsteps come down the stairs.

The guy sailing down them had platinum blond hair, a shirt complete with a scarf, and the tightest jeans I'd ever seen. He glided past me and opened the front door.

I turned to see the guy from the airport, Josh, beaming at me.

"Hey, it's you! *Ooh*, are you my roommate?" Josh beamed, dragging his case behind him.

"Erm, no—I'm sharing with Nancy. You've just missed her…" I mumbled, looking at his case pointedly. "There are no elevators."

The guy with the blond hair just looked bored. "Floor 2. I'm Nicholas."

Josh reached his hand out, to which Nicholas shuddered.

"I don't shake hands. Germs." He sniffed and ran his hand over his perfect hair.

I stared at his waist, which must've been the width of my thigh.

Wow.

"You're kidding me, right? *I'm* rooming with a germaphobe. Brilliant." Josh laughed.

Nicholas glared at him. "I'm *not* a phobe of any kind. I just don't like to take risks with *strangers*."

I smiled secretly, aware that was the second time today Josh had been called a stranger.

Nicholas looked at me disdainfully. "Are you going to sit on that until an elevator magically appears?"

I flushed, standing up quickly. "No. I'm going to break my back getting it upstairs. But thank you for your concern," I replied sarcastically.

Nicholas's eyebrows shoot up at my response. "Oh, you have *spirit*. I like that."

I glared at him. I wanted to dislike him, but his demeanor had something about it I quite liked.

Josh yawned. "Look, Curly, I can take it up for you. Seeing as your *boyfriend* isn't here. You can buy me some beers later. Deal?"

I grinned. "Yes, deal. I can't do this on my own, I hate being such a girl...but I can't drag that case up there. Thank you so much," I gushed.

He nodded; his playful side was suddenly replaced by a serious version. "No worries, Curls. I got this."

He reached down and lifted my suitcase in one hand and his in the other. Nicholas met my eyes, and we lifted our eyebrows up simultaneously.

"How gallant of him. He must be *very* strong," murmured Nicholas, watching Josh as he walked up the stairs effortlessly.

I was grateful as we followed him up the steep stairs because by the second floor, I was out of breath and holding onto the railing for dear life. I heard my phone beep as I pulled it out.

CAL: Raven, don't tell me you are trying to drag that case up three flights of stairs...

I grinned as I typed back.

> GRETCHEN: No, someone else is doing it
> for me. Gretchen 1, NYC 0.

No sooner had I sent the text did a ping come straight back. I smiled knowingly.

> CAL: Who is he? Don't forget, you are mine.
> I do not share.

Josh called me from the floor above. "Curls! Come on, I'm not up here for my health."

Nicholas had disappeared into his room.

I followed the direction of the stairs, my legs protesting. I made it to the top floor and gasped as Josh eyed me with amusement.

"Are you okay? You need to get in shape. You'll be doing this at least twice a day."

I pulled out my key, ignoring his comment as I rolled my eyes. "Thank you, Josh, I owe you."

The door swung open, and Josh pulled my case in for me. "There you are, my lady. Right, I will meet you on the second floor at seven p.m.. You owe me those beers. Ask your roommate to come. Is she hot?" He looked at me hopefully.

"Boiling," I nodded as I walked into the apartment.

"Yeah?" Josh looked interested. "Definitely bring her. Later, baby." He tipped an imaginary hat and smiled as he backed out of the door, closing it softly behind him.

I walked into the main room and saw a mustard sofa with cream throws and cushions tossed over it casually. The floor was natural wood; the windows were bay-fronted and overlooked the street. It was an open plan, so the kitchen was tiny; a coffee machine and a stove dominated the small side.

I smiled to myself and squealed. I am in *New York City*!

I opened a door and saw a small but tidy bathroom,

complete with a mirror over the basin and a shower in the corner.

I walked on and saw what must be Nancy's room. It screamed her: black sheets on the bed and a blood-red chair in the shape of lips. A floor-length mirror with fairy lights hung over it stood in the corner, and a pile of makeup lay messily on the floor in front of it.

I moved along and opened the door to what was clearly to be my room. The bed was in front of the three large windows with a bedside table on each side. A lamp sat on each table, and along the side of the wall near the bed, I saw a wardrobe. A desk was on the other side, with room for my books and my laptop.

I loved it.

I pulled my suitcase in and put my things away.

My phone rang, and I saw it was Cal.

"I wasn't kidding." His gruff voice made my insides melt.

I fell backward onto the bed. "I know. His name is Josh, and he was kind enough to bring it up to my room for me. He is going to be more interested in my roommate than me, so please don't worry. I just owe him some beers."

I twirled with my hair, remembering Josh calling me 'curly' and thought I would leave that bit out.

"Your roommate *cannot* be hotter than you. Are you coming back yet?"

I heard the longing in his voice.

"No, I'm not qualified yet," I teased.

"So, what're your plans, city girl?" Cal asked.

"Well, Josh said I owe him some beers, so he is going to come here at seven. He wants to meet my hot roommate."

There was a silence on the other end, and I laughed.

"I have to get to know people, baby…"

Silence. I rolled my eyes. This was ridiculous.

"Cal?"

"Listen, be safe. Don't be on your own with him, okay? Don't trust anyone. I love you."

With that, he hung up, and I stared at my phone in surprise. I got that he was jealous, but what did he expect me to do, not speak to anyone?

I sat up and hugged my knees. I had no idea where we were heading tonight, but I should get a shower and get ready.

It was five p.m. now.

New York City waits for no one.

31

GRETCHEN

*B*y seven, I was dressed and ready for wherever the night was going to take me. Nancy still wasn't back, so I imagined Josh was going to be disappointed.

I left my apartment, feeling slightly nervous as I made my way down to the second floor. I knocked on the door of the apartment and smiled as the door opened to reveal Josh.

He whistled and ran his hand through his hair. "Looking good, Curls."

I rolled my eyes and told him my name was Gretchen, to which he shrugged. He looked behind me, hopefully, and I laughed.

"She hasn't come home. Sorry…"

We heard the entrance door slam as our eyes met.

"Ooh…" I teased as we watched the staircase curiously.

Sure enough, it was Nancy, but she wasn't alone. An older man followed her in a suit with his tie loosened and his dark brown hair tousled. Nancy stopped, and I smiled, introducing her to Josh and Nicholas.

I stepped back as Josh stepped forward, unfazed by the man at Nancy's side.

Nancy eyed him appreciatively, taking in his muscular body and all-American good looks.

"I'm Josh. You must be Curly's roommate."

Nancy raised her eyebrow at me, then looked back at Josh. "Have you anything to drink in there?" She walked past him into his apartment, to which he smiled wickedly, following her.

The man in the suit smiled, and I looked at him awkwardly.

"I'm Tate, Nancy's brother." His voice was deep and masculine but friendly.

Unlike his sister, I noted.

I smiled. "I'm Gretchen, Nancy's roommate."

His eyes twinkled. "Lucky you." He laughed sarcastically, and I relaxed as I laughed with him. "Shall we follow?'" He gestured into the room behind me.

"Yes, better than congregating in the hallway…" I noticed his eyes on mine a beat longer than they should've been, and Cal's words echoed in my head.

Don't trust anyone.

We headed into the apartment to find Nancy and Josh doing shots of tequila. Josh beckoned us over, and I looked at Tate and Nicholas, who looked as uncomfortable as I did.

"To NYC!" Josh shouts, raising his shot. He nodded to the table where many other shot glasses lay full to the brim.

Tate shrugged and leaned over, picking one up for me and one for him.

Nicholas grimaced as Nancy pushed one into his hands.

We all knocked it back, and I coughed. Josh laughed, handing me another. I shook my head.

No way was I having another of those.

"You owe me, little lady. One more!"

I met his eyes and sighed. I was a student, after all.

I woke to beaming sunlight in my face. I blinked, shielding my eyes.

Ugh.

My head hurt, and my mouth felt like it was filled with cotton balls. I glanced around the room, looking for my phone. It was strange waking up in my new bedroom, but I was happy to have made it home in one piece. We didn't even make it out of the apartment last night. Instead, we ordered pizza and sat drinking. It was enjoyable, but that day, I was meant to be looking for a job.

Nausea swept over me, and dizziness clouded my vision.

I need water.

I groaned as I swung my legs out of bed, opening my door to see Tate lying on the sofa in a pair of navy joggers, his top half bare. I averted my eyes and cleared my throat so he knew I was there and could pull a top on or something.

He tilted his head and smiled. "Good morning. What a night, eh?"

I nodded and walked over to the tap, pouring water into a mug from the drying rack. I drank it gratefully before pouring another. I walked over to the sofa, tapping Tate's legs so he could make room.

He sat up and stretched.

The door buzzer went off, and I looked at Tate, who shrugged as though to say he didn't know how to answer it either. We both laughed as Nancy stomped out of her room and pressed the buzzer with gusto.

"Who is it?!" she hissed.

The reply was muffled as she rolled her eyes and allowed the stray inside the building. She only had her underwear on, and makeup was smeared all over her face as she trudged back to bed.

Tate snorted with laughter, and I shook my head as I covered my eyes.

"Coffee?" Tate asked, getting up to make his way to the kitchen. I checked my calls, and it seemed I had called Cal last night, twice. God, I hoped I hadn't cried. I missed him so much.

I studied Tate and wondered what his story was. He was older than us for sure, in his thirties. He walked over, handing me a mug of steaming hot coffee.

I moaned appreciatively and sipped it.

There was a knock on our door, and I realized that whoever Nancy had let in had finally managed the stairs. I didn't envy them. Tate stood and walked to the door, peering through the spyhole.

"Looks like another of my sister's admirers," he said dryly, and I snickered as he opened the door.

I curled my legs beneath me and watched as Tate greeted the guest.

I almost dropped my coffee when I saw Cal standing in front of me.

He was taking in the scene— Tate half dressed, me with wild, messy hair, dressed in my nightwear—as he looked back to Tate, then me. I stood, placing my coffee on the table.

"Cal?" I murmured in shock.

He studied me for a minute, a frown on his face as his eyes met mine. "Am I interrupting something?" Cal spoke so softly I almost didn't hear him.

My eyes widened and flew to Tate, who looked as puzzled as I was.

At that moment, Nancy came out of her room, heading for

the bathroom. She left her door open, and there in her bed was a very content Josh.

"Sup Curls!" he called.

Cal turned back to me, looking at me with fury in his eyes.

"It's not what it looks like," I said, desperately looking at Tate for help.

He leaned against the counter, arms folded as he watched Cal, refusing to help the situation.

"Tate, this is Cal, my *boyfriend*. Cal, this is Tate, my roommate's brother," I babbled as fast as I could.

Cal lifted a brow at me, his jaw clenched as he tugged me into his arms.

My god, he was so beautiful.

My body screamed for him.

Our lips met, and I felt like I was home. He pulled away from me slightly as his green eyes burned into mine, and his finger stroked my face.

"God, I've fucking missed you."

He picked me up, and my legs wrapped around his waist as he kissed me deeply.

I kissed him back, my tongue exploring his mouth urgently as his hands cupped my ass.

"So, you're who woke me up," Nancy murmured. We broke apart, and Cal turned to see who was talking.

"Looks like it. So, you're Nancy."

I frowned. I didn't recall telling him her name.

She beamed at him. "That's right. The one and only."

A smile played at the corners of Cal's mouth, and I felt a twinge of annoyance.

Did he like her?

It was obvious she liked him.

Josh stood in the doorway of her room as he cleared his throat. "I'm Josh, good to meet you, err…"

Cal nodded at him, "Cal. You too. I owe you for helping Gretchen with her case last night. I take it that was you?" Cal eyed him skeptically.

I snaked my arm around his waist and snuggled close to his chest, hearing his familiar heartbeat.

"Yeah, it's cool. Nancy thanked me, *actually*." He winked, and Cal laughed in understanding.

Nancy glared at Josh. "Ugh. My brother is standing right there. And you can leave now."

She strode past him into her bedroom, closing the door behind her.

Josh stared at the door guiltily. "*Wow*. She was much friendlier last night." He laughed awkwardly. "Guys, I'm beat. I'm gonna hit the hay. Nice to meet you, Cal." He nodded at Cal and Tate as he left.

Cal turned back to me. "Where were we?" He smiled as he leaned down, kissing me softly.

I pulled away and glanced at Tate, who was still in the same position, sipping his coffee.

"Come to my room," I murmured, wanting to be alone with him.

Cal grinned at Tate. "The lady's wish is my command, man; what can I say?"

We reached my room, pulling the door shut behind us.

I couldn't believe he was here, *in New York*!

I couldn't get enough of him. My tongue slammed against his as we fell into bed, and he towered above me.

"Only you could make me come back to this fucked up city." He kissed me in between words, driving me insane.

My body arched towards him, begging for him to just take me.

He trailed kisses down my stomach as he pushed my underwear down with his fingers.

"I didn't like what I saw when I walked in, Gretchen." His eyes found mine as my body shook with anticipation.

"What?" I gasped as he dotted kisses further down as he slid my underwear off with his long fingers.

"You're *mine*, and I don't fucking like him."

His tongue brushed my vulva, and I practically screamed there and then; the electric shot I felt inside when he did that was incredible.

"Who do you belong to, Gretchen?"

His tongue flicked again as he sucked and played with my clit. My hands tugged at his hair, and I tried to find my voice. He slipped his tongue all the way from the top to the bottom of my sex before slowly easing his finger inside of me. My body arched, and I lost my grip on reality. He pumped his finger in and out of me as I gasped. He sat up, loosening his belt as he gazed down at me. I shivered, watching as he rolled a condom onto his dick.

"Gretchen? Who. Do. You—" He entered me roughly, and I moaned loudly. He thrust hard, pulling my hair back as he gazed into my eyes, pausing as I clawed at his back. "Belong to?"

"You!" I gasped as the thrusts grew deeper and faster, his mouth on my neck, his teeth nipping the skin there.

"Say it again. Say it," he commanded.

I would have said anything in the world at that point, but I meant it.

"You! You, Cal, you!" I was yelling now, but I didn't care. I could feel my body building up to the point of explosion.

His mouth met mine, and I felt him release deeply inside of me; at the same time, I gasped, my body shaking and shuddering underneath this amazing man. He panted, still inside of me. He kissed me slowly, and I wanted him so much it hurt.

"Don't leave me. *Please*," I begged him softly.

He raised his eyes to look at me, rolling away from me. I pulled my underwear onto my legs from the bottom of the bed as he slid his boxers on. He ran his fingers down my back as I lay beside him. He was my everything.

"*You* left *me* if I recall?" he teased.

I closed my eyes and wrapped my arms around him. Maybe if I held him tight enough, he wouldn't go.

"Why are you here?" I whispered, looking up at him.

He kissed my swollen lips tenderly. "Other than the obvious? I fucking *love you*. I can't be away from you. If you're in New York, so am I."

Our mouths met again.

"But... I live here. You have a house in Winterburg...how will it work? We said long distance—you said you couldn't be in New York."

He leaned back on his arm, looking at me happily. "The thing is, Gretchen…"

I shuddered when he said my name.

Will this man ever cease to influence me the way he does?

"I want to be with you. You want to be here, so I'm here. Last night you called me when I was at the airport. You were drunk, and I couldn't bear the thought of dirty bastards taking advantage of your innocence," he growled, looking towards the door, meaning Tate.

I shook my head. "No, he's not—"

Cal silenced me by pushing his finger down onto my lips. "If not him, it will be countless others. I am not fucking *sharing* you. You wanna be a student? Do it. But I want to protect you, and I can't do that from Winterburg, baby."

I stared at him, my heart in my throat. "What are you saying?"

He smiled lazily. "I'm *saying*, shall we do New York together? I can sell the house in Winterburg, I can move here."

I panicked at the mention of his house in Winterburg, remembering the reason I could never go there again.

"Verno?" I asked him, my eyes meeting his, my heart pounding.

Cal kissed my fingers, something he had done regularly since the day we met.

My body tingled as I ran my hands through his hair.

"I think I've redeemed myself in his eyes. He took care of the body. He isn't a friend, but he doesn't want me dead anymore."

Relief coursed through my body.

This meant Cal could stay in New York.

Excitement ran through my veins. I sat up like a kid on Christmas morning, and Cal watched me with a bemused expression on his beautiful face.

"Seriously?!" I breathed, staring at him in adoration.

"Seriously." He laughed. "On one condition."

I met his eyes with mine, prepared to do anything to be with this perfect man forever.

"Anything," I said confidently.

"You call me Leo from time to time."

I fell onto him, kissing him all over his face.

"Deal."

His mouth met mine, and I realized that whatever his name, he would always be *my* Cal. I would always be his, and he would always be **Mine.**

PART TWO
(PREVIOUSLY OURS)

DO I DEVOUR YOU NOW OR LATER?
GRETCHEN

I scrunched my eyes up as I repeated the words in my head like a mantra, determined to make them stick. "Procedural memories are memories of motor skills, actions, muscle memories; episodic memories are memories of life events."I groaned as I scribbled it on a sticky note, tacking it to my mirror. I stared at it as though it was a dangerous article, ready to leap up and attack me at any point. I caught sight of myself in the mirror and smiled, my face softening.

The sound of a familiar truck on the street distracted me, making me leap to my feet and run down the stairs, my bare feet carrying me down soundlessly.

This is my favorite part of the day.

"Baby." The door slammed behind him with a bang, his electric green eyes drinking me in.

My breath caught in my throat as it always did when I saw him; the effect he had on me was timeless. His dirty blond hair fell into his eyes as he pushed it back with his long fingers, the leather of his jacket creaking as he moved, his other hand clutching a duffel that told me he was going to be staying over tonight.

"Cal," I breathed with excitement.

He smiled, shaking his head in mock exasperation, moving towards me. My heart thumped in my chest when he reached me, one arm snaking around my waist, pulling me into him.

"*Woman*, when are you gonna get my name right?" He mumbled, kissing the top of my head as I buried myself into his neck, inhaling his scent as though it were the oxygen keeping me alive. His scent needed bottling and distributing around the world.

They would sell out within minutes.

"It's not my fault you have a secret identity," I teased as I lifted my lips to him, closing my eyes as I waited for his lips to crash down on mine.

I didn't have to wait long.

Kissing Cal Fallon held the excitement of Christmas, the thought of how amazing it would be smashed out of the park by the reality of what it was. He didn't kiss me like anyone else ever had before, teasing my tongue with his, not too fast, not too slow. He made my body weak and always left me wanting more.

We kissed with our eyes closed, our bodies pressed together, with the promise of insane lovemaking never far behind. I ran my fingers through his hair before tugging on it slightly, groaning as he softly chewed on my bottom lip.

See what I mean?

"Do you even think we will make it into the house this time?" He growled, trailing kisses down my throat, making me wonder what I had done in a past life to deserve such a slice of paradise. I smiled as I kissed him once more before turning to the house, my hand in his, and walked back up the last few steps, aware I was grinning like a maniac.

I still roomed with Nancy. Cal insisted we moved somewhere safe—his words—and stubbornly refused to accept my answer that the little apartment we had at the time sufficed.

He took to proving us wrong by breaking and entering one time, waiting on my bed for me when I walked into the room, his green eyes flashing triumphantly. I had given in, and we rented a house in the beautiful residential area in the East Village. I should thank him because I was *so* in love with the place.

Cal had lived in New York City all his life until he had to leave, so I should have trusted his judgment.

My stomach grumbled, and I cringed as Cal's eyebrows raised with amusement.

"Is someone hungry?"

"I haven't had time to eat yet; I've been so busy trying to finish this assignment," I confessed as his eyes narrowed.

"No time to eat? *Baby*. There's always time to eat." He kissed my forehead, reminding me of my Mom.

He guided me into the house, dropping his bag at the foot of the stairs as he shrugged off his jacket. "Where's Nancy?" he asked warily as he walked into the kitchen, pulling open the fridge and inspecting it with disdain.

I rolled my eyes as I slid onto the counter, watching him sift through the measly ingredients the fridge offered. "She's with Josh again."

He shook his head at the fridge and shut it before turning towards me, taking in my position on the counter. He walked over, his hands running up my thighs as he pulled me close to him.

"One, you have no food worthy of human consumption in that fridge. Two, you are telling me the house is empty." His green eyes met mine as my heart raced in my chest, excitement building as he moved his hands to hold my face.

"Do I devour you here and now, then take you somewhere delicious for dinner? Or do I just devour you all night long and fuck the food?"

I gasped as he pulled me off the counter in one swift movement, a deep growl coming from his mouth as his lips crashed against mine. My hands were clawing at his top, desperate to touch his skin, a shiver running through my body as he held me against the wall. My legs wrapped around his waist as his fingers roughly squeezed my nipples.

"Oh God, Cal...."

"Shh," he muttered his mouth on mine, flipping me around, pressing my body against the wall.

"Gretch? Are you decent? I see Cal is here!" A voice called as he groaned with irritation, his hands smoothing my top down as he let me go reluctantly.

The door opened and in walked Nancy, followed by a grinning Josh.

"Did we interrupt anything?" Josh asked innocently, his eyes taking in my flushed expression and swollen lips.

Cal nodded at him and turned to gaze at me. "Nothing that can't be continued later." His voice was gruff, and I bit back a smile, knowing he was sexually frustrated.

As was I, my nipples hard and visible through my thin t-shirt, my shorts hiding the fact my panties were soaking wet.

Nancy raised a perfectly penciled brow in my direction as she studied me.

"Did you finish your assignment? She's been so anxious about this damn thing," she directed the last part to Cal, who shrugged.

"Good thing she isn't just a beauty then, huh? Come on, baby, let's go eat."

Nancy sneaked a glance at him as he passed, fanning herself dramatically to me. "Sorry! If someone interrupted me with *that*, I would eat them."

I rolled my eyes, used to the fact that many of the women in New York would kill for a night with Cal.

I still felt jealous, but it was like no one else was in the room when he was with me, plus his eyes followed me everywhere. It was like there was an invisible cord that connected us. He would only have to tug it slightly, and I would fall over trying to get to him.

I know. Cliché. But so true.

He is **mine**, and I am his.

I THOUGHT YOU WERE HUNGRY?

CAL

*D*amn her roommate.

I was seconds away from being balls deep in this delicious woman until Nancy walked in with her jock boyfriend. I felt Gretchen's head on my shoulder as I drove, her sweet perfume mixed with her naturally intoxicating scent making me hard instantly. She kissed my neck, causing me to grip the steering wheel tightly.

What was she trying to do to me?

Her kisses trailed down my stomach as she unzipped me, her hand pulling out my hard cock. Her mouth suddenly wrapped around the tip, her tongue flickering expertly on the shaft as I groaned with pleasure. I managed to pull over, earning myself a couple of horns from the neighbouring cars in the process.

If they only knew why, they would shut the fuck up.

I cut the engine and allowed myself to lean back, her mouth hot and wet as it worked my cock, her hand under her mouth, slowly wanking it in. I grabbed a handful of her hair, pulling it slightly as I felt her moan against me.

I slid my other hand down her back, realising she still

wore those tiny fucking shorts. I caressed her ass cheek with my free hand, moving her soaking wet panties aside.

I love that she gets so wet for me.

I plunged my finger roughly inside of her and she gasped against me. I fucked her with my finger before adding another, expanding her hole slightly. Her juices ran down my fingers and I smiled wickedly, she rocked against my hand, her pussy tightening around my fingers.

Fuck this.

I slipped my fingers out of her easily as she snapped her head up to glare at me as I smirked at her.

"Cal!" She groaned, the urgency in her voice sending me insane.

I pulled her onto me, shifting so her knees were on either side of me. I used my fingers to guide my cock into her as she slowly lowered herself down onto me. She bit her lip as she accommodated my full length, wincing slightly as she moved up and down my shaft.

I steadied her by holding her hips, despite wanting to bury myself inside of her hard and deep. I couldn't understand how she could still be so tight after fucking me for over a year, but she was.

I'm not complaining.

I tried to restrain myself as she groaned, riding me slowly, her hands on my neck. Her curls escaped the loose bun she had it in, her full lips open as she gasped. She was, without a doubt, the most beautiful creature I had ever laid eyes on. She opened her eyes and nodded at me wordlessly as I gripped her hips, moving her easily up and down the full length of my cock, causing her to cry out as I slammed her back down relentlessly.

Her mouth was on mine as she began to orgasm, and I picked up the pace, knowing how she liked it.

"Come for me, baby," I whispered into her ear as she cried out, gasping for breath. I let myself go, growling as I exploded, my balls tightening as I shot load after load deep into her.

She rested her head on my shoulder as we sat there, our bodies throbbing from the intensity of our lovemaking.

"I swear to God, no one in the world has sex like we do," she muttered, and I smiled.

"You're biased," I reminded her in-between kisses. She pouted at me as she slid off me, my cock slick against my stomach. I pulled my jeans back up, the scent of sex hanging heavily in the car. She fixed her hair as I gazed at her, unable to believe she was mine. She pulled at her hairband, and her hair tumbled around her: my favorite thing in the world to watch.

"You're so fucking beautiful."

"Biased, too," she smirked.

I raised an eyebrow in response.

"I like the fact you have nothing to compare it to, Raven," I muttered.

The thought of any man touching her made my blood boil in my veins.

"True. Maybe I should branch out, experiment, and see how it stands then?"

She was teasing, I knew that. But it didn't stop me from narrowing my eyes at her.

"If you ever let another man touch you like I do, the next time you see him will be at his grave."

She laughed and kissed me hard as I wrapped my arms around her. "I love how possessive you are."

I suppose I was. But I just wanted to protect her from all the dangers in the world—slimy bastards included.

"I thought you were hungry?" She teased.

I glanced down at her shorts and smirked.

"I was. Now for food. Best get takeout. Can't sit in a restaurant like that, baby."

She rolled her eyes as she clipped her seatbelt on, reminding me to do the same.

Same argument, different road.

"If you get stopped—" She started, sighing with annoyance.

"Which I won't."

She pursed her lips then, and I held back a smile.

I love winding her up.

"You'll get fined. Then you'll lose your license."

"I'll still drive."

She squealed in exasperation. "You're impossible! What if you are in an accident?"

I rubbed her thigh softly. "Just calm down, Raven. Enjoy the post-sex bliss that is making you glow right now."

She smiled then, and I contemplated pulling over again.

God, she is fucking amazing.

AREN'T YOU...?
GRETCHEN

I woke suddenly, sitting bolt upright in bed.

Instantly, his arms were around me, his voice soothing me. The nightmares were rarer than they were before, but when they came, they were terrifying. I grabbed the glass of water beside my bed and gulped as though it would wash away the memories.

"I'm so sorry, baby," he mumbled from behind me as I turned to gaze at him. His blond hair shimmered in the moonlight that stole in through the window, sadness written all over his face.

"Angel, you saved us. I just sometimes can't get his face out of my mind." I shuddered as I climbed back into bed beside him, feeling safe as he kissed the top of my head.

"I'd do it again in a heartbeat. I will always protect you, *mio amore.*"

"I love you." I slipped into a restless sleep as he held me tightly, whispering that he loved me back.

When I woke up the next morning, I found the bed empty. I reached across the bed, the empty sheet cold now that he wasn't there. I grabbed my phone to see a text from him.

CAL: Morning, beautiful. I had some stuff to do today; sorry I left you. You're fucking stunning. Wear a trash bag to school today. I love you.

I grinned as I swung my legs out of bed, showering quickly. I threw on my skinny jeans and one of Cal's many t-shirts he'd left here, closing my eyes as his scent washed over me. Feeling closer to him, I slicked on some lip gloss and mascara and grabbed my backpack.

It didn't take long to get to class, meaning I had time to grab a coffee on the way.

"Hey, weren't you in my psychology lecture last week?" A deep voice asked as I turned to see Professor Creed gazing at me with his chocolate brown eyes.

I beamed as I nodded enthusiastically. "Yes! I was; it was amazing. I feel like I learned so much from you," I gushed, aware I was gibbering.

He raised his eyebrows in amusement as I heard the barista asking for my order in an irritated tone.

I quickly ordered my usual, asking for extra shots of the sugar-free caramel syrup.

I smiled shyly as Professor Creed placed a blueberry muffin on the side before ordering his espresso to go. I snuck a glance at him, aware he was very attractive for an older man. He wore a white shirt with the sleeves rolled up and grey suspenders attached to his trousers. Thick reading glasses framed his dark brown eyes, his jet-black hair slicked back. He smiled as he paid before he caught my eye.

"What do you want to do when you graduate?" He asked, his eyes alight with intrigue.

"I want to be a therapist," I answered firmly, having known all my life what I wanted to be.

He nodded with approval as he spoke. "Really? What is it about therapy that attracts you?"

"I think it's the fact that I could be the only person that someone may see that day. That simply listening to them will ease their pain somewhat. I could make a difference to their life."

"With that view, you'll make a fantastic therapist. Never give up."

Our eyes met, and I smiled, glancing away as his eyes lingered on me for slightly longer than necessary. I shook off the thought, realizing my lack of experience with men made me feel like every one of them had an agenda. I blamed Cal for that; he suspected that every male on the planet had a plan to woo me.

"It was a pleasure to meet you. If you ever need any help at all, just get in touch."

He held out a white embossed card, drawing my attention to the platinum wedding ring on his finger. I sighed with relief, mentally kicking myself for assuming he was checking me out. I examined the card and nodded gratefully.

"I will, thank you so much."

He hesitated briefly before nodding in the coffee counter's direction. "Your latte is ready," he chuckled as I whirled around, colliding with a woman in a suit who stared at me haughtily.

"I'm so sorry—" I began as she glared at me before walking away. My cheeks flamed with embarrassment as I smiled an awkward goodbye to the Professor, making my way out of the coffee shop and onto the busy street. I realized my heart was racing.

What is wrong with me?

I wasn't skittish or clumsy normally. I shrugged, sipping my latte in delight as I made my way to my first class.

APOLOGIES

CAL

"So, what you're saying is, there's a possibility. It's my girlfriend's birthday, and I'd love to surprise her."

The travel agent flushed as I smiled at her from across the desk.

"Maybe, but you would need to book it today. There are only two seats left on the flight."

I handed her my credit card with a broad smile. "I knew you could do it…" I eyed her name badge with interest. "Beth."

She tapped away on her computer, refusing to meet my eyes. "I need the names as they appear on the passports, please."

After it was all booked, I slid the envelope into the inside pocket of my jacket, stepping outside into the crisp New York air. I lit a cigarette as I watched the tourists snapping photos of everything—the street signs, the sidewalk, and even the damn sky. I noticed a girl watching me with interest from the corner of the street, her long red coat billowing in the wind. I felt my heart slow as my eyes took in her slender frame, her waist-length black hair loose around her shoulders.

It couldn't be her.

I released the smoke I held in my mouth slowly as she gazed at me, her hand covering her mouth in shock.

Fuck.

Lucia.

We stood like that for what felt like an eternity until I noticed a man standing by the side, suited accordingly. He followed her gaze to me as his eyes flickered in recognition. He whispered something in her ear as she nodded blankly, letting him guide her to a waiting limousine by the sidewalk.

He closed the door before making his way towards me.

Michael Salvatore, Lucia's youngest brother. He had the same caramel-colored skin as Lucia, his blue eyes framed by thick dark lashes.

"I didn't realize you were back here, Leonardo."

I winced at his use of my full name. He shook my hand, his dark eyes studying me intently.

"You should join us for dinner this evening so we can extend our gratitude for your help in Winterburg."

This wasn't to be mistaken for an invitation; it was a command, and I recognized it as such.

"Of course."

He nodded as he made his way back to the car, turning back to me briefly before he opened the door.

"Bring your *Amante.*"

My eyes met his as he sent me a chilling smile before climbing into the car. My blood ran cold as it sped away, the dark windows preventing me from seeing the passengers.

Gretchen cannot be part of their world. Ever.

My phone buzzed in my pocket; I answered it gruffly.

"Hey, beautiful. It's so fucking *good* to hear your voice.

What are you doing tonight?"

My heart soared as Gretchen apologized for having made plans with Nicole, a girl from her class.

"Baby, I've got some business to attend to."

She fell silent as she always did at the mention of business, something I'd not mentioned in a while.

"Is it Verno?" She whispered, the fear clear in her voice.

"It's nothing to concern yourself with, my love. Just enjoy your evening with your friend, and if it's not too late, I will call you when I get home. It will be simpler when we live together," I smiled then, knowing mentioning our living situation would distract her.

"Cal, I would *love* to live with you. You said not in New York," I could almost see her pouting.

"You've got what, two years left at school? Then that's it; we can live anywhere we want. But here, I live in Brooklyn. You know I don't want you too involved with my work here." I was met with stony silence, and I sighed. "I'll call you after. I love you."

I heard her voice soft in my ear whisper, "I don't care how late it is. Love you more."

I ended the call and stared up at the sky.

I'm not looking forward to this.

Four hours later, I drove up the long driveway leading to a mansion set far back, surrounded by trees and water fountains. To the left of the property, five black cars were parked in a neat line as a gardener tended to the flowers beside them. Security was tight here, and I would place my bets that even the gardener was heavily armed—looks were deceiving. Having left my gun at the front gate with security, I felt exposed but confident that if needed, I could look after myself to an extent.

If they wanted me dead, I would be by now; that much

was certain.

I exhaled as I slid out of the truck, reaching into the cab to get my suit jacket from the hanger, knowing appearances mattered with this family. A burly man stood guard at the front door, his eyes boring into me as I walked forward, his hand on his gun.

"Leonardo Cape. Here to see Michael."

He pressed the button on his earpiece and spoke in fluent Italian, not taking his eyes from me once. I heard the words *'blond punk'* and tried to hide the anger from my face. I knew some Italian and this dude had just insulted both my appearance and intelligence.

He nodded and opened the door for me, the smell of authentic Italian food wafting out, making my empty stomach grumble loudly. You didn't show up to an Italian dinner without a ferocious appetite, and I'd made sure I was ravenous. I stood in the grand hallway, my stomach churning at the memories this place held.

"Leonardo. Where is your *Amante?*" Michael walked down the sweeping staircase; his arms opened wide as he greeted me.

"She sends her apologies. She is a student and had prior commitments," my mouth ran dry as his eyes narrowed.

It was disrespectful for her to not come, I knew that, but until I had no further choice, she remained in *her* world for as long as possible.

"That's a shame. I was *so* looking forward to meeting her."

I followed him into the dining hall, where a large table had four places set for dinner. The room had incredible paintings hanging worth millions. I nodded at them appreciatively and took a seat opposite Michael as he gazed at me with interest.

"So, tell me how you came to be back in New York with no prior authorization."

Despite the words being spoken softly, I knew the family was not pleased.

I swallowed as the swishing of fabric announced Lucia's entrance to the room, and I stood at once.

She was as breath-taking as ever, her hair curled to perfection as it sat around her shoulders, her deep green eyes meeting mine as the breath left my body. I hadn't seen her since that fateful day when she nearly lost her life.

I bowed my head as she regarded me coolly.

"I heard what you did." Her silky voice was as enchanting as ever. I bowed my head as I felt Michael's eyes on us.

"I am so sorry I didn't do it sooner," I whispered hoarsely, meaning every word.

She'd been my girlfriend, and she had been on the brink of death after an attack.

Her eyes softened as she spoke. "I knew you were there. I knew if you could have done something, you would have. It was the only comfort I had, knowing you were there."

I felt at a loss for words as I gazed at the floor in shame.

"It scared me. I was fifteen," I said as Michael's voice cut through me like a knife.

"Can you only imagine how scared Lucia was? She was also just fifteen. Alas, we shall not dwell on such matters now. We have dealt with it, and my father seems to believe you have redeemed yourself, but it would be fair to say not all of us feel the same way."

"As you said, Michael, we have dealt with it, and my word is final on the matter. Leonardo is our guest, so behave appropriately." The voice was quiet, the words cloaked in the old Italian accent.

"Verno."

TATTERS
GRETCHEN

*N*icole stared at me as she drained her glass of wine. "He gave you his *business card*?"

I ran my finger around the rim of my glass, shrugging nonchalantly.

"You don't think that is odd? He is our *professor.*" She stabbed her fork into her spaghetti, chewing on it thought-fully. She swallowed quickly when she saw the server passing us, flashing him a smile as she ordered another glass of wine. "It's kind of hot. He is super gorgeous. I wish he would have given *me* his card." She pointed her fork in my direction as she spoke.

"He's also *married*, Nicole," I scolded, shaking my head with disapproval.

"True. But anyhow, it's not as if you are single; you and Cal are *practically* married." She rolled her eyes as she finished her spaghetti, rapidly picking up the dessert menu.

"Are you in a rush to go home?" I asked, raising an arched eyebrow at her. Her eyes went wide as her smile gave her away.

"Is it that obvious? Shit. I'm meeting someone at ten," she mumbled without an ounce of shame.

The attendant placed a fresh glass of wine down before her as he removed her plate, frowning as he realized that I had barely made a dent in mine. I ate quicker, annoyed that she had made overlapping plans.

"So, who is it?" I asked with intrigue.

Nicole had a varied sex life, sleeping with both sexes to satisfy her needs. She was such a warm soul, always smiling, and I loved listening to her many tales.

"Someone from Tinder. We hook up occasionally," she let out a dramatic moan as she tapped the menu card in front of her.

"Triple-chocolate chunk brownie with caramel ice cream, you get *me* for dessert," she declared, and I giggled.

"Have you *really* never slept with anyone other than Cal?" She asked for the hundredth time since I had known her.

"No, I *still* haven't; nothing has changed since the last time you asked me," I teased as she winked at me.

"You get so much attention; you are fucking *hot*. I wish he would just let you loose in New York City for a weekend with me. Your pussy would be in *tatters*."

I gaped at her as I looked around us quickly, praying no one had heard her little outburst; tattered pussy didn't go well with spaghetti.

"I don't *want* to be 'let loose,' my love. He is fucking *perfect*; I want to be with him forever," I said dreamily, gazing into the distance as I remembered the first time he kissed me in the rain because he knew it was something I had always wanted to do.

"Ugh, pass me the vomit bag." Her heavy New York accent still tickled me.

"So, what are we doing for your birthday? The big two-oh. We should get a little apartment in Times Square for the night, invite some hot guys and girls—"

I held my hand up to interrupt her. "If I do anything, it will involve Cal, so get the idea out of your head of me spreading my legs like the Lincoln tunnel for every Tom, Dick, and Harry."

She stuck her tongue out at me.

"Ooh, I need to order dessert!" She waved frantically as the waiter held back a sigh, taking her order. I gave him my plate and passed on dessert.

Nicole hugged me close as we parted. "Text me when you get home. I hate these streets after dark when you are on your own."

I promised her I would and walked towards the subway station, wrapping my coat around me for warmth. I skipped down the stairs, tapping my card against the machine as it let me through, the stench of urine welcoming me to the underbelly of the city.

There were a few people milling about as I boarded the train, preferring to stand, considering I wasn't too far away from home. The journey was relatively uneventful, and I hurried up the steps back into the cold air, already dreaming of my warm bed.

I heard footsteps behind me, and I froze, certain no one else got off at my stop. I walked close to the streetlights, my eyes peeled for any sign of life. I wasn't that great at protecting myself, but I had pepper spray at home—not much use there.

"Hey, Gretchen, wait up!" Called a familiar voice as relief coursed through my veins. I turned to see Josh jogging towards me, pulling his earphones out as he approached me.

"For fuck's *sake,* Josh, you scared me to death. Why are

you out running at this hour?" I frowned, and he laughed apologetically.

"Sorry, babe. Couldn't sleep. Nancy still isn't home." His voice was small as he caught his breath.

Nancy and Josh had been having a "secret" relationship that we all knew about but that none of them would admit. Nancy refused to commit to anyone despite harboring feelings for Josh.

Josh only had eyes for her and had stopped seeing anyone else, which I think was his downfall. Nancy liked to be kept on her toes, and getting it handed to her on a plate was not her style.

We reached our street, and he slung his arm around my shoulder.

"What the fuck am I going to do, Red? I know she wants to be with me. She just won't shake off these other guys."

I slipped my arm around his waist and sighed. We'd all been friends for long enough to feel like family, and I hated seeing him hurting like this. "Ah, I feel for you, I really do. I don't even know what to suggest. Have you tried calling her bluff? Like saying you'll end it if she doesn't stop seeing other people?"

He looked down at me with a sad smile on his face. "Yeah, I started to, once. She just shot me down, said if I didn't like it, I knew what to do."

I frowned as we reached my house to see someone sitting on the front porch, drinking a bottle of beer. I stopped and stared as Josh stiffened beside me.

"Who the *fuck* is that?" He muttered as we walked closer.

The figure was male, well-built, and handsome in a rugged way.

I peered at him, and I shrugged at Josh.

"I don't know who that is at all. Was he there when you left?" I hissed, and he shrugged, wide-eyed.

"Of course, he wasn't. The door was locked, though, and now it's open."

Nancy.

"Dude. What are you doing?" Josh asked in a low voice as I wrapped my arms around myself, suddenly cold.

"What's it to you, boy? Hey, pretty lady. Come sit with me," he rasped, rubbing his crotch crudely.

I stepped back, repulsed, and Josh moved in front of me protectively.

My phone vibrated in my pocket, and I saw on the caller ID it was Cal. "Cal, I need to call you back. There's a random guy here, and we don't know who he is." I bit my lip as I whispered into the phone.

"What the fuck?" He demanded. "Define *we*?"

I heard the fear in his voice, and I quickly told him Josh was with me.

"Pretty much on your own, then. Can you go inside? I am on my way; I am almost there." His voice dripped with sarcasm.

My heart swelled with love for him; the fact he was driving to me anyway made me feel weak with adoration. "Not really. He's, like, in front of the door."

Cal growled as he cursed. "I will be there as soon as I can." He ended the call, and I noticed Josh was now arguing with the guy about Nancy.

"Red lips, dark hair, superb dancer. She's hot as *fuck* in the sack. Think I wore her out though, so you may need to wait awhile if you want some." He winked at Josh.

"What the *fuck*? You slept with Nancy?"

The man frowned then, squaring his shoulders as he glared at Josh. "Nancy, that's her. Saucy little bitch. We didn't sleep. Did everything else, though. What's it to you? Is she your little sister or something?" He shifted his gaze to me, leering as he spoke. "Are *you* her little sister? I've got more ammo in the bank if you want to play, baby."

I saw headlights in the distance, becoming brighter as they sped up the road, screeching to a stop outside of our house.

Cal stepped out, surprising me in a suit, his beautiful face flawed with anger. He glanced at me, assessing that I was okay, before storming over to the two men.

"You. Whoever the fuck you are, leave *now*," he hissed, his voice laced with venom as the man shrunk back slightly, taking in the crazed look in Cal's eyes as his eyes fell to his waist.

"*Fuck*, she has some crazy ass family," he stammered, suddenly sober. He pushed past Josh before making his way down the street without looking back.

I felt the familiar anxiety in my stomach as I knew Cal was about to lose his mind.

"Where is she?" Cal snarled at Josh, who held his hands up.

"I don't fucking *know*. I went for a jog. I'd been gone about an hour, max." He stared down at the floor as I put my hand on Cal, his arms taut through the suit as he huffed.

The problem with being with Cal was that he was damaged by experience, which made him react badly sometimes.

"He could have been here when you arrived back, alone," he shot at me without turning around.

"Cal, I'm *fine*," I reassured him as he shook his head.

"You can't live with her anymore. She's a fucking *nightmare*," he pulled my hand into his as he walked towards his car.

"Cal, what are you *doing?!*" I hissed as he swung open the door, gesturing for me to get in. It was then that I saw a glint of silver in the moonlight, and I saw what he had tucked in his waistband.

Was that a gun?

MY FLAW
GRETCHEN

*W*e rode in silence: my face stunned, his wary.

He wouldn't look at me as he drove through the city streets, navigating like the native New Yorker he was.

I looked ahead as thoughts ran through my mind, wondering how much I truly knew about the man I loved.

What is considered enough?

Is it the way he makes me feel?

Did it matter about his life choices? Did I sign up to whatever he is simply because I love him?

I watched as the streets whizzed by, my eyes aching with tiredness, my body alert with suspicion. I had to know, but I wasn't sure he would tell me.

His jaw was set as he drove, moving through lanes without signaling, taking sharp turns abruptly, as I gripped onto the side of the car, biting my lip with annoyance. He pulled into a dirt track I didn't know they had in New York, which led to a small house hidden from the view of the street. He cut the engine and exhaled, glancing at me as he got out, slamming his door behind him. He strode around to my side, opening the door and gazing at me, those fucking eyes commanding that I leave the truck.

"Are you going to explain to me what the *fuck* you are doing with a gun?" My voice shook as he raised his eyebrows, his face otherwise unreadable.

"Come on, Gretchen. *You know* I'm not a fucking shop-keeper." His eyes blazed as he watched me climb out of the car, closing it securely behind me.

I shivered in the night air, and he moved his hand to the small of my back, guiding me towards the house.

I climbed the steps whilst he unlocked the door before me, his broad shoulders hunched as he tugged the door open, stepping back so I could walk in before him. I stood at the bottom of the stairs, smiling softly as I saw the resemblance between the house in Winterburg and this one.

He tossed his keys on the side, walking to the kitchen to grab a beer.

How could he be so composed?

"Cal. Why do you have a gun?" I repeated, refusing to allow this to slide.

His green eyes burned into mine as he bit the bottle top from the beer before tilting it to his delicious mouth, which I tried to avoid staring at.

"So I have a gun," he snapped as he leaned against the doorway, his hair falling into his eyes. "It's not something you need to be concerned about," his tone softened as his eyes traveled up and down my body, causing goosebumps to rise on my arms. "What did he say to you?" He was irritated, and I glared at the ground.

"I don't remember. He was *drunk*. Cal, you could've lost your temper tonight with a gun tucked into your belt." I folded my arms and glared at him then as he smiled crookedly.

"So? If he would have touched you in any way you didn't want, I wouldn't have hesitated in blowing his fucking head off."

"Exactly."

We stared at each other then, his eyes telling me this was a battle I would not win.

"Move in with me." His words fell between us, and I sucked in a breath.

He gazed at the floor, a soft smile on his face. He knew how much I wanted this, yet he had insisted I had tried to live a "normal" life, with us both knowing that was not something I could live whilst living with him.

"You said—"

"I know what I said, Gretchen, because I fucking said it," he snickered then, and I thawed somewhat, a yearning for his arms to be around me. "But you aren't safe there, and I'm tired of sleeping without you every night." He walked towards me then, placing his beer beside his keys, tugging me close to him as his eyes examined every inch of my face, his breath hot on my cheek. "I can't risk anything ever happening to you, Gretchen." Raw emotion filled his tone, his voice caught in his throat.

Where had this come from?

"*Cal.* Nothing will happen to me. I'm just me, a student living in New York with my protective boyfriend ready to turn up and save me with his fucking *gun.*"

He unhooked it from his belt and then dropped it onto the surface with a loud clatter. He pushed me against the wall, his hands beside my face as he gazed at me.

"First, you aren't *just* you. I've met no one like you in my life. You're the air that I breathe. I couldn't live without you." His finger trailed down my face, resting on my chin as he tipped my head up to look at him, my heart swelling with pure love for this man, whatever he was. "Second," he continued, his voice gruff. "Believe it or not, this gun could save our lives one day. Do you think a lion would fight another lion without his teeth or his claws? Of course not. You match danger with danger. Do you understand?"

I nodded, aware he was right. I didn't know who he dealt with. I knew *nothing*. I dropped my head down as he lifted it back up to meet his eyes.

"Third, I don't want you to need saving. I want you to live your life. But you look like that." his eyes flickered down as he stepped back, admiring me. "And you are stupidly fucking interesting, intelligent—not to mention addictive. Who wouldn't want that? I am territorial, and I'm aware it's my flaw."

I grabbed the back of his head then, kissing him roughly as he raised my legs around his waist, returning the kiss deeply.

"Baby, I mean it. Live with me." He rested his forehead against mine; the intimate gesture made me grin, chewing my lip as I pretended to give it some thought. He gently tugged my hair as his lips found my throat, and he murmured into my ear, "Will you say yes already so I can show you my bedroom?"

I didn't need any more convincing. I nodded as he held his hand out toward the stairs.

"Straight up and any fucking room you wish."

Yes, sir.

INVOLUNTARILY
GRETCHEN

*I*t had been an uneventful couple of months. I settled into living with Cal as easily as I had expected I would, and we became even closer. He did little things like cooking my favorite meal when I had been at college late, reading whilst I worked, the distraction of the pages that moved between his fingers as he lay on our bed, his eyes filled with concentration, his bare torso demanding my attention as I groaned he needed to throw a shirt on. We showered together; we slept in each other's arms night after night. I knew little about relationships, this being my second one ever—but I knew that it shouldn't feel this good for so long. College was okay—I had kept up with the demand so far, but I had to admit I wasn't seeing my friends as much. I just didn't feel we were on the same page anymore. It wasn't like I didn't have time either—Cal was out of the house most evenings, and the less said about that, the better.

This evening was no different. After binging on my favorite shows, I rinsed my coffee mug in the sink, turning it upside down in the drying rack as I trudged upstairs, tired from the day.

Cal had texted me goodnight earlier, telling me he wouldn't be long, so it surprised me to hear a dull knock at the front door, as he had a key.

I frowned, wondering who would knock on the door at this hour. I stood on the stairs as I tried not to breathe.

Cal had told me no one ever came to the house, and if they did, to call him straight away.

I lifted my phone from my robe pocket and dialed his number.

He answered on the first ring.

"Someone is at the door," I whispered, my voice low.

He cursed as he ordered me not to answer it. "Ask who it is," he barked, the worry clear in his tone.

I hated that this was how we had to live as I leaned against the solid door.

"Who is it?" I croaked out, my heart pounding so strongly in my ears I didn't think I could have heard a response if there was one, which there wasn't.

"Gretchen? What's happening?" I heard someone from Cal's background call out the name Leo, and I bristled as he snapped back to give him a minute.

The door handle turned, and I clasped my hand over my mouth, terrified.

"They are trying the door, Cal," I whispered, tears in my eyes as he swore again, ordering me to stay calm. My body shook as I tried to do as he said. Every fiber of my instinct was telling me to get as far away from whoever was on the other side of that door.

"Baby, listen, I'm too far away to get there before the police could. Hang up now and call the police, do it loudly, you hear me? Do it *loudly.* I'm coming, but do that," his voice interrupted my thoughts as I nodded. He demanded confirmation that I had heard him.

"Okay," I managed as he hung up.

I dialed the police as the door groaned open behind me, and I fell over in shock. It wasn't possible—I had *locked* the door.

I heard a voice on the end of the line asking what my emergency was as I stood still, afraid to breathe. I cut the call as I slunk backward, my foot catching the table by the door, causing a loud clatter, exposing my location to the intruder.

Fuck!

The door opened slowly, and I saw a man enter, his bulky frame almost as wide as the door, his face menacing as he scanned the room, looking for me. He was bald with scars over his face, and he grinned with satisfaction when his eyes fell on me.

A voice in my head told me to run with every ounce of my being; my feet were like rubber as I tried to dash for the kitchen, which was merely strides away. My heart was in my throat as I saw the knife stand, lunging for it desperately as I felt a hand clamp around my face, a rag pressed into my mouth as a voice whispered in my ear.

"Sssh, *Bella*."

I clawed at the hands hopelessly, fighting with every ounce of strength I had, the Italian accent pouring fear into my veins. The pungent odor from the rag soon had me gasping for breath as my head swam.

This cannot be happening.

The world spun as I sank into the arms of the enemy, and I was aware of my body being lifted into the air with ease.

Cal, I need you.

RAGE

CAL

I couldn't hear anything but the roaring in my ears as I jumped out of the truck, my eyes taking in the wide-open door.

No, no, no!

Where are the sirens?!

The cops?!

I screamed her name, my throat raw with emotion. I ran from room to room, my heart sinking with the realisation that she wasn't there.

No!

I roared her name repeatedly, before I caught sight of her phone on the floor near the table by the door. I felt like someone had twisted a knife in my gut as I saw the crack on the screen.

Gretchen had dropped it.

My hands shook as I unlocked the screen, her favorite photo of the two of us her screen saver. I swallowed a lump in my throat as I checked the last number she had dialed.

The cops.

I closed my eyes as I slumped on the stairs.

Who the fuck has my girl? Who wants to die that badly?

The endless images of the possibilities swam through my head as I grit my teeth in rage.

I hadn't protected her.

She'd called me; and I hadn't got here in time. I ripped my phone from my pocket and began dialing every contact I had.

Someone has to know something.

Eleven hours later...

"You have an appalling track record with caring for the girls you love, Leonardo," Michael said as he lifted his brows at me.

I swallowed down my fury, refusing to lose control. "Michael. I wouldn't be here if I didn't need your help."

He studied me, his dark eyes verging on black as he glanced around his study. "I'll consider your request. Now leave."

I stood swiftly, fire burning through my veins. "Michael, with all due respect, you know as well as I do that the chances of her surviving the first twenty-four hours are—"

"Leonardo. Cal. Whoever you are. Do *not* stand in front of me repeating pointless statistics from the law," he interrupted sharply, his dark eyes meeting my green ones.

I clenched my fists at my sides as he waved his hand away dismissively.

"I said I would consider your request."

Frustrated, I turned and left, slamming the door behind me, knowing he would see it as a lack of respect.

Where is fucking Verno?

Why do I have to deal with this egotistical prick?

Climbing into my car I slammed my hands on the wheel in irritation. Gretchen had been missing for eleven hours now, and I was beyond rationality. I'd contacted everyone I knew in New York, sending them photos of her with a warning to call me if anything came up, and I knew that most of them would have their ears to the ground.

Unfortunately, The Salvatore Family ruled the criminal underground, so I had finally brought myself to ask for their help. Michael had all but laughed in my face, knowing he would rather let her die than help me. The cops were fucking *useless*, telling me she had probably just left me and to come back to them after twenty-four hours.

I didn't have twenty-four *fucking* hours.

I had *nothing*.

My phone rang, and I answered it at once, my voice gruff with hope.

"I'm sorry, man, I'm getting fuck all," the voice apologized as I breathed out. I couldn't let my fear consume me. "Have you spoken with the po-po?"

"Of course I have," I snapped, aware I was being a prick and not caring anyway.

The voice hesitated before it spoke again. "Are you fucking sure it's not Michael?"

It *was* the obvious choice, wasn't it?

My first thought had been that that cunt had taken her. He'd shown such interest in wanting to meet her the other night; I remembered the disappointment on his face at not seeing her by my side. He fucking detested me for what happened to Lucia, too, so I know if he wasn't responsible for this, he would be damn wishing he was.

"No. I don't know that. But I'm sat outside his house right now, and I am going to watch his every *fucking* move," I growled as I stared up at the large windows, the interior of the house hidden by thick drapes.

If she was in there, I would kill him with my bare hands and fuck the consequences.

"Ring Drake," he advised before hanging up.

I groaned, leaning back in my seat.

Of course, Drake. He adores Gretchen.

He answered on the first ring, his voice filled with concern. "Leo? Are you okay?"

"No. I'm not. Someone's taken Gretchen."

"Where are you?" he demanded, his voice hoarse.

"I'm parked outside The Salvatore house." I shook my head when he groaned.

"Why? What the *fuck* have they got to do with it? You need to leave *right now*. I'll get someone to watch the house. Meet me at Ray's in fifteen. Go, Leo."

The phone slid from my hand as I gazed up at the house, my eyes searching every window.

Have I done this to her?

Have my life choices brought her here? Of course, they fucking have.

I reversed slightly, casting another look at the house before I left, praying for a clue of any kind.

It was not answered.

God can fuck himself.

GIOCO
GRETCHEN

y eyes flickered open as I gazed at the ornate ceiling above me, aware I was laid on a soft bed. I lifted my head up as nausea rippled through my body. I sank back down onto the plump pillows, wondering what had happened.

Where am I?

Did I go out?

I was sure I didn't go out. If I had, where was my phone? I rolled my head to the side, glancing at the bedside table, finding only a lamp on the unfamiliar glossy surface. I groaned as I tried to sit up again before hearing a silky voice from the corner of the dark room.

"Hello, Gretchen. Did you sleep well?"

I didn't know who was speaking to me, and as I sat up, my head swam as though liquid was sloshing around in my skull, my brain a mere ice cube.

"Where am I?" I whispered as I tried to focus. My vision was misty, and no matter how many times I blinked, it wouldn't clear. I groaned and focused on the black floaters that danced in my eyes.

"I wondered which question would come first. I thought you'd ask who I was, so let me answer both for you."

A woman stepped out from the darkness, and her beauty captivated me. She wore no makeup but didn't need to: her green eyes contrasted with her honey-colored skin, her dark tresses pulled into a loose ponytail, which swished as she moved. She wore jeans and a high-neck shirt, showing off her flawless figure. She gazed at me then, her eyes searching my face as she smiled wistfully. "I can see why he is so smitten."

Cal.

Adrenaline flooded my veins, and despite not having the gift of sight, I bolted upright. The woman's eyes widened with concern as she held her hand out to me.

"Please, sit. You've had quite an eventful evening, and I would hate for you to fall and hurt yourself."

"An eventful evening? Please, can you explain where I am and what I am doing here?" I breathed, confusion dominating my brain, making it hard for me to think.

"Oh, of course." She waved her hand in the air as she tapped the side of her head playfully.

"*Ma Certo, sono così smemorata.*"

I blinked, unsure what she had just said, but recognized the accent as Italian.

"You are here because I wanted you to be. This is my home." She smiled sweetly, yet I sensed danger lurking behind her words.

Why am I in a strange woman's house?

Why can't I recall getting here?

My head throbbed as I sank back down on the bed.

"This is just a game, really," she murmured lowly as she sat beside me on the bed, her fingers running through my hair as she gazed at me in admiration.

My instincts told me to move away, but her touch held me still.

"What game? I don't understand. I don't even know you," my voice gave away the fear I felt, and my stomach churned as she nodded sympathetically.

"No, that is true, *Bella*. You don't know me. But your boyfriend does."

My eyes met hers then, and I felt bile rise in my throat.

How does she know Cal? Is he here?

"My name is Lucia. I am not sure if he has ever mentioned me to you—"

My mouth dropped open as I realized the woman sitting before me was the reason Cal was so damaged.

The attack on Lucia all those years ago had left him scarred mentally; it was what put him in witness protection and what caused him to kill a man before my very eyes. She was beyond stunning, and my heart ached as I remembered what had happened to her.

She nodded casually, removing her fingers from my hair, and I was thankful she didn't rip it out of my scalp.

"So, he *did* tell you," she mused quietly. "You must be *very* special because he didn't tell anyone else about it. He just ran," she spoke coolly, anger in her voice. "Do you know he was *my* boyfriend first?" She turned to me then, and resentment filled my chest. "I mean, we were young, but he was my first *everything* if you know what I mean. We were besotted with each other. See, one thing that is so attractive about Leo is how fiercely he loves. You know what I mean? I can see it in your eyes."

I stared at the floor, and I thought if she was going to just kill me, she should get it over with. I'd rather have that than listen to her stories as Cal's girlfriend.

"I'm the daughter of a Don, Gretchen. I know how it feels

to be protected. All my life I have been told where to go, where not to go, who to speak to, you get the picture. So, Leo was my world, I fell in love with him so quickly I couldn't be without him. I knew he was a bad boy, but who doesn't find that attractive? I was used to that lifestyle anyway; I figured it would get him a higher favor with my father if he became a successful criminal." She shrugged, then her eyes glassed over, the memories of her attack now surfacing.

I tried to remember my training and how to talk to someone with Post Traumatic Stress Disorder, as I remained quiet, listening patiently.

"I won't give you the details, but apparently, I should feel lucky to be alive. I *don't*," she hissed bitterly, turning to gaze at me.

My heart beat so fast that all I could hear was the blood rushing in my ears.

"I wish I were dead."

I gulped then, not sure what to say.

She stood up abruptly as I heard footsteps coming down the hall, her name being called. Her eyes darted around the room as the door swung open, revealing a devilishly handsome man, his dark hair slicked back as he caught sight of me on the bed, a frown forming on his face.

"Lucia..." he muttered. His eyes met hers as she giggled.

"I know, it's naughty. But I *had* to, Michael."

Michael.

I hadn't heard of his name before, and my cheeks flushed as he moved forward, scrutinizing me. His cologne was strong and delicious, as I moved further back on the bed, not wanting to be in proximity to this man.

"Sssh, it's okay. My sister and I are just going to leave the room to talk for a moment, okay?" His voice was soft as he gazed at me, his dark eyes piercing into mine.

Sister.

I nodded, and they left, hearing their rapid exchange of words outside of the door. I stood, searching the room quickly for a weapon of any kind. I knew I was in a *mafia* house, and I didn't know when I would need to fight for my life.

There was nothing, absolutely *nothing* to use.

I tore open the heavy drapes that blocked the sunlight, gasping when I saw my view. The window could open outwards to a balcony, complete with a small iron table and chairs, overlooking the most beautiful garden I had ever seen.

Am I still in New York?

I couldn't be; I'd never seen space like this in any real estate there.

The door opened behind me, and I heard someone walk in, the door clicking shut softly behind them.

"Forgive my sister, Miss Red. She is not well."

My skin prickled at his voice as I turned to see him leaning against the bed frame, his face etched in annoyance as he glanced around the room.

"Your boyfriend was here earlier, looking for you. Had I known you were here, I would have reunited you at once. Alas, I did not. So, here we are."

I watched him, my arms crossed over my chest, aware I was wearing my stupid pajamas and that I hadn't even brushed my teeth that morning.

The inconvenience of being kidnapped.

He seemed to register my discomfort as he stood, walking over to me slowly. "I am so sorry. I understand if you wish to press charges." He stared at the floor as he rubbed his neck with one hand.

I shook my head. "I won't. I just want to go home."

His eyes met mine as his fingers captured my hand,

raising it to his full lips before kissing it softly. "Then I am in your debt."

Our eyes met as he dropped my hand slowly, his smile dangerous yet seductive. "If you need anything, ever, you just call me. Do you understand? Just call me." His words sunk in, and I nodded as he turned his gaze to the view behind me.

"Care for a walk around the gardens before you leave? It would be a shame to waste an opportunity to explore something so beautiful." He didn't blink as he gazed at me.

My cheeks flushed beneath his gaze, but I lifted my chin and met his eyes. "I'd rather go home."

"To Leo?" He said coolly.

"Yes," I murmured.

"Then I shall get your things, and I will call him for you. I assume he will arrive quickly, but please take a shower and put on some fresh clothes. I will have a maid bring you something in. We have clothes in all sizes, don't look so alarmed. I can guess yours." His eyes raked down my body slowly as he nodded.

"Please." He gestured towards the bathroom and turned to leave the room, his cologne lingering behind.

You couldn't make this shit up.

GET OUT

CAL

I gripped the phone as Michael's words washed over me.

"Lucia brought her here. Come and get her."

I hung up, dizzy with relief as I stared into my brother's eyes. "That was Michael. He said she is there."

Drake whistled with happiness. "Well, thank fuck for that. I'm coming with you."

I didn't have the strength to argue as he followed me to my truck, the two of us attracting attention as we walked. I didn't think it was that obvious we were brothers. I suppose we shared the same stocky build, but while I had dark blonde hair, his was a deep chocolate brown, which showed no sign of fading as he got older. He wore it long, tying it up in a bun in summer. Summers in New York were deadly anyway, the heat bouncing from building to building like a pinball lost in a machine. I don't know how he coped with long hair and a beard, I wanted to shave mine off in the heat.

We got in my car and began the journey to the Salvatore house, my heart in my throat the entire way. Every obstacle that could have cropped up did. The traffic dragged at a snail's pace as I growled with frustration.

"You aren't going to lose your shit, are you?" Drake sighed.

I glared at him. "That depends."

"On?" He pressed.

"How she is. She better be as she was the last time I saw her."

He smirked at me then. "Irrevocably in love with you?"

I didn't answer as we pulled into the street that held my girl captive. The one place in the world I wouldn't have ever wanted her to go to, the place that held my most horrific memories.

Maybe I should burn this fucking house down.

I cut the engine as I jumped out, running up the steps, the door unguarded this time.

Drake caught up with me as the door swung open to reveal Michael Salvatore, his dark eyes taking in my brother and me.

"Come in."

I intend to.

My eyes scanned the room, and I frowned when I didn't see her.

"Where is she?!" I hissed, unable to contain my rage.

Michael narrowed his eyes as he folded his arms, his voice low and deadly. "I think you mean, *thank you*. She's a beautiful woman, I almost wanted to keep her here a little while longer."

White hot fury ran through me as I walked towards him, my face close to his. "She is *mine*. Don't even *think* about her in that way."

The eyes of the soon-to-be ruler of the underworld widened with delight at my words.

"I see. If she was *mine*, *no one* could take her from me. Yet, she spent the night here last night." He leaned back on a chair, goading me to knock his teeth out of his handsome face.

"Because *you* fucking forced her, you *bastard*."

Drake was between us, his eyes on mine as he spoke. "Leo. No. This isn't what she needs right now. She needs to go home. Think of her."

I turned away as Michael chuckled.

"I can assure you, Leonardo. I didn't force her to do anything she didn't want to do."

What the fuck is that supposed to mean?

I moved towards him when I heard her voice, like an angel calling to me.

"Cal?"

I turned as she raced down the stairs, her eyes filling with tears as I caught her in my arms, burying my face in her hair. Her scent filled my nostrils, calming my senses as it always did.

"Are you okay? I'm so fucking *sorry*," I mumbled, aware my eyes were filling up too.

She meant so much to me, and having her in my arms now made me realize how special she was. I held her away from me as I searched her face, her lips moving close to mine—

"Leonardo." The voice cut through our reunion like a knife as I tensed, turning to see Michael grinning at me. "I suggest you take better care of this one. You are lucky to have such a woman."

I noticed him staring beyond me, his eyes meeting hers. I glanced around as she dropped her eyes from his gaze, her cheeks flaming. He had that effect on women; being who he was but also being blessed with those Italian good looks helped him along.

Suave bastard.

"Drake, take Gretchen to the car," I ordered as she made her way into Drake's open arms.

They had met before and had formed a friendship that drove me wild with jealousy until I realized they regarded each other as siblings would. They left, and I twisted towards Michael.

"I appreciate you letting me know she was here. It doesn't mean I owe you a damn thing, though. I know you hate me; the feeling is mutual. I'm sorry about Lucia, but I'm not the one that hurt her. She cannot do this again, Michael. See that she doesn't."

The storm in his eyes forced me to step back, but it was then that I noticed a cigar being lit in the far corner of the room, the orange embers the only source of light.

"You've got some balls, kid. Speaking to him that way, others have died for much less. Lucia was in the wrong, and that is the only reason you are going to walk out of here. Now get the fuck out."

I nodded, glaring at Michael as I left. Verno had spoken, and I respected him. But Michael— he was a different breed.

I didn't trust him at all.

DO YOU REMEMBER?

GRETCHEN

I bit my lip nervously as Cal slammed the door shut behind me, his eyes on mine. I knew he would beat himself up, and I wished there was something I could do. He frowned as he took in the deep red vest I wore over tight jeans, his jaw tensing.

"Where did you get the clothes?" He muttered.

"Michael said he had some clean ones, as all I had were my pajamas."

His eyes narrowed as he nodded slowly, walking towards me. "I don't like you wearing anything from *him*."

I reached down, pulling the top over my head and peeling the jeans from my legs, tossing them on the floor. "Better?" I snapped, annoyed that was all he cared about right now. "I get it. You don't like him. But he was perfectly decent to me, and all I want right now is for you to change the fucking locks."

His eyes widened as he took in my words. "Lucia did this. I'm so sorry."

"*Cal.* She's messed up... she went through so much it's insane." My voice trailed off, aware he was shaking his head at me.

"I know what she went through, Gretchen. But that doesn't give her the right to abduct my fucking *girlfriend*." He spoke through his teeth, and I froze, aware this was probably the angriest I'd ever seen him, but what chilled me to the bone was how eerily calm he was.

"Cal, it could've been so much worse. I'm fine, no one hurt me. Okay?"

"No, Gretchen. It's anything but."

I wanted him to hold me in his arms and kiss me, fuck me, anything but look at me like he was now. His green eyes filled with sadness.

"Cal—"

He held his hand up, silencing me. "I can't protect you against a *woman*. What good am I to you? She could've killed you. Yet the only reason she knew you even existed was because of me. She wanted to hurt you— because of me. I need to consider that."

He moved towards the kitchen, peeling off his hoodie and tossing it to me, his scent wrapping itself around me like a comfort blanket. "I'm going to make you something to eat."

What is going on?

Why is he being so cold?

I followed him into the kitchen, wrapping my arms around myself as I watched him pour oil into a pan. He pulled out vine tomatoes and began chopping them roughly, tossing them into a bowl of salad leaves, his eyes refusing to meet mine.

"Cal, don't shut me out," I whispered, a lump rising in my throat as he dropped steak into the oil, the sizzling filling the silence.

He continued cooking, adding mushrooms and garlic to the pan as though I hadn't spoken.

"*Cal.*" I moved towards him, pressing my body against his back, and felt him tense beneath me. "Talk to me."

He turned the steaks with one hand, the other holding mine tightly.

I trembled as he turned to me, his eyes dark and deadly.

"I'm fine. Just tired and hungry, I guess."

He was lying to me.

Despite everything we had been through, he'd never pushed me away like this. I moved back, hoping he would pull me back to him, but he didn't; he just carried on as though nothing had happened.

"I'm going to take a shower, okay?"

He nodded silently as he grabbed a beer from the fridge, putting him out of my sight temporarily.

Where is my Cal?

After I showered, I dressed quickly, my tummy rumbling at the smell of steak and garlic. I walked into the kitchen to see mine in the pan, with the large salad beside it in a glass bowl.

He'd poured me a glass of my favorite red wine, and I took a sip, closing my eyes as the familiar taste slid down my throat with promises of calm and relaxation not far away. Before I knew it, I'd drained the wine, and I examined the empty glass with surprise. I shrugged, topping it up and taking a large mouthful.

"*I'm sorry.*"

The voice startled me as I jumped, turning to see Cal leaning against the doorway, watching me, his eyes staring down at the floor. He was still topless, and I tried not to stare at his delicious body, tanned and toned in all the right places. His jeans were loose on his hips, as though he had taken them off but changed his mind last minute, meaning I could see the delicious V that led down to his silky cock.

I blinked, aware I was off in a fantasy world whilst he was watching me with a bemused expression on his face.

"If you are *thirsty*, you'd be better drinking something that will quench your thirst, not wine." He nodded at the half-empty bottle in my hand. "But it goes down very well with the steak."

I took another gulp of wine as I slid the steak onto my plate, the mushrooms and garlic falling along with it, making my mouth water. I added salad for the fact it was there more than any intention to eat any. I carried my plate to the table and closed my eyes as the steak fell apart in my mouth, amazed that this man knew exactly how to cook my steak despite only being told once.

Wow.

He grabbed another beer as his phone rang, and I heard him answer as he walked into the hall. I never listened to his conversations because I didn't want to hear the content if I was honest— I knew Cal did business with some unsavory characters, and I liked to distance myself from that as best as I could.

Since being in New York, I hadn't been exposed to any part of that world until now, and it was fucking *terrifying*.

I chewed my food as I sipped the wine more slowly now as it took effect, making my heart beat that little faster and making the day behind me seem almost delightful.

You've got to love wine.

Cal walked back into the room, his green eyes burning into mine as I felt those butterflies flying around my stomach. My mind extracted one of my favorite memories of us, and I watched it play happily in my head.

"What are you smiling about?"

I pushed my plate away as I finished the last piece of

steak, letting out a contented sigh. "I was just remembering the first time you kissed me."

He raised an eyebrow as he walked over to me, pulling me up by my hands. "I don't think I can remember; it was just a kiss," he teased, knowing how much I had talked about it afterward.

I rolled my eyes, secretly delighted he seemed more relaxed. "It was in the rain, remember?"

He nodded, his finger brushing down my face. "As if I'd *ever* forget, baby. I've never wanted to kiss anyone as much as I did that night, standing in front of you in your little dress." He leaned down, his lips smashing against mine as I grabbed his hair in my hands, wondering if I would ever tire of tasting him. His tongue explored my mouth as he held me close, his warm body sending goosebumps on mine as our skin touched.

"I was with someone else then. *Technically*," I mused as we broke apart, our foreheads still touching. He growled as he pushed me against the wall, tilting my face up to his.

"*Fuck* technicalities. You were *mine* the minute I saw you in the hallway, wondering who the fuck I was and why I made you feel the way you did. Admit it, *Raven*," he smirked as I gasped under his grip as he watched me with interest. "We haven't had this conversation yet."

He flipped me so I was facing the wall as he trailed his hands down to my hips, pulling me against him as though trying me on for size.

"Admit what?" I croaked out as he hooked his thumbs through my bottoms, pulling them down in one swift movement and exposing me to him. He pushed my legs apart with one foot as I heard his belt hit the floor, bracing myself for his entrance.

"When I saw you in the bathroom. At Luke's dinner party.

You wanted me to bend you over the sink and fuck you hard, *didn't you*?"

The head of his cock pressed against my wet slit, and I moved myself against him, begging him to enter me.

"Come now, Gretchen, we are having a conversation..."

"Yes. Now fuck me," I demanded as he obeyed, sliding his entire length inside of me. I gasped as he pulled it back out to the tip before slamming it back inside of me.

"Is this hard enough for you? Would you have screamed out, or would I have had to do this?"

As he thrust in and out of me, I moaned loudly, unable to control myself as he covered my mouth with his hand, so no sound escaped me. The only sound was the slapping of his crotch against my ass, the skin hot and slick as my juices wrapped around his cock, spilling out with each thrust. His hand slipped down to my hip as his other hand grabbed a handful of my hair, pulling it back as he used me for leverage, the thrusts becoming deeper and more demanding. I felt myself shudder against his cock as he moaned with approval.

"Fuck, Raven. You're *killing* me."

I smirked; the pain in my hips from fingers that were now digging into my flesh told me he was close. "I'm yours," I gasped as he grunted with each thrust, the grip tightening on my hips.

"You're *mine*," he growled, lust and desire spilling from his perfect mouth.

Then he let go, and I felt him shooting his seed deep within me. He pulled me tight against him as he swore.

"Now *that*," I gasped as I wriggled from his grasp, our juices slowly dripping down my thighs as he sat back on the chair beside him, "Was fucking *insane*."

He laughed, and I kissed him, although we were both out of breath.

"You shouldn't ever mention you and anyone else in the same sentence; you know what it does to me," he warned as I smirked.

"Did I ever tell you about—" I teased as he jumped from the chair, my heart in my throat as I tried to run away from him.

He caught me by the stairs, and I let out a squeal as we kissed; with such desire, I felt him harden against me once more.

"Don't fuck around. You're *mine*," he whispered as he moved my hair from my eyes softly as he gazed at me with adoration.

"I know, and you're mine," I whispered back as I kissed him, feeling him smile against my mouth.

God, I love him so fucking much.

SOMEONE'S SISTER
MICHAEL

*T*he woman bounced on top of me, her tiny breasts barely moving as she made an elaborate show of herself on my cock. I stifled a yawn as the shock registered in her eyes.

"I'm sorry, I guess you just aren't capable of keeping me entertained. Not for lack of effort, though." I lifted her from me as she snatched her clothes up, her doll-like features twisting into a nasty snarl.

"You won't get anyone better. I'm the best in the entire state," she snapped as she walked away, grabbing her cash on the way out.

She was a whore, why was she so offended that she just didn't do it for me? My cock was going flaccid already, bored with the same old pussy. I peeled the condom off and slung it into the trash can with irritation.

You can't even pay for women to fuck you without attitude.

I stood, walking over to the open doors of my room that overlooked the flawless gardens of the home I had grown up in, letting out a deep sigh. It was beautiful here, but like all beauty, it hid a deeper layer, one that was not as pretty to look at.

I had grown up around crime; one of the first executions I saw at the age of eleven burned into my retina. The man had betrayed my father, apparently, by leaking secrets to a rival family. My father told me to watch without fear that this is what happened to rats. The man had begged for his life, but he was tied to a chair with wire and beaten to death with baseball bats. I will never forget the look in his eyes, the way he pleaded for mercy repeatedly as they ignored him. I can still hear the clatter of the bats on the floor as the clean-up guys arrived, someone pushing me out of the door so I could follow my father, who was covered in blood.

My first kill was a tad more brutal, but at least I felt it was for a valid reason.

Lucia.

I will never forget my mother's screams as my father had her sedated, unable to bear her cries of anguish. Lucia had been savagely beaten, raped, and left for dead, yet somehow, she survived. She was a Salvatore, made of intense strength, but no one expected her to live. My father made sure Lucia had the best round-the-clock care, whilst ordering the bastards to be brought to our home. My father, my elder brothers, and I all stood around the deep mahogany table as we wept, our anger demanding revenge.

She was *fifteen*.

None of us were home.

Yet *he* was here.

The intense anger raged through me as I remembered finding out he was her boyfriend, yet he had run like a bitch whilst she was being used by the perverted bastards inside her room, her screams following him through the gardens, I'm sure—yet still he ran.

It made no sense to me.

When I found out, I was sixteen, a mere boy. But I made it clear I wanted in on the revenge. I smiled as I remembered hearing the pleading, the apologizing. How this dirty bastard didn't know she was my sister. I remember wondering how that made any difference.

She would have been someone's sister. Someone's daughter. Maybe, one day, someone's mother.

That would never happen now. The doctor could not salvage her insides enough to let her carry a child if, by any miracle, she conceived.

I took great joy in peeling the skin from his eyelids so he could never close his eyes. I made him swallow his own cock, piece by piece. Finally, I hung him from a meat hook by the rectum until his heart gave way. I was there for his last breath as I told him it was for Lucia.

When he meets the Devil, I hope he passes on my condolences. Even the Devil doesn't deserve such scum for company.

I blinked, realizing I was ice cold. I had been standing outside for longer than I realized, the sun having left long ago.

Even though Leonardo didn't hurt her, he didn't stop them either. My father may have forgiven him by the fact he had killed Andre, but I hadn't. He ran away, and for that, I feel he deserved more than a one-night abduction of his girlfriend.

My mind moved to her then as I recalled seeing her for the first time in Lucia's room. I couldn't deny the attraction between us, but I don't make a habit of stealing wives or girlfriends from other men, even ones as low as Leonardo Cape.

I'm used to women falling at my feet, wanting to marry me, and getting accustomed to the mob lifestyle. Yet she'd wanted to leave. Her fear was attractive, in a sadistic way. I would never hurt a woman, but when she walked down my staircase, it took everything I had not to call for Leo to be killed so I could make her mine, if only for an hour.

But I was a man of my word. I owed her a favor after Lucia's little prank.

I would have to hope she would come to collect it.

FANTASIZING
GRETCHEN

*S*ummer break arrived perfectly on time, and I was looking forward to landing back in Winterburg with my delicious boyfriend in tow. His hand gripped mine as the plane descended, and I was reminded by how much he hated flying.

"Yet again, I'm glad to be out of New York. I wish you could study somewhere else," he grumbled as he tightened his grip on my hand.

I decided it was best to bite my tongue here; this argument knew no end. He knew I had decided where I was studying when he had just upped and left me during my last year of high school. I didn't expect him to return, and by then, I was ready to move. But it was such a great program, taught by the finest in therapy.

The plane distracted me by touching down, a good landing as far as they go. I glanced at Cal, who had his eyes closed, his face a deathly white. "Cal, we've landed, babe. Breathe."

He smiled faintly, his grip relaxing ever so slightly on my hand.

We finally left the plane, the warm summer air greeting us like an old friend. I was giddy with excitement at seeing everyone, as my eyes scanned the airport crowds eagerly.

"You're like a kid on Christmas morning." He laughed as he tugged our suitcases along easily beside him, his sleeves rolled up to reveal those muscular forearms I loved so much.

"Cal, you get to see your parents!" I exclaimed, sad that he didn't have the bond I had with my parents.

He shrugged as his cool gaze fell on someone behind me, a smile creeping onto his face as I followed his eyes to see my parents striding towards us, my mother's arms outstretched as she pulled me close, her sweet perfume instantly comforting me.

My eyes pricked with tears as she whispered, "I've missed you so much."

"I've missed you too, Mom."

She released me so I could hug my dad, who kissed the top of my head as he wrapped his arms around me. I rested against his chest as my mom hugged Cal, commenting on how much of a man he was now becoming. This made my dad chuckle as he shook Cal's hand firmly.

I slid my arm back around Cal's waist as my dad grabbed a suitcase from him, feeling stupidly content.

This is my world, right here.

As we walked to the car, I felt something inside of me relax, and the mindless chatter flowed between us as we drove home.

"How was the flight?" My father asked, his eyes twinkling as they met mine in the rear-view.

Cal shuddered beside me as I stifled a giggle, which suddenly escaped.

"Contrary to anything Cal tells you, it was perfectly fine."

"We nearly died," he pointed out, and laughter filled the car.

"Oh, Cal. You just aren't a flyer; that's okay. I'm not good on boats, so I empathize." My mother's eyes fell on him as she smiled kindly.

My father snorted then, earning him a sharp look from my mother.

"Not good is probably an understatement. The last time you went on a boat, you passed out. Took a good while for you to get your color back, that's for sure."

She rolled her eyes, a smile playing on her lips. He glanced at her, his eyes crinkling in the corners as he smiled. Her hand covered his, and he pulled it to his lips, kissing it softly before placing his hand back on the wheel. They were still so very much in love, even after many years together.

I sighed contentedly as I gazed out of the window, the familiar sights warming my soul.

I love Winterburg.

"I love your smile." The voice broke into my thoughts as he kissed my shoulder softly, his green eyes meeting mine as I turned to him. I noticed sadness pass over his face briefly, but before I could study it further it was gone, replaced by the lazy smile I adored.

"I love you," I whispered, closing my eyes as I leaned against him, tiredness sweeping over me as I yawned.

"Home, sweet home," my mother sang as we pulled into the drive of my childhood home.

The house was simple, but it would always be my favorite. I knew every nook and cranny here, and every corner held a distinct memory. As the door swung open, I suddenly remembered opening the door to Cal years ago, standing before him in just a towel as he had said—

"Do you always open the door dressed like that?" He

whispered in my ear as he passed me, pulling our suitcases into the hall.

I gaped at him as he laughed, running a hand through his hair. How did he know I was thinking about *that* memory?

His eyes danced with amusement as he walked over to me, his mouth suddenly close to my ear. "I know you well enough to know when you are fantasizing about me." He grinned smugly.

I arched an eyebrow playfully. "I wasn't fantasizing about you; I was just remembering something."

His eyes trailed down my body as he bit his lip. "Mm. Me too."

"Is that all I am to you, a sex toy?" I smirked as he frowned, his hands gripping my hips as he pulled me towards him.

"Is that a serious question, Raven?" His voice was low and dangerous, and I chewed on my bottom lip. "I can go without sex if only to prove a point to you. You'd be begging me for it before long."

There was no way in the world I could sleep beside this man and not have him in the most intimate way a woman could have a man. I kissed his lips as he looked at me with a smug expression on his handsome face.

"Just as I thought. Right, let's get these up to your old room." He effortlessly picked up the cases as my mother watched with approval, her eyes misting over.

"The way you look at him is the way I look at your father. It's beautiful to see. He adores you, Gretchen." Her voice was soft as my dad walked in, swinging the keys around his finger.

We both looked at him and smiled knowingly as Cal jogged back down the stairs, aware of the awkward silence. He laughed, shooting me a curious look as my dad said, "I have a feeling they were talking about us, Cal." He raised his eyebrows as my mother let out a girlish giggle.

Maybe my moving out had allowed them to rekindle their marriage in ways they probably didn't realize they needed.

"Ah, good things, I hope."

Our eyes met, and he walked over to me, his fingers lacing with mine. His very touch made me weak, and I leaned against him as my dad cleared his throat.

"There's an event downtown tonight if you feel up to it." Dad furrowed his brow as he rifled through the drawer in the dresser by the door. He let out a triumphant sound as he found a leaflet, which he thrust in my direction.

I cast my eyes over it and saw it was some sort of mini-festival, with food stands and live music. I shrugged as I handed it to Cal, who nodded.

"Sounds good, but as always, it's up to you."

My father grinned as I nodded, causing him to clap his hands together. "Okay, well, we have some time to freshen up before it starts, so shall we be ready around seven?"

"Okay." I yawned as Cal kissed the top of my head, whispering in my ear.

"Let's go lie down for a bit. Don't get any funny ideas, I need a nap."

I swatted his chest as he caught my hand, pulling it up to his lips. "I said no, I'm tired."

I laughed as I walked past him, pulling him up the stairs behind me.

"Stop begging, Gretchen; I said no," he teased as we made it to my old bedroom, sinking onto the bed as I buried my face in his neck.

"Shut up, you absolute perv."

He held his hands up, and his top rose slightly, showing

the tanned skin beneath it. I caught my breath slightly as a smirk played on his lips.

"Now, who's the perv?"

I leaned down and kissed his stomach, trailing kisses down to his waistband. "That would be me."

SHITTY TOWN
GRETCHEN

"What are you planning for your birthday, lovely?" Mom asked as we got into the car.

I scrunch my nose up as I shrugged. "I haven't thought about it, to be honest."

"Well, you'll be back in New York, maybe we could come and see you?" Her voice was excited as I glanced at Cal who was gazing out of the window, his fingers rubbing his chin.

"Yeah, maybe." I smiled at my mom, wondering why Cal looked so lost in thought.

My eyes still watered with how handsome he was, especially with what he was wearing tonight. He had a crisp white shirt on with the sleeves rolled up, dark jeans and boots with his dirty blond hair slicked back roughly.

I remembered him in my bedroom earlier, not a scrap of clothing between us as we explored one another as though for the first time. He was the only man I'd been with sexually, so I know I had nothing to compare it to, but it was truly out of this world the way he made me feel.

The way he always makes me feel.

He must've noticed me staring because a smug grin played at his mouth as our eyes met, my stomach filling with butterflies as he turned away.

"We should book the flights soon. Otherwise, the prices will rise," Mom said.

"I know someone who can sort your flights. Remind me later?" Cal piped up, winking at me as I frowned.

I still felt like there was so much about him I didn't know.

My mother nodded as he shot her a winning smile.

I squeezed his hand as my father parked the car into one of the last spaces in the parking lot. It must be busy; this town was never short of space.

We climbed out, and I straightened my outfit up, a black dress teamed with a denim jacket and my Converse high-tops. I glanced at Cal and realized we didn't match our outfits up at all tonight, but I didn't care.

"You're *so* fucking beautiful," he murmured as he slid his arm around me. I laced my fingers with his, and we walked after my parents, who were also hand-in-hand.

"It's so strange being back here," I said, noticing some familiar faces milling around.

It had been a long time since I'd been back, considering the last time I had just spent with my family and not gone out much.

Cal pulled me over to a little stall that was selling bottles of wine, handwritten labels with unintelligible scrawl written on them. He peered at them as the woman smiled at us broadly.

"Red, white, or rose?" She asked sweetly as her eyes flickered over Cal a little too long for my liking.

He turned to me and held his hand out for me to answer.

"Oh, I like rose." I smiled sweetly as Cal's eyes crinkled up in the corners.

"We have fourteen different bottles of rose, each one with a unique taste. If you like it sweet, I recommend this one." She slid out a pink bottle and poured some into a tiny plastic cup for me to try.

I glanced at Cal as he watched me crinkle my nose up at the smell, and he bit back a smile. I sipped it, the delicious taste of crushed lemons mixed with what tasted like vanilla and melon.

"Wow! That's amazing," I declared as the woman flushed with pride.

Cal ordered two bottles, and we waited as she wrapped them for us. He paid, and we continued our tour of the festival, stopping to sample cheeses and meats.

Fairy lights hung from the trees, making the town appear almost magical under the night sky; I huddled closer to Cal, finding his warmth comforting.

My parents were deep in conversation with some neighbors of ours when I heard my name being called excitedly from behind us.

"Oh, my God, it is! It's Gretchen and Cal!" The voice trilled as we turned to see Rosie squealing as she hurried towards us, running into my arms. She held me at arm's length as she studied me, her eyes widening. "*Wow*, New York suits you; you look *amazing*. Hey Cal..."

She offered him a small smile as he nodded in acknowledgment before whispering to me he would leave us for a moment to catch up. He disappeared into the throng of people, and I looked after him wistfully before turning back as Sienna bounded up to us, gripping me tightly.

"Oh, my God! Why didn't you tell us you were coming back?!" She demanded, an accusatory tone in her voice.

"Surprise?!" I grinned as we fell into a group hug.

We had been close in school, but it had become difficult

towards the end when I got with Cal after my relationship with Luke ended. They didn't want to choose sides.

Ultimately, moving to New York was a good thing; it created distance, and people could move on.

"Tell me about New York! When can we come to see you?" Rosie exclaimed as Sienna nodded enthusiastically.

"Yes, *totally*, shopping trip!"

We giggled as we walked together, our arms linked like old times.

"How're things with you two?" I asked, looking from one to the other.

Sienna nudged Rosie as she blushed, mumbling that she had moved in with Finn, her last-minute high school sweetheart.

I clapped my hands together, elated for her. Finn had been the biggest player in school, always sleeping with a different girl until the night of Prom when he got with Rosie. None of us saw it coming, but they were good for each other.

"Speaking of lover boy," declared Sienna, nodding toward Finn, who was striding over to us, his eyes glued to Rosie. He did a double-take when he saw me before shooting me a dazzling smile.

"Hey there, city girl. Fancy seeing you here."

I smiled as I scanned the crowds for Cal, my eyes seeking his. I felt a pang of disappointment, but then I knew he wouldn't want to be involved in my current social circle.

"Ah, here's Luke and Ethan." Beamed Sienna as two guys joined our group, and my eyes met those of my ex.

Luke's eyes bulged with shock when he saw me, but he soon recovered. He was still devastatingly handsome, and my heart hurt a little seeing him again, but I knew I had done the right thing.

We all stood awkwardly as Finn suggested we go get

some drinks when I felt a hand on my arm, tugging me back. I yanked my arm back in alarm before I realized it was Luke, and my mouth dried as his eyes narrowed at my reaction.

"Whoa, sorry. I didn't mean to scare you. I just wanted to speak to you alone. Are you okay?" His dark hair contrasted with his tight white t-shirt, which now showed rippling muscles and a broad chest.

He's filled out.

"I'm fine, how are you? Sorry, I'm just a little jumpy, I guess," I babbled as he looked on with interest.

We walked together, stopping in between two stalls.

"Yeah, I'm good. You here with your parents?" He asked, his eyes scanning the crowd.

I gulped, still somewhat nervous about admitting I was still with Cal.

He ran his hand down my arm, causing a shudder to run through my body.

"Are you still with him?" He asked, leaning close to me. I could smell beer on his breath as I moved back, becoming more uncomfortable.

"I'm still with Cal, yes," I stammered as he put a hand on either side of me, pinning me to the wall.

"You're still as beautiful as you were then," he murmured, bringing his face close to mine.

I froze, my hands on his shoulders as I pushed him away. "Luke, I'm sorry, but—"

"She's with me," a deep voice interrupted as Luke dropped his hands.

His posture deflated as he turned to see Cal standing there, his arms folded as he glared at him menacingly.

"*Cal/Leo*. What a pleasant surprise."

I gulped as they stood facing one another, true enemies to the end.

"When she was with me, she didn't flinch if I went near her. She didn't jump when she was touched. What the fuck have you done to her?" He hissed as he squared up to Cal, who stared at him with cold eyes.

"Well, I didn't cheat on her for a year," Cal chuckled. "She's not your concern. She's *mine,"* he growled and pushed past him, taking me into his arms.

Luke shook his head as he looked at me, his eyes narrowing.

"I told you he was no good. I tried to warn you." He shrugged as he walked into the crowd, leaving me alone with Cal.

"Was he going to kiss you?" Cal demanded, pushing me against the wall and gazing at me with a deadly expression on his face.

I opened my mouth to answer before his lips crashed down on mine, our tongues dancing in urgency as we kissed. He lifted me up, my legs wrapped around his waist as I kissed him passionately, as though he were my lifeline.

"Do I have to fight every man in the world for your attention?" He breathed.

I gazed at him as I shook my head, my hands still wrapped in his hair as he let me down.

"He's right, though. It's my fault you are like that, all jumpy and shit." He sighed as I held his face in my hands, my eyes searching his.

"Cal, I'd rather live a life of danger by your side than a life of safety by anyone else's."

He smiled then as he quickly kissed my lips. "I'd rather you lived a life of safety by my side."

We kissed again, unaware that we were being watched.

KARMA

LUKE

I finished my beer, slinging the glass bottle into the bin as we passed, wiping the excess alcohol from my lips. I needed another, but considering we were moments away from the town, I knew I could easily score another drink, possibly a decent beer too. I walked beside Ethan as I heard him mutter.

"Well, I'll be damned."

I frowned as I followed his eyes, my heart dropping from my chest when I saw her. It must've been two or three years since my eyes last drank her in, her now waist-length hair billowing around her in the wind as she laughed, one of my favorite sounds in the world, her perfect full lips parting to reveal her delicious mouth as she did. Her startling green eyes turned to meet mine as I forced a smile on my face. She held my gaze briefly, and I noted the regret in her eyes as she quickly looked away. I knew how that felt. I'd thought with my dick when I was with her, and Krystal gave it up when Gretchen didn't. I knew she had slept with my cousin whilst she was with me, no matter what she told me. That hurt more than my little fling with Krystal.

My heart hammered in my chest as I took in her tight dress, her long, tanned legs, and her black Converse.

My God, what I would do to see under that dress again.

Finn suggested we get some drinks, and we all began to follow when I found myself grabbing her arm, softly tugging her back towards me.

She recoiled in fear as she cried out before realizing it was only me. I frowned as I studied her, the fear clear in her eyes.

"Whoa, sorry. I didn't mean to scare you. I just wanted to speak to you alone. Are you okay?"

She seemed to compose herself with a deep breath and offered me a small smile.

Her eyes ran over my body briefly, and a smile played on my lips—I'd been training intensely for the past two years—and it showed. The desire in her eyes was there, albeit for a flash of a second, but it was all I needed to see.

"I'm fine, how are you? Sorry, I'm just a little jumpy, I guess."

Why?

I continued to study her. Years of being her boyfriend allowed me to recognize the signs of fear and anxiety she was currently displaying: the way her eyes darted around us, her tongue wetting her lips as she tried to regain composure.

What the fuck happened to her?

My stomach twisted with the familiar rage I felt whenever I thought of *him*, my fucking punk of a cousin who she was in love with. He was a smug prick who stole her right from under my nose, altering the course of our lives forever. He was a bad apple, and I knew he would end up dragging her into his life of crime and bullshit.

Where was he anyway?

Hopefully, he had died.

"Yeah, I'm good. You here with your parents?"

I scanned the surrounding crowd before my eyes met hers again, her face an open book. I sighed as I realized he was still in the picture—the look of guilt she wore told me that much.

Without thinking, I reached out, my fingertips running down her arm as she shuddered.

Oh, baby, you have no idea what I could do to you.

"Are you still with him?" I asked, not wanting to hear the answer.

I moved closer to her as her eyes fell to my lips, her mouth parted slightly.

Did she want me to kiss her? I would if so, no problem.

"I'm still with Cal, yes." She was breathless as I placed my hands either side of her on the wall, our bodies pressed together.

Fuck, she's already making me hard.

We'd never had a chance to explore one another sexually, but I knew it would be dynamite.

"You're still as beautiful as you were then." I brought my face close to her, leaning in, desperate to feel her lips on mine. I felt her hands on my shoulders as she pushed me away softly, as though she didn't really want to but had to.

"Luke, I'm sorry, but—"

"She's with me."

I closed my eyes and dropped my hands from her sides, feeling the breath leave my body at his voice. I turned slowly to see the bastard standing there with a deadly glare as he took in our position.

"*Cal/Leo*. What a pleasant surprise."

I stood facing him, my blood boiling as though I had lost her a second time. I remembered her reaction to me touching her earlier, and I found myself snapping at him. "When she was with me, she didn't flinch if I went near her. She didn't jump when she was touched. What the fuck have you done to her?" I took a few steps towards him as I stared him straight in the eyes, my fists clenched.

The bastard had the audacity to push past me towards Gretchen.

"Well, I didn't cheat on her for a year," the dickhead smirked at me, his eyes dropping over me with disinterest. "She's not your concern; she's *mine*."

I watched with agony as he pulled her into his arms, her eyes meeting mine over his shoulder. I looked at her as I turned to walk away, my heart breaking again.

"I told you he's no good. I tried to warn you." I shrugged as I walked into the crowd, out of their sight.

I turned and stood by a vendor stall, able to see them through the crowd. He pushed her against the wall as I had earlier, except he got to kiss her the way that I wanted to, more than anything. Her legs wrapped around his waist, and I got a glimpse into how they probably fucked: animalistic and raw. Her hands were wrapped in his hair as they spoke, their heads close together before they kissed again. My jaw tightened as I watched them, my stomach in knots.

I felt violently sick as I watched his hands roam over her body like he owned her.

How did I still feel this way years later?

Something was wrong; it didn't feel right. Maybe I needed to convince her how wrong he was for her. Something had already happened to make her react the way she did to being touched.

I just needed to find out what.

ENVY
CAL

I made my excuse and left her with her friends. I would rather watch paint dry than watch them look at me like I was the guy who broke their adorable Luke's heart.

Hypocrites, all of them.

I still couldn't give a fuck about that; I never meant to hurt him.

You can't help who you fall in love with, and that woman is mine.

I moved through the crowd as I browsed the little stores, stopping at a jewelry hut, antique rings glinting under the fairy lights. I smiled as I studied them, an idea forming in my mind. I moved on, casting my eyes back to where Gretchen was, and saw she had been joined by two guys whose identities I couldn't make out from where I was standing.

I sighed, making my way back over to see she was now being pushed against the wall by the dark-haired one, who I realized with a sickening feeling was Luke.

The worst part was the way she was looking at him.

I slowed, wanting to see what happened next. I shook

with rage as I grit my teeth, determined to see what she did. He was close to her face now, and I saw her eyes on his lips.

If she kisses him, I'm going to fucking murder them both right here in this shitty little town.

I was close enough now to hear their conversation.

"You're still as beautiful as you were then."

No fucking shit, Sherlock. The slimy bastard.

He went in to kiss her, and I held my breath as her hands went up to his shoulders, the pain in my heart crippling. But then she pushed him away, and I heard her delicate voice speak.

"Luke, I'm sorry, but—"

I'm done.

"She's with me," I growled as her eyes flickered to me, wide with surprise and relief. I folded my arms across my chest so I didn't punch the cunt in his throat.

"*Cal/Leo*. What a pleasant surprise."

I didn't trust myself when he spoke again, his eyes narrowing as he looked at me with disgust.

"When she was with me, she didn't flinch if I went near her. She didn't jump when she was touched. What the fuck have you done to her?"

He squared up to me, and I bit back a snarl as I pushed past him, determined not to disappoint Gretchen further by ripping his head off at the local festival. Hardly the scene any of us wanted.

When she was with him, she wanted *me*.

When she was with him, she didn't know what love was.

When she was with him, it was fucking practice for meeting *me*.

"Well, I didn't cheat on her for a year," I smirked at him. "She's not your concern; she's mine." I pushed Gretchen against the wall softly as he spoke.

"I told you he's no good. I tried to warn you."

I ignored him as he walked away into the crowd, my rage still bubbling deep inside of me. I closed my eyes as I breathed, desperately trying to remain calm.

"Was he going to kiss you?"

I stared at her with a mixture of lust and envy as she opened her sweet mouth to answer me. I smashed my lips against hers as she pushed her body against mine, my hands hoisting her legs up around my waist as I kissed her deeply. "Do I have to fight every man in this world for your attention?"

She gazed at me, her clear green eyes framed by dark, thick lashes.

Fuck, she was killing me.

The thought from earlier drifted back into my mind, blending with what I was feeling now.

I knew what I had to do. I had to make her safe, and I had to make her mine, for good.

LUST

GRETCHEN

*W*hen we got home, we feigned tiredness, heading straight for my bedroom. As soon as we were in there, I dropped to my knees, tugging at his jeans eagerly as he swore under his breath.

"*Jesus*, Raven."

His cock was already hard as I took it in my mouth, my eyes on his as he bit his lip and slid his hands into my hair as he thrust in and out of my mouth with ease as I sucked and licked with expertise, his cock growing harder in my mouth as he struggled to remain silent.

"*God*, you're so fucking *good*, baby."

I used my hand around his shaft to pump his cock, causing him to growl with desire as he pulled out of my mouth, lifting me onto the bed.

He threw my dress up around my waist as he fell to his knees, his tongue lapping at my core. I threw my head back as he brought me to the brink of ecstasy before I felt his warmth leave me, causing me to sit up on my elbows as I looked at him with desire.

"I need to fuck you *now*," he said hoarsely as he searched

for a condom. I needed him inside of me, and I wasn't prepared to wait.

"Cal, just fuck me. I'll get the morning-after pill. Please, I need you in me, *now.*"

He blinked as he looked at me as a wicked smile played at his lips. "If by any chance you forget to get it, and this is how our child is conceived, I need to make it memorable," he whispered, his lips meeting mine, his cock pushing inside of me simultaneously.

I gasped into his mouth as his mouth moved to my ear.

"Be quiet, baby. You'll need to scream silently this time."

He flipped me over with ease as he slammed back inside of me, pumping hard.

I moaned as his hand clamped around my mouth. I shuddered around his cock as he moaned, my core tightening around him as I came.

He released my mouth, and I gasped into the pillow as he picked up his pace, his fingers digging into my hips as he exploded into my belly.

I vowed to go on birth control just so we could fuck like this regularly.

He pulled out slowly, cupping his cock in his hand as he stood, grabbing the tissues from my desk and handed them to me.

I cleaned myself up as I stared at him, unable to believe he was mine.

"Maybe we need to bang into my ex more often," I quipped as he looked at me darkly, his t-shirt held under his chin whilst he finished cleaning our juices from his body.

"Don't talk about him," he ordered, coming to lie next to me on the bed. He moved my hair out of my eyes as he kissed my nose, our fingers lacing together.

"I love you," I whispered as my eyes closed.

"You have no idea how much I love you," he whispered back, his lips on my forehead as we drifted into a peaceful sleep.

RIGHT?

GRETCHEN

*C*al had to fly back to New York after briefly seeing his parents. *Apparently*, there was business he had to take care of. I was disappointed, but helped him pack anyway, and he lifted my head up to his.

"Hey. I'll be back as soon as I can, okay? Don't forget that morning-after pill," he reminded me with a wink, and I nodded in response.

Would having his child really be so bad?

He must've read the question in my eyes as he sat on my bed, pulling me close to him. "Unless you don't want to. I'd love you to be the mother to my children."

My heart hammered in my chest as I gazed up at him, his eyes full of adoration. "Cal, I'm not even twenty-one," I pointed out as he tilted his head and looked at me seriously.

"As I said, baby, it's your call. I don't think I am ready to share you with anyone just yet anyway, not even our child."

I sighed as he kissed me, and he stood, pulling his suitcase next to him.

"Will you be okay flying?" I asked, aware of how he felt about it.

He grimaced as he ran his hand down my cheek. "Yeah, I'm a big boy. I'll go there, sort this shit out, and I will be back before you know it. I *really* fucking love you. Will you be okay without me?"

I lifted my eyes to him as I shook my head. "*No*, so stay."

I felt anxiety in my chest as I did every time we parted; he had left me once, and I had been so depressed that it was like my world had ended.

"*Baby*, I'll be back. Two, three days—tops. Call me anytime. Go see your friends. Relax, you're safe here." He kissed me deeply as I sighed into him before walking down the stairs to where the cab was waiting to take him to the airport.

"Oh," he called over his shoulder as he walked away. "Keep away from my cousin." He raised his eyebrows at me as I rolled my eyes.

"*Goodbye.* I love you."

"I love you more." He threw his case into the trunk of the taxi before climbing in, giving me one last look before he closed the door.

A lump rose in my throat as the cab pulled away, his green eyes on me until he was no longer in sight. The sound of the engine faded down the street as I stood hugging myself, trying to cling to his scent from where he had kissed me earlier.

I turned and walked into the house, aware of how empty it was. My Mom and dad were at work, and I hadn't expected him to leave so suddenly.

The phone call must've been serious, though, because he packed up immediately.

I sighed as I flopped onto the couch, flicking Netflix on to see Vampire Diaries was back up. I decided to settle in for my Stefan fix when my phone beeped with a text.

CAL: Don't make any plans for your
birthday.

As I dropped the phone back onto the table, I wondered what he had planned.

Cal's behavior was unpredictable from one minute to the next, so I had no way of predicting what gift he would get for me.

The Vampire Diaries distracted me for a delightful couple of hours before boredom set in, and I fired off a text to Rosie, who called me back right away. We agreed to head to The Lounge.

I texted my parents, explaining Cal had left for a few days with work and that I was heading into town with Rosie.

When I heard her car honk outside, I smiled, seeing the familiar car at the end of the drive. It felt just like old times as I slid into the seat next to her, her eyes wide with excitement.

"Oh, *God*, it's so good having you back here. It's such a drag with just Sienna for company. I've missed you so much."

We chatted about her college course in childcare as we pulled up, my eyes falling on a familiar Ford Ranger. My stomach sank as Rosie looked over at me with worry in her eyes.

"Do you want to go somewhere else?"

I shook my head, aware that I needed to get used to seeing Luke, considering I was spending the entire summer here. It may be easier without Cal around, I suppose. It didn't stop my heart from racing when we walked in, my eyes automatically scanning the room for him.

He was leaning against the bar with a soda in his hands, his football jersey still on from practice. I knew he was now playing football professionally and that he was fantastic at it.

I smiled as he raised his soda in my direction before turning to Rosie, who bit her lip nervously.

"Are you guys good? I don't want any drama."

I found an empty booth at the opposite end and made a beeline for it, grateful it was out of his eyeline. I gave her a reassuring look as I pulled my phone out to see if Cal had texted to say he had landed yet.

Nothing.

"We'll be fine," I stated, my eyes flickering over to the direction he was in.

We ordered our usual lattes, and Rosie listened as I regaled her with tales of New York, leaving out the part where I was kidnapped.

"Your life is so interesting, and mine is so boring." She moaned as she slid out of the booth. "I'm just heading to the ladies." She flashed me a smile as she walked away, and I sipped my latte.

"No Cal tonight?"

I looked up, dread coursing through my veins.

Luke studied me, his electric-blue eyes burning into mine. "I just wanted to ask if we could catch up; I feel bad about the other day." He looked at the floor before he met my eyes, and I saw the sincerity in them.

I swallowed, knowing I should say no, but it *would* make things easier around here if we were cool. Plus, Cal wasn't here, and he wouldn't know about it.

"Okay, sure. Is tomorrow any good?" I offered, and his eyes lit up.

"Yeah, you still have the same number? I can come and pick you up if you like, say ten a.m.? If you still get up early, that is."

I chewed on the inside of my lip as I nodded. "Yeah, same number. Ten is fine. Thanks." I realized I was talking like a robot, and I tried to relax as he turned to see Rosie heading over to us, concern on her face.

I felt for our friends, it must be hard for them when we were all together.

It was fine, I decided. I was going to smooth this over so we could *all* have the best summer ever.

Right?

AGREED
GRETCHEN

J was glad my parents were at work, for if they'd seen Luke pulling up, they would have had a heart attack, I'm sure. I pulled the door shut behind me, glad I had dressed down. I wasn't about to give him any ideas, so I had my grey joggers on with a loose hoodie, refusing to even wear makeup. No way was he thinking there was more to this than there was. I took a deep breath as I switched my phone to silent, making my way to the Ford Ranger.

He sat in the driver's seat watching me with a smile on his lips, wearing a dark red leather jacket that oddly resembled the one Brad Pitt wore in Fight Club.

Don't stare, Gretchen.

He was hot, there was no denying that, but just as I had hurt him, he had hurt me. Cheating on me for an entire year was shitty, and my heart was with Cal, who would always be my one and only. I suppose it was usual for exes to still admire each other as long as nothing was done about it.

"How can you still look so beautiful in your loungewear? Man, girls must hate you." He laughed as I climbed into the truck, pulling the door shut behind me.

I clipped my belt in as I shot him a warning smile. "Less of the beautiful. You said no funny business."

He held his hands up as he pushed the car into drive, pulling away easily. "So, New York," he said, glancing over to me as we drove through the familiar streets, my heart aching with memory after memory.

"Yeah, it's a big ass city."

This was ridiculous.

When were we going to just get to it?

He seemed to read my mind as he sighed, turning onto the freeway.

"Okay, Gretch, here's the thing. You know I still love you; there's no denying that."

His bluntness surprised me.

If he had loved me in the first place, then he wouldn't have cheated with Krystal, I thought with annoyance. But I guess either way, it didn't matter anymore. I stared straight ahead as he continued to speak.

"You're with Cal; that's just how it is. But that doesn't mean I can turn off how I feel for you. I haven't seen you since we left school, and I just handled it badly the other night. I apologize."

I nodded, relieved by the direction the conversation seemed to be taking.

"Thank you," I said as he smiled at me reassuringly.

"I thought we could head to that little cafe overlooking the sea." He pointed toward the hills that rolled in front of us, and I nodded. I knew the place; he used to take me there when we were dating.

"That's fine."

I wanted to say more, but the guilt at even being in his presence alone made me feel sick with nerves. Cal would leave me after sawing Luke's head off with a rusty blade. We drove in silence for a while until he pulled into a dirt track that led to the cafe, his tires guiding us toward the parking lot despite the gravel.

"Ah, man! I've not been here since I last came with you," he admitted sheepishly as I lifted my eyebrows in surprise.

Surely there had been other girls?

"Not even Krystal?" I said.

Luke narrowed his eyes then as he shook his head. "It was never like that between me and Krystal. I'm sorry I was such a jackass, Gretchen. I majorly fucked up…"His words trailed off as he waited for me. He swung his keys around his finger as I climbed out, landing on the floor with a thud.

"It's in the past, Luke. We've all moved on," I said pointedly as we walked into the cafe.

Luke grunted in response, and the conversation ended there.

It was quiet—few people knew of it. You had to be a local. We got a gorgeous window seat overlooking the bay, and I sighed happily. It was nice to be here, even with Luke.

"I'm going to ask you a question, and I want you to be honest with me," he said seriously, and I raised an eyebrow at him suspiciously.

"If it's anything about you and me—"

He cut me off with his hand in the air, blinking slowly. "It's not."

I sat back in my chair and clasped my hands together. "Okay, go on then?"

He sat forward, his hands meeting in a steeple motion as he gazed at me. Our eyes met as he spoke, and he held my gaze as he watched my reaction. "What happened in New York? Tell me."

I dropped my eyes from him and gave a short laugh. "I don't know what you are talking about, Luke."

The waitress brought our coffees, and I watched her with interest.

Luke, however, kept his eyes on mine, murmuring thanks as she left. "Why are you lying to me?" His voice was low, and I sighed, irritated.

"What does it matter to you, Luke?" I snapped. "I thought we were here to remedy our shit, not create more."

He sat back as he studied me, his fingers pressed to his lips. "Did he hurt you?" His voice was hollow as I screwed my face up in response.

"*What*? No, don't be absurd."

"That's what abused girls say."

I stared at him, my mouth agape. "Luke, you have this wrong. It wasn't Cal." I sipped my latte, wincing at the heat. "Cal would never hurt me."

"If it wasn't him, who was it?!" He demanded, refusing to let the matter drop.

I folded my arms as I gazed at him. "If I tell you, you need to swear not to tell a soul."

He made a cross over his chest as he stared at me, his expression hardening as though he was preparing himself for the worst news he'd ever received.

I took a deep breath and met his eyes. "I'm fucking *serious*, Luke; I will *never* forgive you if you tell anyone. If you care for me at all, you won't."

"Gretch, you're scaring me now. *What the fuck happened*? I won't tell anyone."

"I was kidnapped."

His eyes widened as his mouth fell open, his hands reaching for mine over the table. "Are you being fucking serious right now?" he hissed quietly as I nodded. "Who the fuck by? What did they do to you?"

He sat listening to me as I poured it all out, and I had to

admit, it felt so good to speak to someone about it who wasn't Cal.

"What did Cal do about it?" He asked through gritted teeth, his eyes wild with anger.

"*Do*? He came and got me. What more can he do, Luke? It's the fucking *mob!*" I exclaimed as he sat back in his chair in shock, gazing out of the window whilst he rubbed his chin.

"I don't care. What did he *do?*"

His voice had a hardness to it, and I blinked in surprise.

Cal had done the right thing, left it alone. I knew that, yet sitting here in front of Luke, I suddenly felt like someone *had* to do something in my honor. I shook my head as he met my eyes again; hatred filled his eyes.

"This is *his* fault. You can't see it, I know that. But listen to me, it is." He sighed as he reached for my hand, gripping it. "I'm going to tell you this once, and I want you to remember it for the rest of your life. If you *ever* need me, *ever,* I don't care if I'm married with kids, you ring me. Okay?"

I nodded slowly, and he released my hand, the warmth of his touch gone.

"Mob or not, I'd bury anyone that touched a hair on your head."

"Thank you, but I've got Cal and—"

"Yes, he's a vicious fucker. But he isn't the only one who loves you, and sometimes you may just need someone else to turn to."

I nodded as he smiled at me.

"We can be friends, you know. It means I can't have you the way I want, but at least I have you in some capacity. Agreed?" Luke said, and I nodded.

"Agreed."

NYC
CAL

*W*hen it's cold in New York, it's fucking freezing. It jumps from one extreme to the other here, with blistering summers leading straight into icy winters. I shivered as I made my way into the damp basement, my eyes accommodating to the dark. I heard a whimper from the far corner of the room, followed by the sound of a steel boot cracking into bone. I winced as I walked in, my fingers running along the wall as I searched for the light switch I knew was there. I felt the smooth plastic under my fingers as I flipped the switch, the room illuminated by a harsh light.

"Johnny," I intoned as I took in the man hunched on the floor in the corner, his knees drawn up to his chest as he sobbed. "Hey, Johnny, look at me."

It was a difficult thing to ask of him, considering both of his eyes were swollen so much he couldn't open them, let alone see. I smiled as I leaned down next to him, my rage burning through my veins. "I just wanted to talk to you. Why have you been so hard to find?" My voice hid my anger well as I whispered, almost soothingly.

"Leo, I'm *sorry*—"

"Sorry? For what?" I asked as I leaned closer to him, my ear close to his mouth.

"For taking her. I was just following orders."

I nodded as I stroked his hair, matted with blood and sweat. "You broke into *my* house. You took *my* girl to a fucking mob pit, and you have the audacity to think an *apology* will cut it?"

There was silence as he sobbed, knowing he'd sealed his fate.

I met the eyes of Eugene, his captor, as he watched me. Eugene was a wiry man, with the strength you wouldn't assign to him or his frame—but he was an absolute psychopath. I knew that Johnny had suffered already despite the orders to leave that to me. I nodded at Eugene, who grinned sadistically as he pulled the silencer out of his pocket.

"Eugene here is just following orders, too. Good talking to you."

I glared at him with disgust as I stood, commanding Eugene to make it quick and as clean as possible. The last thing I needed was blood all over the fucking walls again. I climbed the stairs, my shoulders tense with anger.

Johnny had to pay for taking her.

Nothing was forgivable. I understood that Lucia had suffered, but that had nothing to do with Gretchen. I left the house, whistling as I skipped down the steps. The wind bit into me, icy fingers curling around my body as I jogged back to midtown. I checked my watch and smiled when I saw I hadn't wasted too much time with him, I'd make my appointment in plenty of time.

Excellent.

TWENTY-FOUR HOURS LATER

"How are you doing cuz?" The voice drawled down the line as I rubbed my brow with irritation.

What does this little shit want now?

I tightened my jaw as I sighed, preparing myself for his bullshit.

"What the fuck are you calling me for?" I growled down the phone as he tutted, making me want to smash his face into next week. Sadly, that was yet to be invented. As advanced as technology was, a punch couldn't travel over the airwaves.

Pity.

"I've just had breakfast with our beautiful Gretchen; she's like a fine wine, my man; she seems to get better with age. But I'm worried about her."

I tightened my grip around the phone as I closed my eyes, regret filling my chest at the thought of him anywhere near her.

Our Gretchen?

"You better be lying," I said through gritted teeth, my eyes scanning the airport for an update on my flight. They had delayed it by an hour, and I was getting restless.

Now I have this punk giving me grief.

"No, I mean this whole kidnapping shit," he waited, enjoying every moment of proving what he knew.

Fuck.

"Keep away from her. Do you understand me?" I muttered, my voice trembling with rage.

"But don't you think it's time you admitted I was right all those years ago? I'm better for her than you. She would have a simple life with me, marriage, pop out some babies—Fuck, I'd enjoy making those though—no kidnaps, no mob. Just a picket fence and warm apple pie."

I pulled the phone away and almost snapped it as I ended the call; my vision blurred with anger as I dialed Gretchen's number.

"Hey baby!" She sang down the phone as I tried to speak calmly.

"Why did you tell him, Gretchen?"

I heard her suck in her breath, and I knew then that she would never have told me about meeting him. My heart hurt, knowing she could betray me.

"Just like that, huh? I've been gone a day, and you are with him."

Her voice broke as she cried, and I held my head in my hands.

"Come back, Cal," she begged, sobbing. "I just needed someone to talk to—"

"Yeah? You've got *friends*, Gretchen. You've got *me*," I growled as I noticed my flight being announced over the speaker. "I have to go." I hung up, making my way to the departure gate. I was in two minds: whether to drown my sorrows at a bar or go back to that shitty town and blast my cousin's fucking head off. The latter idea appealed more than whiskey, so I boarded the plane. As I jammed my seatbelt on, a slender brunette slid into the seat beside me, her eyes running over me appreciatively.

"Wow, looks like I won the seat lottery," she smirked, her tongue sliding over her full lips as I studied her. She didn't turn me on like Gretchen did, and that annoyed me even more. I considered fucking her in the tiny toilet just to destroy every aspect of my relationship, but I decided against it.

"Lady, with all due respect, I don't wanna hear any more noise from your mouth," I muttered as she narrowed her eyes at me, her mouth forming a perfect 'O'.

Fucking women.

NOT AGAIN

GRETCHEN

I'm going to kill Luke.

I called an Uber and went straight to his house, banging on the door. I didn't care if his parents were in or not; I wanted to kill that piece of shit.

He opened the door lazily, his eyes lighting up when he saw me. I pushed him hard in the chest, causing him to fall back slightly as his expression changed to that of surprise.

"What the fuck?" He grunted as I pushed him again, rage brimming in my veins so much I was shaking.

Tears fell down my face as I pointed at him, my finger close to his face.

"You *fucking* bastard. You told Cal," I spat as he folded his arms in front of him. "You made me a promise, Luke."

"Yes, I told Cal. Because I'm worried about you." His face softened as he gazed at me.

"*Worried* about me? If you were so worried about me, you wouldn't have told Cal I had been with you when he had been out of town for one day!" I screeched, aware I sounded like a crazy person. I wanted to punch the smirk from his face as he rubbed his neck.

"Babe—"

"*Don't* fucking call me babe," I snapped.

"Okay, *Gretchen*, you need to understand something. I care about you a lot. It's *his* fault that you were in that situation. He deserves to be fucking *told.*" He stepped closer to me as I moved backward, holding up my hand in a way of warning him not to come any closer.

"You also need to ask yourself why you were with me the day after he left town."

I blinked, his words hitting me hard.

He thinks I'm still in love with him.

This was too much; the man was insane.

His blue eyes burned into mine as I struggled to speak, suddenly very aware that whatever I said made no difference; he wouldn't listen.

"I'm leaving." I turned on my heel and strode towards the door as he swiftly grabbed me, pressing me against the door.

He searched my eyes briefly before he pressed his mouth to mine. He drove his tongue into my mouth as I tried to shove him away, adrenaline giving me strength I didn't know I had.

I was no match for Luke, though.

"How fucking *dare* you!" I tried to push him away as he slammed me back against the door, his arms gripping me close to his body, his mouth near my ear.

"Do you know what? Maybe I'm done with fucking *asking*," he rasped as he smothered my mouth with his, pushing me against the wall as his hands roamed over my body.

I tried to push his hands off me, as he pushed his hands up my top, his fingers tugging at my waistband.

"Don't deny it, Gretchen, you want me," Luke smirked,

pressing his hardness against me as he tried to force his hand down my jeans.

"I don't *want you!"* I cried, bringing my knee up to his crotch hard.

He doubled over in pain as I shoved past him, running out of the door.

I gasped as I ran down the street, terrified he was going to chase me. I didn't look back as I ran, streets whizzing past me, adrenaline keeping me going. I slowed after a while, a stitch crippling my stomach as I pulled my phone out and called an Uber, my fingers trembling. I couldn't believe what Luke had just done. I couldn't believe I let myself fall for his shit, and he'd gotten worse as he grew older. My stomach turned as I remembered his hands all over my body, and I closed my eyes.

I just want Cal.

I dialed his number only to hear the voicemail, and I cried fat, salty tears that I wiped away with the back of my hand, still scanning behind me for Luke. I knew Cal would be *incensed*, and I feared he wouldn't come back for me. I half-hiccupped and half-snorted when I tried to breathe, my heart aching as my stomach churned.

Why did I meet up with Luke?

After what felt like an eternity, my cab arrived. I climbed in, slamming the door shut with relief. I tried Cal again and sent him a text.

GRETCHEN: I know you are mad, but please call me. I'm so sorry.

The cab reached my house, and I climbed out, exhaustion weighing me down suddenly. I made my way inside and made a beeline for my bedroom. My head hurt from thinking, and my heart ached from loving. I was furious at myself for doing this to Cal and me. Tonight could have gone down a darker path had I not gotten away. I shuddered, burying my head beneath the covers.

I needed Cal.

I cradled my phone as I fell asleep, waiting to hear it ring or beep with every fiber of my being. I woke later, the room now dark. Something had woken me up, but I couldn't figure out what. I grabbed my phone as I sat up to see no missed calls or texts. It was two in the morning.

"Hey." Came a voice from the corner of my room, and I shrieked, jumping from my bed as I ran for the door.

Arms circled me as I recognized the scent, my heart jumping from my chest.

"Cal?" I moaned as fresh tears fell down my face.

He's back!

"*Jesus*, baby, calm down. Where's the fucking light switch?" He mumbled as I flicked it on, revealing his intense green gaze, his eyes filled with concern.

"I'm so *sorry,* Cal," I cried as he held me, his hands in my hair as he kissed my head softly. I buried my face in his chest as I inhaled his scent, masculine and strong.

"Do you still have feelings for him?"

I pulled away and met his eyes as I shook my head wildly.

"Absolutely not. I just wanted to make things right, and instead, it went *very* fucking wrong."

He frowned as he watched me, his hands pulling me away from him slightly.

"How wrong?" He asked, his voice dangerously low.

I swallowed, my mouth dry. I couldn't tell him. I knew for a fact he would probably kill Luke, and I didn't want to carry the guilt around with me forever. Instead, I just explained that I felt terrible for betraying him and that I thought he wouldn't come back. That much was true, I just left out the fact Luke tried to assault me.

"I won't ever leave you again. You need to remember that I love you, Gretchen, *so much*."

I never grew tired of hearing him say that to me, but tonight, it seemed to hold more meaning. I wasn't sure why; maybe it was something to do with the fact I felt I had nearly lost him again, but something felt different.

He wiped my tears away with his thumb before kissing me softly on the lips, a smile on my face as he did. He had the ability to remove any stress from me just by being in the room. His sheer presence calmed me.

I climbed into bed and threw back the covers for him to join me as I yawned, feeling deliriously happy that he was back where he belonged—with me. I lifted so he could slide his arm beneath me, pulling me close to his bare chest as he sighed contentedly.

"I'm so glad you weren't gone long. I hate sleeping without you," I mumbled sleepily as he ran his fingers up and down my arm, the comfort it gave making my eyes close with delight.

"I'm sorry I had to go. But I'm back now. We'll talk more tomorrow, okay?"

I nodded as sleep took hold of me, my body racked with fatigue and emotion. In the arms of Cal, I slept deeply, unaware that for most of the night, he lay awake.

TRUTH
CAL

*T*he house was empty, except for him. I made my way into the house, walking boldly through the front door.

I'm family, after all.

Thuds from the bedroom above me told me where he was, yet I stood still briefly, listening to the sounds of the house.

Yes, Luke is definitely home alone.

As I walked up the stairs, I didn't bother to disguise my footsteps.

Let the fucker know I'm coming.

I pushed open his door as our eyes met; his filled with confusion, mine wild with anger.

He sat up from his push-up position on the floor and sat on his bed, scowling at me. "What the fuck do you want?" he snapped as I imagined snapping his neck. "Who let you in? Your name is scum in this house—"

"I'm going to ask you this *once*. What happened with Gretchen?" I said, my eyes locked on his.

He smirked at me, and I counted backward from ten, aware I would be useless to her in prison.

"You mean when she went out for breakfast with me or last night?"

I had learned a few tricks working for the mob. One was to always keep quiet if someone gave you information you didn't know already, like now, for example. I had no fucking idea what he was talking about, but pieces were sliding into place.

"She didn't tell you about last night, did she?" He smirked at me again, and this time, I moved towards him, comforted by the fear that flashed in his eyes.

"No. But now you're going to. Or I'm going to remove your fucking teeth one by one, Luke, and I'm not fucking playing." I reached into my pocket and felt the smooth metal of the pliers against my skin, and I smiled lazily.

"I'm not fucking scared of you, you prick," Luke scoffed as he squared up to me.

There it was: the invitation. Not that I needed one; he'd had this coming for years.

Luke lunged for me, thinking years of lifting weights would make him a match for me. It was more to do with balance and knowing your enemies. I moved swiftly, my fist connecting with his jaw with a loud crack as he fell backward into his bed, blood gushing from his mouth.

The silly bastard must've bit his tongue.

"What did you *do*, Luke?" I didn't want to hurt him again, but I would if he didn't start giving me some answers. He spat blood out onto the floor and looked up at me, realizing I meant business. I toyed with the idea of pulling a couple of teeth out to prove a point, but that was just cruel.

I'm not a thug.

"She came around shooting her mouth off. Things got carried away, one thing led to another—"

The color drained from my face as I grabbed him by the

throat, pulling him to his feet. The thought of this prick kissing my girl was enough to make me slit his throat. My temples throbbed as I tightened my grip on his throat, my eyes narrowed into slits.

"You fucking *what*?"

My voice didn't sound like mine, and I remembered how she jumped last night. I thought it was the after-effects of the kidnap, but it seemed my suspicions were right. She was on edge because of this cunt.

"Relax, she didn't go through with it; she kicked me in the balls and left." He confessed as his shoulders deflated.

I also knew Gretchen wouldn't just kick him in the balls for no reason. She must've had a reason, so I squeezed his throat a little tighter, enjoying watching him gasp for air. Just before he lost consciousness, I released him, and he fell to the floor in a heap. I kicked him hard in the balls, then the stomach, making sure the message was received loud and clear. "I don't want you to *ever* speak to either of us again. If you do, you better come and kill me before I fucking find you. Do you understand? This isn't a game, you little cunt." I glared at him as he whimpered on the floor, my blood boiling to the point of no control for leaving him alive.

I couldn't go around killing people, not all the time anyway. I fucking hated him, though, and I hesitated at the doorway as he apologized.

"Your actions speak louder than your words. Don't fucking insult me, you piece of shit. Keep the fuck away from us." I walked away then before I did something I would regret. I lit a cigarette as I stood outside, trying to calm myself down before I saw Gretchen again. She was already a bag of nerves; she didn't need to see me all fired up.

Inhale, exhale.
Repeat.

SURPRISE
GRETCHEN

"Three more weeks and we will be back in New York." I shielded my eyes from the sun as I turned to look at Cal, his hand on the steering wheel as he drove. I felt the familiar lurch in my stomach as he turned and smiled at me before lacing his fingers with mine.

"I thought you hated New York."

"It's not too bad with you in it. I'm happy wherever you are, baby."

I sighed happily as I rested my head on my hand, feeling tiredness wash over me. I yawned as he glanced at me, a frown on his face.

"You can't possibly still be tired. All we've done is sleep."

I stuck my tongue out at him, and he laughed in response.

"Alright, it's not *all* we have done," he smirked as the visions of the past week clearly filled his mind.

Cal had surprised me with a trip to the coast, insisting we needed some time alone by the sea. It had been amazing, but now we were driving back to my parents. I was sad that we had to go soon, but after the fiasco with Luke, I was secretly relieved.

Luke.

If Cal ever found out what he had done to me that night—what he had *tried* to do—I shuddered at the thought. But I hadn't heard from him since, and Cal promised he wasn't leaving my side whilst we were here.

I stared at the scenery as it changed from barren to green, a road sign informing us we were now in familiar territory. I closed my eyes, the hum of the car beneath me rocking me into sleepy security as Cal drove steadily.

"*Raven.*"

His voice made me stir as I looked at him through sleepy eyes. I sat up, becoming aware that the car had stopped, blinking slowly when I realized we were parked at my parents.

I'd slept all the way home.

"Maybe you need some vitamins or something. It's not normal to sleep that much." Cal studied me through concerned eyes as I sat up, tiredness still holding me prisoner.

"My period is overdue. That's all."

He nodded as he swung open his door, pulling our bags out of the back seat. "Go and have a bath, babe. Do you need anything?" He called as I walked up the steps, turning to shake my head.

I walked into the empty house, the familiar scent of home greeting me. A bath sounded like a good idea, so I made my way upstairs and began running one.

I heard Cal's voice echoing through the hallway as he spoke on the phone, hearing his delicious laugh as he thanked whoever it was, promising he would see them soon. I felt a stab of jealousy as I listened, annoyed he was speaking quietly now.

"Yeah, do that. Send it to me. Thanks so much, Beth, you're amazing."

I stood bolt upright, my fingers gripping the stair rail as he walked back out to the car.

Who the fuck is Beth?

I realized I was shaking with jealousy, a rage racing through my body like fire. What was she sending? Why was she *amazing?*

I stepped back, aware that my bath was running.

I need to check his phone.

If I asked him, he would never admit it, but I knew he was hiding something from me.

Something important.

I usually turned a blind eye to his work at his request. He insisted the less I knew, the better and safer it was for me. But now I just felt stupid. I heard his feet on the stairs, and I dashed into the bathroom, not wanting him to find me lurking on the stairs.

"Babe. I'm going to grab us some food because there's nothing in. I thought we could cook for your parents tonight. I can do it if you don't feel up to it?" He stood in the doorway then, his hands holding on to the top of the frame, exposing his taut stomach. He frowned as he gazed at me, his deep stare boring into my soul. "Gretchen, what's wrong?"

Despite my intentions, the words slipped out of my mouth in an angry snarl. "Who the *fuck* is Beth?!"

I noticed the color drain from his face as my heart raced, causing me to hold onto the sink.

"What?" he whispered in disbelief as I nodded at him.

"Answer me! Who the fuck is Beth?"

I stood close to him now, unable to imagine that this man could hurt me this way. But in his eyes, I saw the secret, and I sucked in a breath.

He closed his eyes as he exhaled, a look of frustration on his face.

"If I say nothing and no one, will you leave it?" His tone was pleading as I laughed harshly.

"Absolutely fucking not! Are you fucking her?! Is that why you went back to New York?" I was shaking as I asked him, visions of him with some scantily clad whore burning through my retinas.

I'll kill her. Then him.

He raised his eyebrows as he gaped at me in stunned silence before I fixed him with a deadly gaze.

"You need to fucking answer me right *now*, Cal Fallon, before I rip your balls off and ram them down your throat."

To my horror, he began to laugh, and I shoved him in the chest angrily.

"I'm not fucking anyone else, princess, come on! I swear, it's nothing like that."

I folded my arms as I waited. He sighed as he put his hands on my shoulders, which I shrugged off angrily. "I'm waiting."

"You're going to ruin the surprise," he said quietly.

"Oh, I'm surprised, alright. Spit it out, Cal."

"I'm taking you away for your birthday. Beth is the travel agent, and she's sending the tickets over to my email as we speak. Enjoy your bath." He turned and walked away, disappointment on his face as I stared after him with a mixture of disbelief and regret.

Oh, fuck.

SLEEP

GRETCHEN

"*Y*ou really don't trust me, huh?"

I shifted from one foot to the other, squirming under his gaze. How could I possibly explain my overreaction? My cheeks burned as he slid his phone over the table to me, opening his hands out.

"Read the email, if it puts your mind at rest. Her name is there, her contact number too, if you want to call her." He sounded wounded, his voice full of disappointment. I shook my head, not wanting to further spoil the surprise. "Gretchen, have I ever given you a reason to doubt me?"

I chewed on my lip as I considered his question. "Well—"

"*Seriously*?" He interrupted, his hands on the back of the chair as he frowned at me.

I swallowed and shook my head no.

No, he hasn't.

"I'm sorry. I just heard you speaking to another woman and—"

I looked up to see a smile playing on his lips as I struggled to finish the sentence.

"I just didn't like it. *Argh*, now I've ruined my surprise." I folded my arms as he walked around the table, pulling my arms apart and wrapping them around his waist.

"This isn't like you. You know no other woman compares to you." He kissed me softly and I sank into his arms gratefully.

"I'm so sorry," I mumbled into his chest as he rubbed my back tenderly.

"It's fine, just act surprised when it happens," he growled into my ear as I giggled. "How was your bath?"

"Angry and short," I grumbled as I yawned again. "I'm going to lie down for a while, are you coming with me?"

"You sleep, babe. I'm going to go get some food to cook for us all, do you want anything?"

I shook my head as I walked up the stairs, my head suddenly feeling too heavy for my shoulders.

What the hell is wrong with me?

Snapping at Cal, falling to sleep constantly, now headaches.

I frowned when I realized I had barely eaten that day. It dawned on me that I was probably dehydrated and hungry. I mentally checked in with my stomach, my brain showcasing food for it like a damn buffet whilst it churned in protest. Maybe I was getting ill. I pulled back the duvet as I slid between the sheets, my limbs embracing the coolness of the bed as my eyelids dropped.

OH...

GRETCHEN

*T*he flight back to New York was relatively painless. Even Cal managed to doze most of the way back, which gave me the opportunity to reflect on the summer. I realized that I had grown so much in the time away from my childhood home, unable to believe that I had once thought I was going to marry Luke and spend my life in that little town without ever really wanting anything more.

Luke.

Even thinking his name made my skin crawl. I couldn't help but pity him, I had hoped he would have changed a little in the time I'd been gone. But he was still a creep, playing football and hanging out at The Lounge. He lacked ambition but had buckets full of sleaze—what a combination.

I stole a glance at Cal, and my heart physically ached with the love I felt for him. The difference between Cal and Luke was astounding—but then again, the difference between Cal and any man was. I didn't need to travel the world to know there would be no one like him, no one who could look at me the way he did, make me feel like I was the only woman in the world like he did.

I couldn't imagine my life without him, and *that* terrified me.

His eyelids fluttered as the pilot announced our descent into New York, and I was greeted by those captivating green eyes.

"Did I really fall asleep on a plane?" He mumbled in disbelief as I littered his face with soft kisses.

"You did. You slept like a baby."

He yawned as he stretched, the cabin stewardess pausing by our seats to remind us to wear our seatbelts. I was used to the effect he had on women, the way their eyes widened at his breathtaking good looks, the way they would struggle to compose themselves when he shot them that panty-dropping smile. But this one was greedy, her professionalism slipping as she gazed at him openly, her eyes locked onto his body until he finished stretching.

"Sir, your seatbelt."

He nodded as he waved her away with disinterest. "Yeah, lady, I know. But if this plane comes crashing down, do you really think this sliver of fabric will keep me alive?"

I bit back a smile as a flash of annoyance crept into her doll-like face. "I'm just doing my job, Sir."

He nodded without speaking, turning to me. "How are you feeling?" He murmured against my hair as he kissed my head softly.

"Tired?" I offered with exasperation as he grimaced.

"Go and see a doctor. It's not normal to feel this tired for weeks. Tell him you're losing interest in your boyfriend, too," he teased as I turned to look at him, kissing his mouth before he could say anything more.

"Shut up, Mr. Fallon."

He grinned as the plane began to pick up speed, his hands now gripping the side of the seat so hard his knuckles turned white. I laced my fingers over his as the pilot executed a near-perfect landing, and I turned to see the relief in Cal's eyes.

"Thank *fuck,* that's over."

"I've missed our bed so much," I groaned as he sent me a wicked look.

"The three of us will reunite shortly."

"Do you ever think about anything else?" I laughed as we left the plane, the wind whipping my hair around my face.

"I think about you in every capacity. All of the time," he said seriously as we entered the terminal building. I felt a shiver of delight at his words as we made it through customs unscathed. I was a U.S. citizen on an internal flight, yet I still felt like a criminal under the suspicious gaze of the border officers.

As we waited for our luggage, I felt a wave of nausea overtake me as I searched for the toilets with desperation.

"I need the toilet," I managed to get out before racing to the nearest restroom, which happened to be an accessible one. I didn't have time to consider that as I reached the toilet bowl, emptying my stomach contents into it. I gasped as I retched, aware that something was wrong with me. I wiped my mouth as I stood, listing my symptoms in my head. I washed my face in the sink, noticing how pale I looked.

Tiredness...

Irritated all the time...

I must be due on my period soon. But that had never made me sick before.

Sickness...

I stared at my reflection as it hit me.

Where was my period?

I closed my eyes and jumped when someone tried the handle of the door, opening to reveal Cal.

"Are you alright? You've been in here a while—"

"I think I'm pregnant," I whispered as his eyes met mine slowly.

"What?" His voice was low as he dropped the bags he was holding onto the floor beside him.

I didn't speak, but to my horror, I began to cry.

"Hey, Raven, don't cry." He strode over to me, taking me in his arms.

"I can't remember when I had my last period and—"

"Sssh. It's okay. Let's just get out of the airport, then we can talk okay? We've got this baby, don't worry," he said soothingly as he kissed me softly.

I nodded as I sniffed, watching as he gathered our belongings onto a nearby cart. He slid his arm around me protectively as he guided me out of the airport and towards a waiting cab, barking an address at the driver, who scurried to the driver's seat as Cal put our luggage into the trunk.

I lay against him as we drove, aware that we were nearing home. Cal paid the driver as he handed me the keys to our home, watching me carefully.

"Don't carry anything," he ordered as I leaned down to drag my suitcase.

"*Cal*," I sighed as he looked at me sternly, and I knew better than to argue.

I walked in, the familiar smell of our house greeting me as I made a beeline for the kitchen, grabbing the wall calendar. I searched with my finger until I saw the little red dot that showed my period's due date.

Cal stood in the doorway, watching me intently.

"I've missed my period," I whispered as my eyes widened, realizing it was more than that.

Being away distracted me; how did I not remember?!

"*Fuck*. I've missed two."

WHATEVER IS RIGHT.
GRETCHEN

"You need to keep calm, my love." Cal rubbed my knee reassuringly as my leg jigged with nerves, my eyes glued to the black screen above the reception, waiting for my name to scroll along in red pixels.

I was sweating and chewing on my lip, yet Cal was an oasis of calm.

He was flicking through a home magazine, turning it this way and that to assess the photographs with interest.

I felt bile rise in my throat, and I sipped my water, praying that I would be seen soon.

Suddenly, there was a soft ping, and there was my name, Miss Gretchen Red, swirling on the screen as I felt dizzy with fear.

"Do you want me to come in with you?" He asked, and I shook my head.

"I'll be fine."

"I'm right here," he said, kissing my hand as I nodded numbly, walking down the pale corridor to the room shown on the screen.

I knocked softly out of courtesy and heard a firm voice call me in. I pushed open the door and smiled while my legs felt like jelly.

The doctor was in her fifties, soft grey hair curled under her chin as she glanced at me with kind eyes. "Hi, Gretchen. What can I do for you today?"

I swallowed and held out my first urine of the day bottle, my hands shaking. "I have missed two periods. I think I may be pregnant," I whispered as she nodded, turning back to the screen.

"Okay, what was the date of your last period?"

I answered her questions robotically as she took the sample, dipping a thin stick into it and then placing it on top whilst she stood watching it, her hands on her hips.

I stared at the floor, feeling about ten years old suddenly, sitting in the headteacher's office about to be given a dressing down.

"You are indeed pregnant."

I closed my eyes as I heard her shuffling over to the desk, tapping into her computer as she glanced at me.

"Is this good news for you?" She smiled kindly as I looked at her in shock.

"I'm not entirely sure how I feel."

She held her hand up as she turned a calendar in her hands, then looked up at me.

"That's an entirely normal reaction. From my calculations, you are approximately eight weeks pregnant. A scan will confirm that, though, but we don't offer them until twelve weeks. Are you in a relationship?"

"I am, yes. He's in the waiting room."

She nodded as she handed me some leaflets, her eyes crinkling as she smiled. "Okay, well, you will receive an appointment from the obstetrician when you reach twelve weeks. If you need any further information from us just call. Is there anything you want to ask now?"

I shook my head as she smiled.

"Okay, then, congratulations."

I turned and walked out of the door, my heart in my throat as I walked back down the corridor.

I was pregnant? I was going to be a mommy?

Cal had his hands laced behind his head, jumping up when he saw me.

"Are you okay?" He asked gruffly, and I nodded, pulling him to the exit.

When we got outside, I began to cry, and his eyes filled with worry.

"Baby, whatever the doctor said, we can get through it. I swear. Come here." He held me in his arms, and I cried before pulling away from him, looking up into his eyes, my heart thumping in my throat.

"You're going to be a daddy, Cal."

He blinked, a broad smile spreading over his face. "No *fucking* way."

I nodded as his eyes searched mine anxiously.

"Are you happy? Whatever you want—" He began his supportive spiel, which I interrupted suddenly, kissing his mouth.

"I want it. I'm in shock, but Cal, a mini us."

Suddenly, I felt the floor disappear from beneath my feet as he lifted me into the air, swirling me around.

"Oh baby, I'm so fucking happy right now, you've got no idea."

I bit my lip as our lips met, a new feeling enveloping me as I saw his eyes gazing at me like they did the first time he saw me.

"I couldn't wish for anyone better than you to be a mother to my child."

I felt tears fill my eyes again as he pulled me close, kissing my head as his arms circled me protectively.

"The baby is due in seven months, Cal! What am I going to do about school?" I chewed on my fingernail as he sighed, guiding me towards his car.

"We'll speak with the college and see what your options are. What are you thinking of doing?"

I couldn't think; my head was too busy with images of our unborn child.

Would they have my eyes or Cal's?

"Oh *God*, our parents…" I groaned, but he smiled, almost as though he had already thought it through.

"I need to be honest. I have booked to take you away to Paris. I'm not entirely sure that it's the best idea, considering how ill you have been. I'd rather not take you on a flight over the Atlantic to a foreign country." He grimaced as he thought about it, his eyes filled with anxiety.

My heart swelled with love for him, and I reached for his hand. "You're so romantic! *Paris*?! For my birthday?"

His lips kissed my hand softly, his green eyes piercing into mine and making my skin heat up instantly. "You'll have many more birthdays. I'll take you and our baby around the world if that's what you want." His hands fell to my stomach, caressing it softly.

I didn't think I could have felt more love for him than I did right then, and I threw my arms around him.

"Shall we get you home?" He opened the car door and gazed at me as I climbed in gingerly, suddenly aware I was carrying a tiny human in my womb. He shut the door carefully before making his way to the driver's side, climbing in beside me and grinning inanely at me. "I'm so fucking *happy*, Raven. I want to go and buy a whole new nursery for the little bean."

"*Bean*?" I laughed as he drove, his hand on my thigh lovingly.

"Yeah, it's like the size of a kidney bean. I looked it up last night whilst you were sleeping." He looked over at me and blushed as I laughed.

"Seriously?"

"Yeah, you said you had missed two periods, so I guessed you were about two months pregnant. Either that or a whole host of other terrifying things that could be wrong with you." His jaw clenched as I watched him drive, his thumb now running circles on my thigh.

"Is our house big enough for a baby? Is it in the right area?" I suddenly panicked at the thought of being a mother in New York. I had visions of me hauling a screaming baby onto the subway whilst sweating buckets, everyone sneering at how bad a mother I was.

A smile played at his lips as he glanced at me, before focusing back on the road.

"Listen to me, Gretchen. You and this baby will want for *nothing*. Anything you want or need, you've got it. Just tell me."

"What if it means no more mafia stuff?" I blurted out, biting my lip as his eyes hardened, his posture deflating as he let out a sigh.

He pushed his hair back in irritation before answering me. "Whatever is right for us. As a family."

Relief coursed through me as we sat in traffic, my eyes darting around the streets surrounding us, looking for babies and mothers. Cal would be as good as his word, that I knew. I just also knew that there was a side to him that I was either going to have to accept that I didn't know it or decide if he needed to change it.

If that was even possible.

ANYTHING
CAL

I'm going to be a daddy.

I had always known I'd want a family at some point, but I didn't expect it to be so soon. I couldn't be happier, though; the most incredible woman in the world was going to have my child.

I watched Gretchen sleep, her full lips parted slightly as she breathed, her chest rising and falling with a steady rhythm. She was so pale though, and it was killing me seeing her suffer through something that was supposed to be natural. She didn't want anyone to know until the scan proved that everything was okay, which meant she didn't have any other women to talk to. I wanted her to tell her mother at least, but she was stubborn. My eyes trailed down her chest to her exposed stomach, my chest aching with love and adoration for what was growing in there. I stood and quietly walked to the window, staring out at the city.

I don't want our child growing up here.

I didn't want our child to be a target for all of those who had issues with me—and there were many.

The only reason I was here was because of Gretchen and

her studies, but she could study somewhere else if she wanted to. I glanced back over at her, the moonlight from the window falling on her in the darkness, illuminating her like an angel.

Too much had happened to her already.

If it was up to me, she would be on bed rest for the rest of her pregnancy. She'd addressed my line of work a few weeks ago, and at the time, I was filled with shame. This woman deserved an honest man, who worked his fingers to the bone to put food on the table, not someone who pulled the trigger on a gun when someone needed to pay a debt.

It was this city. When I was here, this is what I did. She deserved better.

"Cal?" Her soft voice broke into my tormented thoughts, as I turned to see her rubbing her eyes sleepily.

"Go back to sleep, baby; it's early." I made my way over to the bed as she yawned, looking at me with those beautiful eyes. She still gave me those damn butterflies in my stomach, and that's how I had known she was *The One*. Many girls were beautiful, and kind. Most are great in bed too, and eager to please.

But Gretchen was different. She made me want to be a better man.

"I'm hungry," she pouted, and I laughed.

"At three a.m.?" I couldn't hide the disbelief in my voice as she nodded enthusiastically.

"Yup. Bean must be hungry."

I leaned over her, my lips brushing against the soft skin of her tummy as I addressed Bean. "What would Bean like? Waking mommy up for food and all."

"Bacon," she declared, her hands on my hair as I looked at her in surprise.

"Bacon at three a.m. Okay, Bean, I'm going to cook some bacon. Anything Mommy wants, Mommy gets." I pushed up onto my forearms as she held her hands out, pulling me into an embrace.

"Thank you."

I kissed her tenderly as her tummy rumbled.

Our eyes met and I did a mock salute before climbing off the bed, pulling my thin hoodie over my head as she watched me hungrily.

"Then can I have you for dessert?" She bit her lip as I winked at her.

"As I said, anything you want."

INFINITE
GRETCHEN

*T*he craving for coffee was ridiculous. I pushed open the doors of Starbucks, my nostrils inhaling the intoxicating scent.

Cal wouldn't approve, but I'd done my research.

I can have a small coffee.

I almost ran to the barista who blinked at me in surprise as my order tumbled from my mouth hungrily. I spied the lemon muffin and demanded one of those, too. I paid and went to sit at a table by the window, feeling giddy that I was finally going to get my caffeine fix. The nausea was starting to fade now, but cravings were kicking in big time.

My phone vibrated on the table and I saw Cal's name with a message asking where I was. I considered lying for a moment as I wondered where I could say I was. The barista called my name and I stood eagerly, only to see someone standing in my way.

Someone heavenly. Who smelled amazing.

"You didn't reply to my text," he said softly as he turned to get the coffee and muffin from the gazing barista.

"*Cal*," I squeaked as he examined my cup.

"Decaf?"

I shifted on my feet as I snatched it from him, holding it to my chest protectively.

"It's small," I snapped defensively, as he chuckled softly.

"But strong. Like you." He guided me back to my table, sitting in front of me as he watched me carefully.

"I'm *not* a Faberge egg."

"You're pregnant with my child, in New York City. Yes, you are."

My eyes met his then and my heart swelled with love for him. Suddenly, I frowned.

"Why are you here, though? You're always busy." I pushed the muffin into my mouth eagerly as the citrus flavors exploded on my tongue. Why had I not had one of these daily prior to pregnancy? It was delicious.

"Because I've considered your request." He spoke quietly, his eyes on me whilst I swallowed, sipping the coffee and shivering with delight.

"Oh, my God, that's so good."

He folded his arms as he watched me with interest. "Oh? Better than sex?" He asked innocently as I laughed in response.

"Almost?" I offered as he scoffed, clearly offended.

"Bullshit."

I laughed as he ran his hand through his hair.

"Baby, listen. I've been thinking."

My breath caught in my throat as he studied me.

"How do you feel about moving back to Winterburg? I could find work locally; you'll be close to your family. It's up to you entirely; I know we moved here so you could study—"

"Yes," I said instantly, tears welling up in my eyes. "I would love to move back there with you. It would be a whole different existence for you though, Cal. I can go back to school there after the baby is born." I shrugged, having already done my research. I could study therapy anywhere, but New York had the best program. I could graduate with a good enough grade to allow me to finish studying when our child was born. It would mean squeezing my lectures into fewer days, but my tutor had been fantastic.

"We have the scan soon." Cal smiled, and I smiled back.

"Three days until we get to see Bean."

"Do you want to move? If so, when? I don't want you traveling when you are really pregnant. I don't want you in New York City pregnant *period*, to be honest."

I stared at him as I ran a hand over my stomach. He was right, as always. I had been kidnapped barely three months ago. But could he really give up the life he was accustomed to for me? He was never without money, and I didn't work. Not yet. I voiced these concerns to him, and he grabbed both my hands in his.

"You and this child are *everything* I have in this world. Money isn't an issue; I have a lot of it. I just won't be making it illegally anymore. I've got the sale from the house so I can buy us a home easily. Don't worry. I'll get work locally; I've got *all* kinds of skills."

Our eyes met and I realized he meant every word. He was going to change his ways, and I couldn't wait for us to begin our new life together.

But first, I needed to break the news to my parents.

SONOGRAPHY
GRETCHEN

"*T*he gel is a little cold, so I do apologize." The lady smiled kindly as she squirted the gel onto my bare stomach as I inhaled sharply.

Jesus!

It was like ice, was there really any need for it to be so cold?!

Don't they know they are putting it on pregnant mothers not using it in a recipe?

The sonographer gently pushed down on my lower stomach with a probe, the TV screen beside us flickering into life. It was difficult to make sense of it at first, and I realized I wasn't even breathing as she used a finger to point at the screen.

"This is your uterus, and this area is the amniotic sac where your baby is forming." She was pointing to a white rim around a clear center, whilst the rest of the screen was a grainy black-and-white image. "*This* is your baby."

My eyes focused on the center, my heart pounding as I recognized the circular head and a tiny body attached to it.

Cal squeezed my hand as I gazed at the screen in wonder.

"Everything looks as it should be, and I am just going to measure the little one to see how far along you are for sure." She zoomed in, clicking on various buttons until she nodded with satisfaction.

"You are approximately thirteen weeks, which would make your due date around March. Your obstetrician may be able to give you a more exact date. You can clean the gel from your stomach now. You will have another scan in about seven weeks which may be able to tell you the sex of the baby, should you want to know."

She printed us a couple of scan photos and I dabbed at my stomach, turning to see Cal sitting, completely stunned. He was staring at the photo, and I saw him gulp, a lump in his throat.

"Finally, we meet. Hello, Bean. *Wow*, Gretchen." He flickered his eyes over to me, and I blinked back tears. Panic flashed over his face as I grabbed his hand in reassurance.

"Happy tears, Cal."

He nodded as I pulled my top back down and swung my legs down, standing slowly.

I was starting to show a tiny bit, but I must confess I was more excited than ever at the idea of having a large baby bump.

We left the hospital, and Cal drove us to a little Italian restaurant we both loved. he even ordered me a coffee without me asking. I ordered the spaghetti carbonara with extra cheese and a side of garlic bread, and Cal watched me in awe.

"What?" I smiled as he gazed at me.

"I just really love you right now. I can't believe our baby is in your tummy, listening to us. I want us to go and view some houses soon and stay with your parents until we find one. We need to leave New York, honey."

I nodded sadly. I'd become so fond of the city, despite having recently only spent time with Cal, I had made some friends.

My parents were shocked but elated when we told them about the baby, but more so, they were ecstatic we would be moving back to Winterburg. They had offered for us to stay with them until we bought our house for when the baby was born.

My stomach lurched when I thought about becoming a mother, but I had no real fear. I would be bringing our child into the world at the same hospital I was born in myself, going to the same schools I had, growing up in the same town I did. I wanted that for them; my childhood was idyllic.

"Have you considered names?" Cal asked, his eyes flickering with amusement. I had already gone through about a hundred baby name websites and still was no closer to choosing one for either sex.

"I can't decide on any. What about you?"

"If it's a girl, she will need a plain name like Margaret. Or Beryl. She won't need an attractive one." He scowled as I suppressed a giggle.

I would really feel for Bean if it was a girl.

"I like names like Grey, Thor, and Theo for a boy," he continued.

I scrunched my nose up and shook my head.

This is going to be hard work.

Luckily, we had six months to argue about it.

The food came and we both dove in, unable to speak with how delicious the food was. When we had finished, Cal turned to me.

"I think we should spend your birthday in Winterburg. Shall we move out next week? I can have things shipped over to us, so I'm not concerned about that. Then we can get looking for our forever home."

I nodded enthusiastically, dragging my hair into a loose bun on my head as I yawned.

"You still take my breath away, Gretchen. The most beautiful girl I've ever laid eyes on. Shall we get you home?" He signaled for the bill, and I sank back happily into my chair.

"Cal, are we sticking with Cal or Leo? You said you wanted me to call you Leo, but you're always gonna be Cal to me," I shrugged, and he smiled.

"Cal Fallon or Leo Cape. It's still me, whichever way you look at it. But I think I'm going to stick with Cal. My old name has too much trauma attached to it." His eyes turned dark as he gazed behind me as though peering into a memory. He paid the bill, and we left, walking to his car.

The tiredness was overtaking me now, my shoulders slumped as I tried to keep my eyes open. I slid into the seat and watched as a huge truck drove by with a holiday promoted on the side.

"Summer," I mused aloud as Cal studied me.

"What?"

"Summer. It's a nice name."

He nodded as he smiled.

"Whatever you say, darling. Your choice. Always."

BUSINESS
CAL

"So, you're leaving us, boss?" Eugene studied me, his black eyes darting around as he shifted uneasily.

I sighed as I slid the whiskey glass towards him, watching as he threw it down his throat with incredible speed. Sometimes, I wondered how this man was still alive; if he wasn't drinking, he was smoking. He was always angry, which is what made him a brilliant executioner, I guess.

"You've got Carl. He will take over from me. You'll be fine," I tried to reassure him, and he nodded thoughtfully.

"So, you're gonna leave just like that? What's the Don say?"

I lifted my eyes to him then as Mark and Teddy glanced at each other nervously. I knew that Eugene would be the nosey bastard he always had been, but he was right to ask.

Just not respectful.

I decided not to dignify it with an answer, my glare telling him to shut the fuck up. I rubbed my chin as I stood up, nodding at Carl who sat on the chair in the corner of the room smoking, watching me intently. He had wanted my job for as long as I could remember, so I knew he was more than happy with the cards he was being dealt. Unfortunately for the others, he had even less tolerance than me. He nodded back at me as I left the room, knowing my next conversation wouldn't be a pleasant one.

The Don was informally known as Paul Gasio, a man with such charm that he could smooth-talk a man into swallowing his own tongue.

I'm not kidding, he fucking had once.

I guess the alternative was too much.

I waited outside his room for about twenty minutes, until a man walked out with soulless eyes. People came to ask the Don for favors of all kinds, and many were in debt to him. He called me in with a deep Italian accent which had thickened from a recent visit to Sicily.

"Leonardo. Sit down."

I sat on the hard leather chair, my eyes meeting his as he studied me carefully. He looked like you would expect him to —slicked black hair and a thin mustache on his tanned face. His eyes were dark, and his tone intrigued. "I hear you are going to be a father soon. There is no greater gift than children, Leonardo. I have four boys. They keep me young." He smiled as he lit a cigar, leaning back on his chair as he waited.

"Indeed, I will be. That's why I am here." I cleared my throat as I braced myself for the questions, but he waved his hand dismissively.

"You came to me in a strange way. You had avenged a family member, and I respected that. You work hard, follow commands, and execute them seamlessly. Yet you want to be a picket fence guy, no? You want to be at the football games, the charity cookie sales?" He raised his eyebrow at me, and I remained very still.

"Carl is in your shoes already. That doesn't concern me. Everyone is replaceable," he said simply as I waited for him to finish. He took a drag on his cigar as he gazed at me, exhaling the thick smoke slowly. "But you did go into witness protection, did you not? Given a different name to that your mother gave you?"

I nodded, dread causing the knot in my stomach to tighten as he dragged on his cigar again while eyeing me. His long fingers tapped on the desk as he considered his next words, and I refused to break eye contact with him.

"I did. Because I was innocent, I didn't hurt that girl at all," I stated, the facts tumbling out of my mouth.

"No, that is true. You avenged her. I respect that, as I said earlier," he repeated slowly. "However, the fact remains, people don't just *leave* the family, you understand? If they do, it's because they are fucking useless or they leave in a body bag. We have too many secrets to be fucking letting people work out notice periods." He chuckled softly as I felt my jaw clench.

"So, you're gonna kill me?" I demanded, the anger clear in my voice. I should have felt ice-cold fear at this exact moment, but I didn't. However, when he narrowed his eyes at me, I lost all sense of bravado.

"Don't be fucking stupid, kid. Don't ever raise your voice to me again. *Capisce*?"

"I didn't mean to offend you."

He nodded, watching me carefully. "I've considered this prior to you coming in here today. You're a good kid, and we all like you. You can be with your family. But let me tell you, if you ever leak anything about our business, Leonardo, you will not have a family or a heart to love them with."

I nodded slowly, keeping my anger in check. He was threatening my family, but this was business. "So, go. As you know, you are no longer under my protection; certain people may wish to...seek you out. Always watch your back. Oh, and leave your gun on the way out. You can go now."

I stood, offering my hand out to him, and he shook it, not taking his eyes off of me.

"I'd leave this city as soon as you can. People are like fucking vultures. God bless." He turned away from me, the conversation clearly over.

I didn't know if he meant it, but there was only one way to find out.

Make it out of New York alive.

EPILOGUE
CAL

"*D*addy, you *promised*!" It was that voice again. The one that wrapped me around her little finger by putting on the damsel-in-distress tone.

I sighed as I wiped my brow, fully aware from her giggle that I had just wiped oil over my face. "You laughing at your old man, kiddo?"

"Yup. *Please* can we get ice cream now?" Summer whined as I closed the lid of the truck, admitting defeat.

I turned as I heard the car pulling onto the drive, a smile on my face as I waited to greet the love of my life. She didn't disappoint.

"Mr. Fallon, get those greasy hands over here and help me get these bags inside. Hey baby girl, have you been good for Daddy?" Gretchen leaned down to drop a kiss on her head as she passed, arms full of groceries. I went to help her, but she scolded me, telling me to get the other bags.

"Caleb wasn't good, was he Daddy?"

"Summer, what have I told you about snitches?" I teased as I followed Gretchen to the house, Summer at my heels.

She pouted at me and sighed. "Snitches get stitches."

"Yeah, so shut up, *Summer*," drawled Caleb, pushing open the screen door as he glared at his sister.

They were twins but couldn't have looked more different. Caleb had blonde hair and deep green eyes that he clearly inherited from me, whilst Summer had chocolate brown curls and blue eyes. We joked that Summer was added last minute, being the smaller twin and a complete surprise at the second scan.

"*Enough*. Inside," I commanded as we walked into the open-plan kitchen where Gretchen was unpacking the bags.

"Daddy..."

"Raven, I've got to take this little lady for some ice cream. She's clearly experiencing severe withdrawal. It's been what, a day since you last had ice cream, squirt?" I ruffled her silky hair as she held her arms up to me, her tiny frame as light as a feather in my arms as I hoisted her up.

"Why'd you call Mommy *Raven*?" She asked, her eyes wide as she studied me.

I gazed at my wife as she glanced at me over her shoulder, a smile playing on her lips. The swell of her belly was now becoming obvious, and my heart skipped a beat.

"I don't know, kid. I just do. Go get your shoes. Caleb, you want ice cream?"

She slid down my leg as she ran to get her shoes, pushing past her brother who glared at her.

"Nope."

"Where's your manners, young man? "I leaned down, my hands on my knees as I gazed into a pint-sized version of myself.

He thrust his chin up to me and smirked. "Someone needs to stay and look after Mom."

I kissed his forehead to his disgust as I smiled at him. "Yeah? You got everything you need there?" I nodded behind him to where he had the Avengers lined up ready for battle. He nodded seriously as he patted my back.

"I've got this, Dad. You go get ice cream."

Laughter burst from Gretchen's mouth as she gazed at us lovingly. "He's a mini you."

"*Daddy*!" Yelled an impatient Summer from the doorway.

"She's—" I began as Gretchen held her hand up.

"Nothing like me. She's a diva. Go get our diva some ice cream."

I strode over to her, taking her into my arms as my hands slid around her stomach. "How's my littlest bean?"

I kissed her throat as Caleb made sick sounds from the living room. I smirked at him, proud that he got to see his parents in love. I hoped one day he would appreciate it.

"Fine. Busy kicking a soccer ball around today." She placed my hand on her stomach, and I waited patiently before I felt a tiny foot against the palm of my hand.

"He has quite the kick."

"She does."

I rolled my eyes as I kissed her again, allowing her to win the eternal argument about who was right about the sex of the baby.

"*Daddy*!"

I chuckled softly as I reluctantly pulled away from my kryptonite, pointing a finger at Caleb. "Look after your Mama."

He grabbed Captain America and forced the toy arm into a salute.

"Coming, baby girl," I called as I grabbed my truck keys and, of course, my wallet. A man didn't get to have kids and a wife and not need his damn wallet twenty-four hours a day.

Summer stood at the doorway, hands on her hips as she glared at me. "You're late."

"My bad, baby. An extra scoop of ice cream coming up."

She ran impatiently out the door, her curls bouncing as she reached the truck, her eyes narrowing as she saw a bike on the drive, blocking our exit. I followed her gaze to see a boy of about seven years old if that. He was inspecting his knee, which was oozing with blood, having clearly fallen off his bike.

"Can you please move?" Summer asked, a cold tone to her voice. Nothing stood between her and ice cream. She was five, and she was fucking relentless. I can't imagine her in ten years.

"Summer, where are your manners?" I said sharply as she folded her arms in irritation.

That's right, my five-year-old does that. Folds her arms in irritation.

Pity me, won't you?

"Hey kid, you alright?" I asked, crouching down to his height, noting the cut was deep.

"Yeah. Just a scrape." He was gazing past me at my daughter, his eyes wide as though he were seeing an angel for the first time.

Not on my watch.

"Off you go then. Get up and get back on that bike." I helped him up as he climbed on, his face etched in pain but a strong determination not to show it prevented it from staying on there for long.

"I'm Gabriel," he threw over his shoulder to Summer who watched him leave with a strange expression on her face.

I had a feeling it was going to be a long fucking ten years.

THE END

**READ ON FOR THE SECOND BOOK
IN THE SERIES:**

THEIRS

THEIRS
CHAPTER 1

ALEB

"Caleb!"

Oh, fuck.

"Caleb Fallon, I suggest you stop pretending you can't hear me and stay right there, young man."

Fuckity fuckity fuck. With a cherry on top.

I slowed, tugging out my earphone in mock surprise as my principal's face came into view—a terrifying reality at the best of times, least of all when you are me.

"Would you like to hazard a guess at why I may need to speak with you?" Her voice boomed down the corridor as she marched up to me, her spindly legs somehow sturdy enough to hold up her giant upper torso, complete with the saggiest tits I'd ever seen. Her eyes danced with delight at my obvious discomfort as I pretended to wrack my brain to piss her off even more.

"Was I running in the corridor? I didn't think I was—"

Too much?

She cut me off with a fierce glare, baring her teeth at me like she was a wild animal. Her chest puffed out, and her cheeks deepened in color as she bellowed so loudly I thought my eardrums were going to burst.

"Caleb Fallon! Don't think your little jaunts out of school during class are going unnoticed. I'm going to call your mother and let her know that you've been sneaking off to smoke, destroying what little brain cells you have left, instead of going to class. One more slip up, Fallon, and I will suspend you. Are we clear?!"

Not my mom.

"Crystal." I smiled as she nodded her head briskly, walking in the opposite direction. "Mrs. Potts?" I called as she whirled on her heel, glaring at me.

"What now, Mr. Fallon?"

"Could you call my dad? My mom's snowed under with work and—"

Her face turned into a sneer as she spoke. "I'm afraid not. I will call your mother first. My apologies."

Fuckity fuck.

Mom will bust my ass big time.

I dragged my sorry ass to class, wondering if I could fake choking or something drastic to get out of English Literature. The last thing I wanted to do was fall asleep in class, but it was just so... bland.

Who cares about characters in books? Why poets write what they do?

It baffled me how people could sit and spend hours with a book filled with words, not when there were so many other things to do. I pushed the door open, a broad back blocking my view of the class. I cleared my throat as Josh Harley turned to see me, his eyes lighting up.

"Dude. Where have you been? I thought you were skipping class again."

He clapped me on the back, and I winced. Built like a brick shithouse, he towered over most of us in our year by a good five inches, at least.

"Nah, I thought I'd make an appearance." I yawned as I slid into the seat near me, dropping my bag to the floor. Curling my head into my arms, I rested my eyes for a minute. Maybe if everyone just let me be for once, I could get some shut-eye.

"Caleb?"

Oh, hell no.

"Caleb, is this seat taken?" Her voice was sickly sweet. I opened one eye, squinting, so it wasn't overly obvious I was checking who it was.

Sasha Adams.

Otherwise known as the girl I call when I'm bored.

Which I wasn't, not at the moment. I was fucking tired.

She slid into the seat, the sound of her chewing on the gum that never seemed to expire irritating me beyond belief. Her hand crept onto my thigh, and I moved it away abruptly, throwing her an apologetic smile.

"Not in the mood, kitten. Sorry."

I heard a guffaw in front of me, and I noticed Josh's shoulders shake as he tried to disguise it. I sighed as Sasha tensed up beside me, her eyes boring into me.

This was the problem with shitting on your doorstep. Girls expected things, started demanding things. They got territorial without due cause, making out they were all for the casual loving but demanding a fucking Facebook relationship status as you pulled your dick out of them.

Nah.

I had made it clear to Sasha it was just a bit of fun—I had

zero intention of settling down anytime soon. I couldn't stick to the same girl for long, so there was no way I was going to make promises I couldn't keep.

A woman walked in, and I sat up a bit straighter, as did most of the guys in the room. My stomach flipped over as she brushed her hair out of her eyes nervously, biting on her full lips as she shuffled some papers on the teacher's desk.

She wore a navy dress with black tights and high fuck-me heels. I exchanged a glance with Gabe, my best friend since our diaper days. He gave me a knowing smile, and he cleared his throat, making her dark brown eyes flash up at him, confused.

"Excuse me, Miss, where's Mr. Frazer?"

She blinked before she blushed, darting a look at the door. As if on cue, in walked Mr. Frazer, a mountain of a man who let his gaze linger on the woman's legs longer than necessary.

Pervy bastard.

"Sorry I'm late, class," he drawled, not the least bit embarrassed. I couldn't tear my eyes away from the broad in the navy dress, the way she stood innocently, staring down at a ring on her hand as she twisted it around her finger. She didn't look old enough to be a teacher, and she wasn't a student—I'd remember seeing her.

"Class, we have a student teacher in with us today—her name is Miss DeQuincy. She's here to observe and help me. You can go about your business as usual," Mr. Frazer answered my silent question as I sent him a thank you with my eyes.

Miss DeQuincy swallowed as the entire room gawped at her, and when she lifted her eyes, they met mine. It was as though static electricity bolted from her to me like a hairdryer dropped in a bath of water.

What the fuck?

I couldn't take my eyes away from her, but she glanced away, focusing her attention on Mr. Frazer, who puffed his chest out like a pigeon in heat.

"So, today we start our new book. I know you are all incredibly excited." His voice dripped with sarcasm as he dumped a pile of textbooks onto the table with a thud, beaming at us.

"ROMEO AND JULIET!" he roared with enthusiasm as we all stared at him.

Wonder-fucking-ful.

THEIRS

CHAPTER 2

*C*ALEB
    Somehow this DeQuincy chick made English bearable, but it was still fucking bullshit.

I hate school.

I wasn't a jock either; I couldn't *stand* sports. I didn't get what was so exciting about chasing a ball around a field with a group of sweaty guys—plus, it would eat into my private time.

Dad had humored mom when she put me in all kinds of after-school clubs when I was a kid—until I came home with a black eye when the ball hit me square in the face because I wasn't paying attention. He said I was made for different things, and he was right.

Dad was *always* right. We just didn't tell Mom.

The bell rang, signaling the end of class and giving me freedom, albeit temporarily. I didn't need to gather my shit because I didn't even take anything out of my bag, so I was the first one at the door. Miss DeQuincy tidied the books away, leaning up to stack them on the shelf beside me. She was small, even in those heels. Her tongue darted across her lips as she reached, and I realized I was staring.

"Can I help you with something?" She asked me coolly, stretching to push the books onto the shelf.

"No, but maybe I can help you with those books?' I offered as she shot me a look of indifference.

"I've got it, thanks."

She turned away, but not before I caught a whiff of the perfume she was wearing, an intoxicating scent of sweet vanilla mixed with something I couldn't place.

"Yo. Some of us want to leave class," muttered Gabe from behind me, shooting DeQuincy a dazzling smile.

Gabe was my favorite cunt.

A star football player, an all-around American dream. You only had to look at him, and you imagined apple pies and hot dogs on the Fourth of July. He made you want to sing the national anthem proudly as you drove a Mustang through Route 66. Tanned continuously, as though we lived in fucking California, with a Hollywood smile, complete with the bluest eyes you've ever seen. His blonde hair fell into his face as he slung his beefy arm around my shoulders, still staring at DeQuincy.

"So, how old are you, Miss?"

She stared at him, blankly before her eyes darted over to me. "Haven't you got another class to get to, boys?"

Ouch.

"Oh, we do, Miss. It's called gym. We get real sweaty and end up taking our shirts off—do you want a sneak preview?" He lifted the bottom of his top as he revealed his toned abs. Even I snuck a peek.

"I'm afraid not. Run along now. You don't want to be late." Her tone was flat as she turned away, disinterested.

"Lesbian," muttered Gabe, shoving me out of the door, but not before I caught her rolling her eyes.

Bodies filled the hallway, along with their odor—not everyone here showered. I grimaced when someone pushed by me, stale sweat invading my nostrils.

"You are going to gym, right?" Gabe drawled as we weaved through people, greeting friends with nods, and brief handshakes as we did.

"I kinda have to. Potts is calling my fucking mom."

Gabe winced in sympathy as a flurry of red and white fabric smashed into him, hairspray and perfume replacing the general odor we were swimming in.

"*Baby*! I've missed you *so* much. I feel like it's been forever!"

The little blonde in his arms littered his face with kisses as he shot me a 'save me' look, pleading with his eyes.

Kennedy Hall.

"Uh, it's been like, an hour?" Gabe wrinkled his nose up, and I held back a snigger, earning myself a glare from the head cheerleader.

"Get fucked, Caleb," she snapped, throwing her hair over her shoulder as she gazed lovingly at Gabe.

I held my hands up in mock defeat, unable to suppress a smile.

"Are you still coming over tonight?" she purred, and he sighed, jamming his hands into his pockets.

"Yeah, probably."

She threw her arms around him as she kissed him again, and I turned away, bored. I didn't get why Gabe was riding the relationship wave—it wasn't as if he was into it. Sure, Kennedy was cute, but her voice irritated the fuck out of me. I don't even think I could fuck her—well, maybe if she were quiet.

"Hey, Riley." I offered to the petite girl beside her, who shot me daggers before muttering an inaudible response. She was a past conquest, but I had been nothing but polite to her since. Just a drunken fuck at a party, but again, she expected so much more.

Gabe stood a little straighter suddenly, his eyes staring at something beyond me. I followed his gaze to see a familiar wave of chocolate brown hair that skimmed just above my twin's waist as she pushed her books into her locker. I noticed JT, a jock friend of Gabe's, leaning up against the locker beside her, chatting as he checked her out.

"Summer!" I called out as JT narrowed his eyes at me before he realized who I was.

Does he need fucking glasses?

I strode over, my green eyes locking onto the ice blue ones of my sister.

"Hey, womb-hogger," Summer said, her lips curling into a smile. I was slightly older than her and weighed much more when we were born. Mom didn't know she was having twins until her second scan as my bulk hid Summer.

Hence the joke.

"Alright, man?" asked JT as he met my eyes. I glared at him without responding, and he shifted uncomfortably.

He needs to fucking leave. Now.

"Catch you later, Summer," he muttered, having received the message loud and clear.

"He was just trying to talk to me," Summer sighed as she closed the locker, leaning against it as she spoke.

"That's not all he wants to do either. Asshole," I retorted, watching him greet Gabe, who made a beeline for us, having shaken Kennedy off.

"I'm not *stupid*, Cale," she scolded as I rolled my eyes.

"No, but you're not immune to their charms."

"Hey, Summer." Gabe smiled as Summer nodded at him before turning back to me.

"Based on what evidence?" She demanded as Gabe's brow furrowed in confusion. I glanced at her as she raised her eyebrows questionably. "I've hardly fucked the entire school now, have I?"

"*Summer*," I warned as she shook her head.

"No, I haven't. So why do you think I can't tell when a meathead is trying to get in my pants? This one does it regularly." She jutted her head to Gabe as his mouth opened, then closed as I narrowed my gaze at him.

I knew he liked my sister; he always had. But she wasn't interested in anyone, and I wasn't complaining. It sure made my job easier.

Gabe held his hands up, his eyes wide with alarm. "I'm just a flirt. It's nothing personal!" he exclaimed, his eyes darting from me to Summer.

I watched him briefly before turning back to my twin. She was giving Gabe a look that made me wonder if something had gone on between them, but as she turned her blue gaze to me, a commotion came from the bottom of the corridor. I turned to see two guys squaring up to each other, both pretty equal in size, both looking pretty pissed off.

Gabe frowned as he studied the guys before turning to me. "Ten bucks on Rodgers."

I scoffed as I checked out the other guy, Hanson. There was no way Hanson would beat Rodgers.

"Nah. Rodgers looks pissed off as fuck." I leaned back on the locker as Summer looked from me to Gabe, shaking her head.

"Instead of placing bets, why don't you break up the fight?" she hissed, pushing past us and striding towards the circle that had now surrounded the group.

Oh, for fuck's sake.

Gabe nodded at me, and we followed Summer, pulling her back by the arm as she strode forward, determined to stop the fight. She hated violence, yet I knew these guys had tension that had been bubbling up for weeks. I didn't want her getting a right hook on my watch. My dad would murder some fuck. Probably me.

"Summer!" I tried to pull her back, but she tugged her arm away, pushing herself between the two guys.

"Stop! It's not worth it, whatever this is!" Summer pleaded with the two boys.

Daniel Rodgers had smoke coming out of his ears as he panted, his finger pointing over Summer's shoulder to Liam Hanson. "You're a fucking dead man."

Liam smacked his hand away in anger and snarled back at him. "Fuck you. It's not my fault your girl is following me around like a lost fucking puppy. If you fucked her right, we wouldn't be here."

Gabe strode forward, wrapping his arm around Summer's waist, and I heard a fist crunch against bone, and blood spurted from Liam's nose.

"Gabriel! Put me the fuck down!" Summer screeched as I smirked at her anger, knowing Gabe was in for it now.

Gabe put her down, his eyes fierce as he held her shoulders still. "You're fucking welcome."

Summer turned and clasped her hands to her mouth in horror at the two guys throwing punches at each other on the floor. Suddenly, the teachers came round the corner, strolling forward like a bunch of garden gnomes.

"Summer, stop being a dick. Don't get involved in other people's shit. You could've got hurt," I snapped as she threw a hateful look in my direction.

"If we don't stop shit like that, Caleb, what sort of fucking people are we? It's not entertainment. It's barbaric."

God, she was so fucking sensitive. She used to cry if someone stepped on a bug when we were little, insisting on holding a funeral for its squished carcass. I turned and left, content she wouldn't get bitch-slapped into next week.

DeQuincy tapped away on her phone near the office, a smile on those fuckable lips of hers. I stood watching her, my heart beating much faster than it needed to.

She was so fucking curvy it was killing me. She had these incredible legs and the perfect hourglass figure, her hips wide but her stomach flat. The blood rushed to my dick as I imagined fucking her over the desk in our English class. She could recite Romeo and Juliet to me or some shit.

Fuck.

AFTERWORD

Thank you for reading my book!

If you loved it, would you be so kind as to leave me a review? Even one word helps!

Thank you.

Leave a review here if you're in the UK

Leave a review here if you're in the USA

ABOUT THE AUTHOR

You can find out about Linzvonc on her website below; she'd love to hear from you, too, if you want to get in touch!

www.linzvonc.com

Made in the USA
Columbia, SC
28 June 2024

37832581R00214